NICOLA MARSH

THE SOLAR SNATCHERS SERIES

SCI☉N
OF THE SUN

Scion of the Sun by Nicola Marsh.

All rights reserved. Published in the United States of America by Month9Books, LLC. Month9Books is a registered trademark, and its related logo is a registered trademark of Month9Books, LLC.

Summary: A teenage supernatural misfit enters boarding school for the freakishly gifted, discovers she can teleport to a Druid parallel existence and battles coming of age issues while embarking on a quest to recover an icon that can change the world and her family as she knows it.

ISBN 978-0-9850294-3-2 (tr. pbk) 978-1-939765-53-6 (ebook)

For information, address Month9Books, LLC, 4208 Six Forks Road Suite 1000, Raleigh, NC 27609.

Visit us online at www.month9books.com

eBook and print Cover Design by Georgina Gibson
Cover Art Copyright © 2013 by Month9Books

Praise for

SCI⊛N
OF THE SUN

*"Scion of the Sun is packed with action, mystery, romance, and suspense.
It's not to be missed."*
– Jennifer L. Armentrout, #1 New York Times and
USA Today bestselling author

For my amazing boys, who are already asking when they can read this book.
I'm sure the years will fly too fast and you'll be reading this before you know it.
You're my inspiration.
I love you more than words can say.

NICOLA MARSH

THE SOLAR SNATCHERS SERIES

SCI☀N

OF THE SUN

CHAPTER ONE

I always thought cults were for crazies.

Until I joined one.

Let me clear up any misconceptions. I'm not crazy. A freak, but not crazy. Which is why I'm here. Freaks R Us. A *boarding school for the intellectually gifted* tucked away in the back streets of Wolfebane, New Hampshire.

Intellectually gifted? Yeah, right.

We have a pristine lake surrounded by majestic mountains. We have lush green fields that turn into fabulous groomed ski trails in the winter. We have upscale restaurants and thriving businesses and fancy homes—city pizzazz with small town coziness. We even have our very own homegrown C.U.L.T.

The *Clique of Unique Luminary Telepathies.*

When the average person searches this place on the Internet, the home page reads *Co-Ed for Unified Learning and Teaching,* a New Age school for the hippest of the hip. It appears to be a rambling English manor, sandstone and massive latticed windows and French doors, surrounded by a cottage garden gone wild.

All very civilized for a place of learning, but what I'd learn would scare the crap out of me.

"Going in sometime this century?"

I glared at Colt, sitting smug in his beat-up Chevy, eager to get rid of me. I'd been thrust on his family, Nan's only neighbors, when she got carted off to the hospital. I hated staying with his uptight family as much as they hated having me.

"Nah, think I'll hang with you a bit longer. It's so much fun."

He pointed at the door. "Get out."

I didn't budge. Colt didn't scare me. C.U.L.T. did.

"I had no choice staying with your folks. What's your excuse?"

His expression turned stubborn.

"How old are you anyway? Nineteen? Twenty, tops?"

"Twenty-one," he gritted out. "Too old to be babysitting dorks like you."

"Dork? That's mature for a guy tied so tight to mommy's apron strings he's still living at home."

His hands clenched on the steering wheel and I jiggled the door handle. The door opened on the third try.

"If you were this smart-assed with your Nan I'm not surprised she had a stroke."

Low blow. That's what it felt like, like he'd kicked me in the guts. His words inspired the same nauseating feeling I'd had when I'd told her what I'd seen. When she'd uttered five mysterious words—*she took the wrong one*—and keeled over.

"And she's in a long-term coma?" He drove the boot in harder. "She'd probably do anything to stay away from you."

I grabbed my backpack, slung my messenger bag over my shoulder, and slammed the door. I couldn't get away from him fast enough. It wasn't what he'd said as much as the possible truth behind it.

He leaned across the bench seat and leered out the window. "Enjoy the lock-up. It's a perfect place for psychos. You'll fit right in."

"Screw you."

Colt gave me the finger, gunned the engine, and squealed away from the curb, leaving me standing in front of my prison.

Wolfebane High had sucked, but *boarding* school? Fine for my fictional faves Zoey Redbird and Rose Hathaway and Cammie Morgan. Me? I wasn't the kickass heroine so much.

I stiffened as a group of girls exited the school gates. No uniforms, just a motley mix of preppy and prissy mixed with cheerleader chic. In my faded jeans, striped hoodie, and worn pink ballet flats, I stood out like the nerdy bookworm I was.

One of the girls, a tall blonde with shiny hair to her waist, stopped and glanced my way. I half smiled. She scrutinized me from head to foot before giving me the cheerleader welcome.

She turned her back.

Humiliation heated my cheeks as Cheerleader Chick said something to the group and they tittered, gawked at me, and snickered.

Not one of them smiled. Most did the same flick-over dismissive thing before turning away and heading up the street toward town, leaving me as helpless and mortified and angry as I'd been at Wolfebane High.

There, too, I'd tried to pretend the princesses didn't get to me, that my grades were all that mattered. But with every condescending smirk, every haughty glare, I'd wanted to smash my fist into their conceited faces. Not that I was pro-violence. Unless provoked.

Who needed all that perfect hair, perfect makeup, perfect outfit crap anyway? Who needed friends?

As I watched the tight-knit group stroll down the street in all their trendy glory, confident in their place in the world, a small part of me yearned to run after them, to be part of their shared secrets, their out-there prettiness, their inner circle.

"Cliques are the same the world over, huh?"

I stopped staring at the princess posse and mustered a tight smile for the girl who'd voiced my opinion. A girl who looked about twelve, wearing a bizarre outfit of a saffron-sequined halter top, camouflage pants, and patent leather Mary Janes.

"You go to school here?"

She nodded, her baby face losing years by the second. "Third year."

I'd never been good at small talk so I scrambled for a semi-polite response. "You like it?"

"Yeah, it's not bad."

She pointed at my bags. "First day?"

"Uh-huh."

She glanced at her watch. "Gotta run. Good luck."

Great, even the youngest, worst-dressed kid in school didn't want to hang around me. And how could she be in third year when she looked like she belonged in preschool? I must've been staring, because she pointed to her face.

"Don't let this fool you. I can conjure up a good spell like the rest of them."

Just like that, my bubble of normality burst. It had been thin to begin with, but it had been there, an illusion that this place was like any other high school, complete with an in-crowd tailor-made to ignore me.

But nothing about C.U.L.T. was normal, as I'd soon find out.

As if my crappy day couldn't get any crappier, one of Wolfebane's legendary storms decided now was as good a time as any to dump a sky full of rain on me.

I scurried for the nearest shelter, a towering oak that could've protected an entire football team. I could've entered the school and huddled under the huge stone arches flanking the path leading to the main building, but the longer I could delay the inevitable, the more in control I felt.

Of course, the Cheerleader Crew chose that moment to come back, balancing their diet sodas and umbrellas and delicate egos without missing a step. They glanced in my direction, their nerd-radar working overtime despite the storm, and did the derisive quick-look-away in unison before dashing into school, making a mockery of my "I'm cool and in control" mantra.

Hard to appear cool when you're a drowned rat huddled under a tree, clutching your messenger bag to your chest to protect your precious books. I glanced up at the sky, hoping for a reprieve so I could make a run for it.

"Room for two under here?"

I jumped and spun around, wondering where the biker dude had sprung from. A few years older than me, he wore head-to-toe black—black jeans, black T-shirt, black leather jacket—and had enough facial piercings to create his own magnetic field.

"Whatever."

His lips curled into a surprisingly nice smile at my answer. "Let me guess. First day?"

Not interested in making small talk but stuck here until the rain stopped, I shrugged. "What gave it away? My unbridled enthusiasm?"

He laughed. "You've got the look."

"What look?"

"This look." He frowned, making his eyebrow and lip rings

jiggle. "I call it the get-me-the-hell-outta-here look. All the newbies get it. Makes it easy to spot you a mile away."

I jerked my thumb at the school. "You're a student?"

"Not anymore." He kicked a khaki duffel at his feet. "I'm done."

"You graduated?"

This time, there was nothing remotely nice about his smile. His top lip curl was positively evil. "You could say that."

I took in the slouch, the bad boy outfit, the piercings, and the sneer. "Expelled?"

He shook his head, his long brown ponytail flicking over his shoulder. "Not that lucky." He kicked his duffel again, harder this time. "I'm tired of all the New Age crap, so I quit."

Intrigued by a school that allowed its students to decide how long they stuck around, I pretended I didn't care about his answers when in fact I wanted to play twenty questions with the rebel before he hit the road. "Why were you here?"

His dark gaze swept me from head to foot as he took a step closer. "You really want to know?"

I shrugged, determined not to show his proximity intimidated me a tad. "Hey, if I'm going to be stuck inside this freak show, pays to be in the know."

He studied me as he slugged me on the shoulder like an old buddy, and I struggled not to wince. "Pity I'm leaving. I dig you, new chick." He stuck out his hand. "Drake."

"Holly." I shook his hand, a little disappointed when some greater force didn't zap me. As if. Drake didn't seem so bad for an ex-student. Hopefully the rest of my classmates would be okay too.

Leaning against the tree trunk, he folded his arms. "So you want to know what I can do, huh?"

"Yeah."

He pushed off the tree so suddenly I took an involuntary step back. "I burn things." He leaned into my face. "Want a demo?"

I knew he wasn't referring to using matches or kindling and my heart twisted in fear as his eyes glowed red.

"Sure." Maybe Drake would fry me to a crisp and save me an entire term of freaky lessons?

He invaded my personal space, but I didn't move. I'd faced bullies like him at Wolfebane High and had learned the hard way: if you show fear, you go down. I stiffened when a crimson circle spread around his irises. I braced myself to be nuked, staggering in relief when he punched me on the arm again and stepped back.

"You're cool, Holly. Pity I can't stick around and show you a few party tricks."

"Yeah, pity," I said, almost peeing my pants in relief when he hoisted his duffel, slung it over his shoulder, and saluted.

"I'd say break a leg, but with the weird stuff that goes on in there, it'll probably happen." His eyes flared red again before he blinked and the scarlet vanished, his smile back to benign. "Don't say I didn't warn you, kid."

He took two steps before turning back. "Almost forgot. A little friendly advice. Don't trust the principal. She's one serious psycho."

Not a problem; I never trusted principals as a rule. Except Nan knew this one and had said Brigit Smith could help me. Considering what had been happening lately, I needed all the help I could get.

As he bolted into the rain, which had eased to a light sprinkle, I swung back to school with dread turning my feet to lead.

If a freak like Drake couldn't make it there, what chance did I have?

CHAPTER TWO

Outside the school gates, I plucked at the string of my hoodie, twisting it around my finger until it turned numb. I had to do this. I just didn't want to.

The way I saw it, I had two options.

Drag my sorry ass into school and go meet the principal, or run screaming back to Nan's where social services would haul me away. Some freaking *options*.

I had to figure out why I'd started having visions so I'd be safer taking my chances with the head freak, despite Drake's weird warning, than ending up in some scary foster home.

Decision made, I marched through the long stone-arched entryway, the gloom of the stones at odds with the welcoming appearance of the main building. *Way to go with the Stonehenge look.* Once I turned onto another pathway free of the odd-shaped stone arches, I glanced around. Not a student in sight. Odd. Then again, what did I expect at a C.U.L.T.? They were probably all tucked away with their magic wands, trying to transform Fs on their term papers to As.

Harsh, considering the bulk of the student body was *normal* apparently. From what I understood, the kids attending here were *intellectually gifted students with an interest in New Age studies to complement their high school diploma.* Whatever that meant.

Guess the name Nan knew the place by, the *clique* and *luminary telepathies* thing, made me imagine a school filled with levitating, spell-casting freaks. If Drake was anything to go by ...

I could live with the *intellectually gifted* tag, but the visions, the telepathy? I could do without.

I mentally rehearsed what I'd say as I followed signs to the principal's office, housed in the front of the massive sandstone building sprawling across an acre.

Nan said you could help freaks like me.

You see, there's this thing, I see stuff. Weird stuff.

With no idea what I'd say when I met the head freak, I stopped outside a thick wooden door with a brass nameplate reading *Brigit Smith, C.U.L.T. Principal*, nerves knotting my stomach as I shook out my hands.

"Come in, Holly, I've been expecting you."

My hand, raised to knock, dropped to my side. First lesson: head freak had ESP. Or cameras. I glanced around and saw no evidence of recording devices. *Spooky.*

"I haven't got all day, Holly."

11

This time, steel threaded through the command, and as the door creaked open—adding to the surrealism—I shoved my hands into the pockets of my hoodie to stop the tingling and bumped the door fully open with my hip.

I glanced around the room, surprised by the normalcy of it all. Gold-embossed wallpaper, wood-trimmed french doors, marble fireplace, antique furniture, with an impressive crystal chandelier overhead. I'd imagined something along the lines of Hogwarts with a healthy dash of nuthouse thrown in, not this staid, simplistic drawing room taken straight from Jane Austen's era.

Then I caught sight of America's preeminent parapsychologist and my preconceptions, along with whatever Nan had told me about Brigit, flew straight out the barred window.

"Don't stand there gawking. Come in and join me."

A plump, snowy-haired woman with apple cheeks, owlish eyes, and a striking widow's peak stirred a miniature bubbling cauldron on her giant mahogany desk. If she thought I'd join her for a quick incantation in this freak show, she had another think coming. "And call me Brigit. We don't stick to formalities around here."

I stopped a few feet short of the desk and tilted my chin up, waiting for her to say something, anything, to give me an excuse to turn around and storm out without looking back.

"I'm sorry about your grandmother."

"Thanks."

Nan had raised me after Mom abandoned me. *Vanished*, Nan said. Whatever that meant. Like Mom had gone up in a puff of smoke when the reality was probably far harsher. Rhiannon Burton

obviously hadn't wanted a squalling kid, so she'd run c
my ass.

I kept a photo of Mom next to my bed. Because, who knew,
maybe if I stared at the picture long enough, she might show up
one day?

So I could say to her face, *screw you.*

Nan was the only person I trusted in this world, and she now
lay in a vast bed hooked up to machines to keep her alive, her
vegetative state so frightening I ached every time I visited. A sliver
of pain, as sharp and niggling as a splinter lodged under a
fingernail, stuck in my heart, and wiggled, intensifying the
throbbing ache until I could barely breathe. I didn't need Brigit's
trite condolences. I needed her help with my problem. I needed her
to make it go away.

"She'll recover." I didn't add *and when she does, I'm so outta here.*

"Yes, Rose is a fighter." She clicked her fingers and the
cauldron switched off, the suddenness surprising me. She waved at
it and gave a wry smile. "A party trick I use to tease newcomers.
It's like one of those noise-activated lamps. Clap or snap your
fingers, and *poof,* gone."

I revised my earlier assessment. I'd be damned if I stood there
with the chief crazy and her props. I was bitter and resentful, but
even I knew you didn't put new students through bizarre
initiations.

She pointed to a worn suede couch while she settled into a
mismatched chintz chair opposite, her paisley caftan draping over
the arms and cascading to the floor. "Sit. We'll talk."

I stood, torn between wanting to flee and the unrelenting, irrational, unstoppable hope she could deliver what I wanted most in this world: answers to questions too convoluted to contemplate.

Brigit didn't say anything else; she sat back, clasped her ringless fingers in her lap, and waited, her nonjudgmental gaze edged with sympathy.

I was unnerved by the comforting warmth seeping through my body, as if she'd reached out and enveloped me in a squishy hug, the kind of hug Nan used to give me whenever I aced a test, whenever I said something to make her laugh, just whenever.

Tears stung and I swiped at them. I was angry—furious, in fact—that I'd ended up here through my own stupidity. I'd never given Nan cause to worry about me, had always striven to be the model granddaughter from some deep fear that if I didn't, she'd end up leaving me just like Mom had. Irrational, considering she'd never given me one moment to doubt her.

Anger was good. It helped me banish the tears. Crying wouldn't get me what I wanted. Maybe Brigit could. Plopping ungraciously onto the couch, I folded my arms and assumed my best nonchalant I-don't-give-a-crap slouch while my heart pounded with expectation.

"I need answers."

Brigit inclined her head. "That's what I'm here for, to help you on your journey of self-discovery."

I rolled my eyes and refrained from sticking two fingers down my throat in a gagging motion—just. "I'm not so much into the journey as much as the destination. Where I'll get *answers*."

Her lips compressed at my rudeness, but I didn't care. She'd done nothing but antagonize me with her stupid tricks and condescending calmness since I arrived. "When's the last time you spoke to Nan?"

"A few weeks ago."

"What did she say?"

She frowned at my tone. "Nothing, other than boarding here for a while may be a good option for you." She paused, and her eerie stillness made me squirm. "Though maybe she should've told me how antagonistic you'd be. I would've pulled out more tricks."

I managed a tiny smile, a twitch at the corners of my mouth. More than I'd managed lately.

She was right. It was wrong, taking my anger out on a woman I'd just met, a woman Nan recommended when I'd had my first *episode*. Nan loved all the spooky woo-woo crap: aura readings, tarot, horoscopes, even had the odd hit-or-miss premonition. It didn't surprise me when she told me she knew Brigit from a few seminars she'd attended. While she'd never mentioned me attending C.U.L.T. before, I'd seen the way she lit up when I mentioned my visions and she'd picked up the phone to discuss my boarding with Brigit.

I unfolded my arms, slumped into the couch, and sighed. "I've had visions."

She didn't blink, didn't seem surprised. Then again, considering America came to this woman for expertise in all areas wacky, I was probably her least complicated student yet.

"How many?

"Two."

"What of?"

"The first was a car accident involving kids." I'd told Nan about the first one—I'd freaked out when I saw a bunch of joyriding drunken teens crash into Lake Wolfe, down to the exact date and time. Nan put in a call to 911. The kids were rescued, but seriously shaken. I'd laughed it off as a coincidence.

Nan hadn't laughed. She'd rung Brigit immediately. An old mentor, she'd said, someone who'd know what to do with *this kind of thing*. An old mentor who'd advised Nan to offload me here for a year.

"Tell me about the other."

It was the second vision that freaked Nan out and induced her stroke. Frustration curled my fingers into fists, the sting of nails digging into my palms a welcome relief from the constant ache gripping my heart.

"I saw my mom."

With a monster. A shrouded, hooded black figure exuding evil. Holding her hand.

Brigit didn't question the validity of what I'd seen or ask questions about my mom as expected. She merely nodded, clasped her hands together, and rested them in her lap. "You've had visions before?"

"Never."

"Tell me exactly what you saw."

I closed my eyes, willing the disjointed scene to flash into my mind again.

Nothing.

I pinched the bridge of my nose, pressed thumb pads into my eyes until red spots danced with black across my lids.

Nothing.

"Don't force it. Tell me what you remember." Brigit's soothing tone washed over me, soft, low.

I opened my eyes before she could hypnotize me or perform any of the other weird crap she was probably into. "My mom. Wearing some long hippie dress. And a guy. In a Grim Reaper get-up so I couldn't see his face … "

I swallowed, glad I couldn't remember that part of the vision in too much detail. The cloaked figure had flashed across my mind's eye for a split second, gone before I could identify him, but that fragment in time was all I'd needed for terror to snap me out of whatever I'd seen.

"What else?"

Dragging a breath into my constricted lungs, I closed my eyes again. "A room, possibly underground, the size of the gazebo in Market Square. Dark. Damp."

Like the caves on the east shore of Lake Wolfe I'd explored as a child. I'd liked the cool darkness and the sandy floors, but I'd never ventured too far in for fear of getting lost and being gobbled up by a faceless cave dweller. Nan had teased me about my imaginary boogieman. Not so funny now that I'd seen his adult counterpart.

"Good. Go on."

"No furniture. Though some kind of stone slab, like an altar."

The altar was off-putting. Though I'd never been religious, I knew altars were sacred. The altar in my vision didn't give me that feeling. Its lack of reverence made me want to run as far away as I could get from that cold, lifeless stone.

Brigit remained silent. I had to remember, had to have answers to why this was happening to me, and why now. But the further I delved, the uneasier I became. Poking my nose into mysterious corners as a kid had only ended in spider bites and bee stings, and I had a feeling that I was going to end up in the same pain.

"And there's another person in the far corner, hidden in the shadows."

"Male? Female?"

"Can't tell. Too dark."

That's what bugged me the most, that maybe, just maybe, I'd inherited some of Nan's gift, but couldn't use it well enough to discover what this was all about. A small masochistic part of me hoped I was getting a glimpse into what happened to my mom. That probably explained why I blocked the rest out.

"You want to know more because this involves your mother."

I nodded and opened my eyes slowly this time, blinking to adjust to the sudden light.

"She's fine."

"How would you know?"

"Because the gift of precognition is just that. Allows you to see forward, to foresee future events, not look back." Brigit drummed her fingers on the spare tire around her middle. "Your grandmother has limited precognitive powers which may now be blossoming in you. She doesn't have post-cognition, which means you don't either." My confusion must've shown, because she explained, "The ability to know facts of an event after it has occurred."

She leaned forward so fast I jumped. She placed a hand over mine, its cold clamminess revolting. Her narrow-eyed glare was tinged with ice. I snatched my hand back, spooked by her momentary malice, before she blinked and eradicated any hint of malevolence I might've imagined.

"That vision is leading you to your mother."

My relief at having my flashes analyzed evaporated as the implication sunk in. Mom was in that dark, dingy hole with a monster. Why? The thought of her holding hands with that *thing* filled me with dread.

That's when it happened.

I froze.

Cold seeped beneath my skin, a rimy trickle that started at the nape of my neck and spread frigid fingers outward. I shivered despite the mild day, despite the claustrophobic confines of the room.

The first time this happened two weeks earlier, I'd been terrified. The second, horrified yet curious. This time, I just wanted answers. I willed the image to come.

A damp cave. Sound of a constant drip. Faint screech of nails scrabbling against hard, unforgiving stone.

A girl in the far corner? Thin chain circling her neck. A medallion ... gold ... an engraved sunburst ...

Mom touches it, traces the outline and the sun's rays, before the monster extends a hand, clamps on her shoulder.

He yanks Mom back, hard.

She stumbles, falls onto jagged rocks, slices her hand, blood everywhere ...

I gagged and grabbed my throat, gasping. Brigit stilled my clawing hands, her stable monotone urging me to breathe and relax. Easy for her to say. She hadn't just seen her mom being manhandled by a monster.

"Your mother?"

I nodded, panic threatening to engulf me again. "With someone else. A girl, I think? And him ... " My breath hitched as I rubbed the spreading ache in the centre of my chest, willing the last image freeze-framed in my brain to vanish. "Mom fell. Cut her hands. There was a lot of blood."

"Don't worry. You're here now. We'll get to the bottom of this."

Maybe I didn't want to get to the bottom of anything. Maybe I was happy being a sixteen-year-old with a passion for books and ballet flats and Ben and Jerry's Chunky Monkey. Maybe I wanted to ignore the fact I'd just had my third vision in two weeks and I absolutely hated every freaking second of it.

But I couldn't turn my back on Mom no matter how much I'd vilified her over the years. I was desperate to ask her *why*. Perhaps I'd finally get my chance.

"What can you do to help me?" What I really wanted to know was what they did at C.U.L.T. And, if any of it could help me understand what was happening with my messed up mind.

"We can hone your gift."

"Gift?"

"What would you call it?"

"A pain in the ass."

Brigit's smile bordered on patronizing, as if she knew something I didn't. "Would you prefer power?"

"Makes me sound like a superhero," I muttered, back to my ungracious best.

Brigit stood. "Precognition is a gift. Accept it."

She waddled toward her desk, leaving me to slouch along behind her. She'd told me nothing so far. Nothing I didn't already know.

"I can help. But first, formalities." She handed me a bland beige folder from the mess on her desk. "Your schedule. You have a week of spring break, and then your classes will begin."

I flipped it open and saw the usual breakdown of hour-long lessons: English, history, chemistry, biology. The subjects alongside the basics were far from usual: psychic scrying, divination, parapsychology—and that was just for starters. "Why all the blank study periods?"

"Because once you start the basics, students discover they want to specialize."

She opened her mouth to elaborate before clamping it shut. That made two of us. I wanted to blurt out my misgivings about being here, about these visions, about everything. Instead, I focused on the schedule and tried to pretend I was back at Wolfebane High starting a new school year.

"Classes aren't allocated by age." She pointed to my Year One

21

level, the equivalent of beginners, and I almost fainted. "We use a different method here."

"But I'm sixteen!" I blurted, horrified at the thought of being dumped in with a bunch of freshmen.

"You look younger."

Bane of my life, resembling an underage pixie. Scruffy blonde hair, wishy-washy blue eyes, pale skin, skinny—unremarkable in every way. Except the visions, and thankfully, no one could see that particular attribute.

"All newcomers start in Year One," she continued. She sounded arctic, as if she didn't like being questioned. A tiny frown line appeared in her creaseless brow. "Your talent is raw. You need to start at the beginning, learn the basics, learn control." She paused to give me her best intimidating glare. "There are no exceptions."

Yeah, that's me, not exceptional in the least. "Fine," I mumbled, flicking through the rest of the info. I needed time alone to assimilate it all.

"Do you have any other talents?"

Considering what this place was all about, I assumed she wasn't talking about my speed-reading ability or snowboarding skills, though I thought they were pretty impressive.

"No."

Her astute gaze bored into me and I eyeballed her back, not giving an inch. She might have thought she had all the answers, but I hazarded a guess Chief Crazy would be glad to see the back of me when I was through asking questions.

"Our learning is intensive and exhausting. You'll have limited social time."

Didn't bother me. I hadn't exactly been Miss Prom Queen at Wolfebane High. I'd been an outcast, one of those brainy nerds who didn't go in for all the rivalry-for-popularity crap. I'd steered clear of the cheerleaders, the goths, the jocks. The Loner, they'd called me, in one of their nicer moments.

"That's fine."

"Good. New term starts next week, so you have some time to settle in, orient yourself, and get a jump on some of your new subjects." She tapped a stack of textbooks on her desk for emphasis and I stifled a groan. Studying in my last week of freedom before I became a compulsive clock-watcher? Principals were the same the world over.

"That's it? Has Nan paid fees? How long will I need to stay? When do I—"

Distracted, Brigit peered at the door. "Quinn will answer any more questions you have while he shows you around."

There was a knock and Brigit barked, "Come in." Maybe her power involved seeing through doors—first me, now the newcomer Quinn. However, when the door opened and in walked a tall, cute guy with spiky caramel hair and deep green eyes, it wasn't Brigit's undisclosed powers that intrigued me as much as what a hottie like him was doing in a place like this.

He swung toward me, slowly, fluidly. I stiffened as tiny prickles of electricity zapped my skin in awareness of something not quite right, something scary, something supernatural.

"Hey, I'm Quinn." He held out his hand, his smile warm and welcoming.

I mentally shook myself for imagining anything strange a moment ago. "Holly."

As I placed my hand in his, I got more than a polite introductory handshake. His fingers closed over mine, strong and secure. I met his peculiar gaze and my world tilted. Staring into his fathomless green eyes was like peering into the deepest, darkest depths of my soul.

I snatched my hand out of Quinn's and barely resisted the urge to swipe my tingling palm down the side of my jeans, seriously spooked. I'd had the same reaction as I'd had to Drake. What was it with the freaky guys in this place?

"Let's go." His deep voice held a hint of amusement, like he sensed my horrified reaction and found it funny.

"Thanks, Quinn." Brigit dismissed us with a wave, though I couldn't shake the feeling she'd expected more from me, the way she kept staring at me like an experiment in a Petri dish. The principal of the New Age school was as offbeat as I'd expected, but I couldn't forget Drake's warning: *Don't trust the principal, she's one serious psycho.* While I had no reason to take anything he said seriously, after meeting Brigit I had a suspicion there was more behind her apple-cheeked enthusiasm.

I wanted to ask a thousand questions, wanted to demand clarification on what I'd actually be learning, wanted to ensure I'd finish with a normal high school diploma, wanted reassurance that I wasn't going insane and everything would be okay. Instead, I got a tight smile and a "Welcome Holly. I'm sure you'll fit right in here." And she turned her back on me with a swirl of mauve paisley, effectively ending further communication.

In a daze, I followed Quinn out into the corridor. Before I could speak, he laid a hand on my shoulder and I stiffened, expecting more peculiar tingling, my gaze firmly fixed on my ballet flats, refusing to meet his spooky, all-seeing eyes.

"Don't be scared. That buzz you felt back there? Part of my aunt's bizarre little initiation process."

Screw scared. I'd moved straight on to terror courtesy of the nut-jobs here. I risked another peek at him; thankfully, all I saw this time was pity.

"You've got some kind of power, haven't you?"

Not wanting to give away too much, but desperate to discover more about this crazy school, I nodded.

"Figured as much. That's why Aunt Brigit projects some of her hocus-pocus on me when I greet new students, to see how you react."

"Sicko," I muttered, belatedly pondering the wisdom of dissing the principal to her nephew on my first day. Defiant, I jabbed a strand of hair behind my ear. "And you can tell her that, what with the principal being your *aunt* and all."

"Don't remind me," he said, his expression less than enthusiastic. "It's mortifying being her stooge when she does that weirdo stuff."

Curious, I shot him a glance. "Aren't you into the New Age crap here?"

"No way."

"So you just hang out at freak school for the hell of it?"

With a grimace, he pointed down the long corridor. "Come on, I'll tell you all about it on the grand tour."

With a resigned sigh, I fell into step beside him, my curiosity outweighing my urge to run screaming from this place and its freakoid occupants.

"Much to my aunt's disappointment, I'm perfectly normal. No sign of any supernatural gifts, not even a flicker, which is why she insisted I attend school here for the next two years 'til I graduate." He made cutesy quotation marks with his fingers. "If you open your mind, Quinn, immerse yourself in New Age subjects, who knows what may manifest?"

I chuckled at his perfect imitation of Brigit's voice. "What do your parents think about it all?"

Discomfort flashed across his face, darkening his eyes to emerald. "Mom's a hippie. Never knew my dad."

"Me either," I said, wary of any guy who was the principal's nephew but happy to find some common ground with the first "normal" person I'd met all day. "How long have you been here?"

"Three months."

I winced, hoping Nan would snap out of her coma soon and I'd be back in our cottage by the lake, away from visions and bad dreams and suspect principals. I couldn't imagine spending a week here, let alone months.

"It's a drag, but I'm making the best of it."

Something I could empathize with one hundred percent, but I

didn't want to bond with him, didn't want to feel anything other than resentment at being put in this position, placed here with the rest of the freaks. What would he know, anyway? Mr. *Normal* wouldn't understand what I was going through: the confusion, the fear, the anger, the hope I'd learn to control whatever was going on and not feel so utterly helpless.

"So what can you do?"

"Precognition," I admitted reluctantly. He'd find out from Brigit anyway.

A newfound respect gleamed in those enigmatic eyes. "Visions?"

"Uh-huh."

"How long?"

"Two weeks." Fourteen days too long. If I hadn't had those stupid visions, Nan wouldn't be in the hospital and I wouldn't be here. "Anything else you'd like to know? Like what I saw? If I can levitate? What I eat for breakfast?"

Some of my hostility waned as I noted his pained expression, his awkward stance of hands shoved in pockets and his body half turned away like he didn't want to be near me. This guy wasn't the enemy. He could be a potential ally in whatever I faced here. It would be smarter to befriend him rather than alienate him. "Sorry for being a pain."

"No worries."

Our gazes locked, and this time when I saw the flare of awareness in his eyes, it had nothing to do with his aunt's projecting energy.

Off-kilter, I gestured around us. "Aren't you supposed to be filling me in on details during the grand tour?"

"Right." He ticked points off on his fingers. "Some students find the New Age hippie thing isn't for them, so they only stay a term or two, but the school offers the normal subjects through to graduation."

So I got to excel at my favorites, English and biology, while flunking Read-the-Crystal-Ball.

"No boarding fee since we're funded by the Parapsychological Society, who would love to find more students willing to undertake post-grad work at college. You pay for incidentals. You choose elective classes, with the option of one-on-one tutoring, and take any classes you want on an accelerated program."

It all sounded very civilized. What he hadn't answered was the important stuff: how many other freaks like me were here, who the powerful freaks in charge were, and what they actually taught us.

Quinn was oblivious to my insecurities as he prattled on about practicalities. "No curfews, no uniforms, free rein of resources, access to whatever you need to get your high school diploma while honing your skill, if you have one."

"Just like summer camp, goody," I muttered. While the freedom didn't sound so bad, he didn't need to sound so damn peppy about being here. He was practically a walking, talking brochure.

"You wouldn't have come here if you were hoping for a vacation."

I smiled at the irony. This place was far removed from any

vacation spot I'd ever choose. Who would want to come here voluntarily?

Eager to finish the tour, I picked up the pace. When he fell into step without a word, I thought that maybe he'd underestimated his normality and possessed a hint of clairvoyance.

"How many people study here?"

"Ninety." My eyebrows shot up and he chuckled at my surprise. "About seventy are like me, magic wannabes, hippie kids interested in mysticism and paganism, nothing out of the ordinary. The rest are like you, gifted." He paused outside an elaborately carved oak door, his hand on the doorknob. "From what I've heard, some people have been here a while, but haven't gotten far."

"Why?"

He shrugged. "Because they're too scared to know."

I knew the feeling. Part of me wanted to gain control over the visions, wanted to use them to find my mom and maybe get the answers I deserved. But delving into my so-called power—what did that mean? I didn't want to know the future. The present was freaky enough. Besides, I wanted to be normal.

I'd always laughed at Nan's *second sight* and scoffed at her vague predictions. Some had come true, some hadn't, but they'd been so general, like horoscope stuff, and I'd never paid much attention. Yet when I'd confided in her about the visions, Nan hadn't been surprised. She'd merely nodded, picked up the phone, and called Brigit.

Quinn touched me lightly on the shoulder. "It's okay to be

scared. I guess it's better to know what you're dealing with, huh?"

Finding his touch comforting rather than spooky, I nodded. "I guess."

With that half-crooked smile that made my synapses zing, he turned the doorknob. "Come meet the rest of the crazy crew."

I stepped into a cavernous room lined with floor-to-ceiling bookshelves and ergonomic desks and chairs. The quiet hum of computers warred with the subtle murmuring of students. The heads bent over textbooks brought some normality to my otherwise abnormal day.

It also felt like the first day at high school when about twenty curious gazes swung my way: coolly assessing, openly inquisitive.

"Study hall," Quinn announced unnecessarily, beckoning me into the room. "Come meet Raven. She's a newbie too. Started last week."

Stares prickled the skin between my shoulder blades as we wound our way between tables, quickly reaching the far side of the room, where a girl around my age sat alone, her black hair shadowing her pale face and her snub nose firmly buried in a worn novel with a vampire on the front.

"Hey Raven."

The girl didn't respond and Quinn snatched the book out of her hands. "Listen up, bookworm. Newbie alert. Stop reading for a sec and meet Holly."

Disinterested dark eyes, almost as black as her hair, swept over me before she managed a tight smile. "Hi." She held out her hand to Quinn. "Book, please."

With a wicked chuckle, Quinn held it overhead. "Come and get it."

I liked Quinn, liked his ability to joke around and fit in and be at ease when he'd only been here a few months longer than I had. Considering how on edge I was, I could spend a lifetime here and I still wouldn't feel comfortable.

Raven rolled her eyes. "Child."

Before I could smile at Quinn's mock indignant expression, Raven did some fancy wrist maneuver while pointing an extended index finger at the book. I watched, dumbfounded, as it sailed out of Quinn's hand and landed back with its owner.

"Show off," Quinn said, his amused tone laced with admiration.

Raven arched an imperious eyebrow. "Just practicing."

"Like I said, show off." Quinn turned to me, his smile teasing. "Telekinesis is much more impressive than the stuff you can't see."

I mumbled a noncommittal response, curious as to how much *practice* newbies had to do and when I'd get to start. The faster I learned to control my precognition, the faster I could get out of here.

While I wasn't here to make friends, the fact that this Raven chick barely looked at me rankled. Who did she think she was? Some clichéd semi-goth in head-to-toe black, with the regulation long black hair, alabaster skin, and ebony nail polish? She probably changed her name just to sound authentic.

As if sensing my silent animosity, she shut the book with a loud snap and glared up at me. "What's your thing?"

"Precognition."

"Visions. Cool." Her disparaging flyaway comment implied it was anything but. She flipped open her book again.

Quinn swung his head between us, frowning. "We should hang out. You two can practice together in the vain hope it'll rub off on me."

Raven ignored us and flipped to the next page, while I shrugged. "What do we get to practice? Vampire-hunting skills and befriending werewolves?"

My snark captured Raven's attention long enough for her to look up from her book. "Have you had your version of the Sorting Hat with Brigit yet?"

"You mean the shortest interview on record, where I got told nothing before being handed over to Quinn with that weird hand buzzing thing?"

She laughed. "Yeah, same thing happened to me. Don't worry. You get used to it."

"Really?"

"Hey!" Quinn butted in, tapping his watch. "Cut the mushy female bonding stuff, I've got things to do."

Raven snorted. "You'd think he'd been here a year rather than three months."

"Guess it pays to be confident."

Quinn blushed at my backhanded compliment before waving toward the door. "Come on, let's go."

"See you 'round," I said, pleased when Raven smiled at me again.

I needed all the friends I could get in this place.

The rest of the tour proceeded without incident, and as much as my imagination had built boarding school up into some kind of haunted house for crazies, the reality was surprisingly tame.

The ancient sandstone building sprawled over an acre and consisted of long, cool corridors, several large conference-style rooms, a library, a cafeteria, a fancy dining hall, classrooms, and a dorm.

All very conventional, discounting the one class I'd peeked into that had books hovering over desks. Scratched that one off my subject list. Levitation 101 held little interest unless I could levitate my mom directly out of that dreary cave and away from the monster.

"Your room's this way."

Quinn pushed through a heavy wooden door and we stepped out into another stone archway linking the main building to more dorms.

I pointed overhead. "What's with the rocks? These stone arches are everywhere here."

He shrugged. "Stones were prominent in the megalithic period, supposed to be powerful in casting magic. Guess it stands to reason this place would have them." His half-crooked smile managed to be adorable and bashful at the same time. "I'm kind of a nerd for facts."

"Me too."

He stared at me for a long moment, something more than admiration in his eyes. "If you ever want a study partner, I'm your guy."

"Thanks."

Neither of us moved, and a slow blush crept into my cheeks. *I'm your guy.* I'd never had a guy want to study with me, let alone come near me, and the fact someone as cute as Quinn was offering made me think this place wouldn't be all bad.

"Hate to run, but I've got a bus to catch after I show you your room."

"Oh, right," I mumbled, mortified I'd misread his attention. The guy wasn't interested in me. He was being polite. All part of the grand tour, probably. *Schmuck.* Me, not him. I practically ran along the flagstone pathway, desperate to get to my room and away from the embarrassment of taking up too much of his time.

Quinn didn't speak as we walked, though I caught him sneaking a few confused glances my way.

"This one's yours."

We stopped outside a thick wooden door devoid of numbers and I frowned.

"No numbers, because we're supposed to be intellectually gifted, remember?" He laughed and I managed a tight smile.

I shuffled my feet, anxious to get inside before I made any more blunders. "Thanks for the tour."

His slow wink had me blushing again. "Anytime."

I opened the door and slipped inside, ready to close it, when he placed his hand in the doorjamb.

"Holly?"

"Yeah?"

"It's going to be cool getting to know you."

His lazy smile set my body buzzing all the way down to my toes, making me grin like a goofball. I watched him stride down the corridor, purposeful long legs eating up the yards, a guy going places, a guy knowing where he wanted to be. I envied him that, because right now, after the confusing, crappy day I'd had, I had no idea where I was headed, let alone what I'd find when I got there.

CHAPTER THREE

My plan to grab a quick snack from the cafeteria and head back to my room to eat in peace hit a major snag the second I stepped into the huge room and ran into someone. Literally. Not a little "oops, sorry" bump, but a full-on slamming into the back of a girl who appeared from nowhere as I entered. My apology died on my lips as she swung around to face me.

"What the hell do you think you're doing?"

She jabbed me in the chest, hard, and I struggled not to wince. Like I'd give the troll with the magenta Mohawk, ten eyebrow piercings, and a nasty lower lip bar the satisfaction. Usually, I'd walk away from confrontation, but after the day I'd had? I needed to let off a little steam.

Hoping I'd keep all my teeth intact on my first day here, I tilted my chin up, eyeballing her. "Me? I'm just getting some food. You, on the other hand, need to visit an optometrist."

"Are you implying I can't see where I'm going?" Her nostrils flared, making a tiny diamond stud twinkle in false friendliness.

I shrugged and waved my hand in front of my face as if shooing away an annoying fly. "Not implying anything. Stating a fact."

She bared her teeth and I inadvertently found myself searching for fangs. "So that's why Drake was all over you earlier."

"Drake?"

What did scary biker dude have to do with magenta Mohawk? "Don't know where you get your intel from, but you're wrong."

Her vicious leer made me wish I'd apologized and backed away. "I saw you cozying up under that tree." Her dismissive glance flicked over me. "You're so not his type, but I guess that badass attitude you got going on kept him amused for a few seconds."

Her possessiveness clued me in. Mohawk was biker dude's girlfriend. "You and Drake are together?"

The rings in her right eyebrow quivered in outrage. "What of it?"

I tapped my lower lip, pretending to think. "I guess that makes you the Duck?" I swear her eyes glowed crimson just like Drake's, and I braced, realizing too late that antagonizing people on my first day probably wasn't the way to go.

To my amazement, she let out a ripping laugh akin to a braying donkey, drawing the attention of every student in the cafeteria. She planted hands on her hips and cocked her head to one side. "Don't go getting any ideas, 'cause you and I are never going to be friends. But you're okay for a newbie."

It wasn't until she'd spun around and clomped away on her purple Doc Martens that I realized my hands were shaking. Swiping the clamminess down the side of my jeans, I headed for the fridge. I grabbed a strawberry milk and an apple, keeping my head down the whole time. I didn't want to run into possessive psychos or even the tentative friends I'd made in Quinn and Raven. All I wanted was to head back to my room, curl up on my bed, and process the monumental first day I'd had.

After chugging back the milk, I lay on my bed and crunched the apple, brooding with every mouthful. I might have survived my first day at boarding school for nutcases, but I felt just as isolated here as I had at Wolfebane High. I'd hated having to come here, but a small part of me had hoped a new start would make me feel different. Like I fit in or belonged or *something*.

Yeah, like I was desperate to fit in with a bunch of kooks. I lobbed the apple core in the trash and swung my legs over the side of the bed. I sat up and let the silence wash over me.

I don't know what I'd expected from this place, but it certainly wasn't anything this civilized. Apart from the few odd ones I'd encountered, the rest of the students appeared fairly normal. The facilities were classy, and my dorm resembled an eighteenth-century hotel room, complete with rolltop desk, fancy bookcase, and a bed designed for late mornings and skipped classes.

I reached for my iPod, jammed one of the pieces into my ear, and ramped up the music, my heart doing a weird little turnover as the first strains of Michael Bublé's latest song filtered through. Not my choice in music, but he was Nan's favorite—a good stand in for

Frank Sinatra apparently—and listening to his soulful voice and soppy music made me feel close to her at a time I needed her most. I wished my life could go back to the way it had always been, before the visions, before Nan's stroke, before cute guys I couldn't stop thinking about.

If Nan were here, she would've been overjoyed I was showing interest in a "boy," as she called any guy under forty. She'd urged me to date, to go out with my friends. And therein lay the problem. I didn't have any. My cell? Textless. Email account? Bare except for the usual spam for drugs and enlargements.

Sure, I'd had study partners and a spot at the nerd table at lunch if I wanted it, but nine times out of ten, I'd preferred eating outside under Wolfcbane High's oldest oak tree, my nose buried in a book, effectively shutting out the world and how damn lonely I really was. I'd never spoken to anyone at my old high school the way I'd spoken to almost every person who'd crossed my path today. I'd stood up to them all: Colt, Drake, Brigit, Mohawk. And what had happened? They respected me for it.

Maybe that was my mistake. Being a smartass wasn't conducive to flying under the radar, like I usually did. Here, guess it was hard to go unnoticed when I was considered *gifted*. Gifted, my ass.

These visions were a crock. I didn't ask for them, but I had to put up with them regardless, kind of like a toothache. As Michael continued to croon, I slipped off my ballet flats, lay down on the covers, and closed my eyes.

One day down.

I hated to think how many to go.

CHAPTER FOUR

After seven days at C.U.L.T. I felt like a fraud.

I hadn't had a single vision or weird dream all week, I hadn't started official classes, and the antagonism I'd expected from other students for being the new kid hadn't materialized. Maybe because the term didn't start until Monday, everyone including the teachers I'd met seemed laid back. We could wear anything we liked, do anything we liked—within reason—and were generally treated like adults rather than a bunch of kids with odd talents or those dying to acquire some.

Not that I'd seen evidence of any of these fabled talents yet. Not a flash of unexplained lightning or exploding books or levitating lunch trays. Nada. For now, boarding school was just like Wolfebane High but for the new textbooks on subjects I couldn't comprehend. All very tame and boring.

Until Quinn came back from a week's vacation.

Sliding into the seat next to me at the library where I was trying to get a head start on divination, he leaned in close. "Party. My room. Tonight."

My first response, an instinctual refusal, died on my lips as I caught the spark in his green eyes. I'd never had a boyfriend, let alone a male friend, but something in the way Quinn acted around me, friendly with an edge, clued me in perhaps he'd like to be both. "What time?"

"After dark." He wiggled his fingers in front of my face and made ghostly noises, making me laugh.

"Good break?"

His smile instantly faded. "Not bad." He tapped the stack of textbooks in front of me. "I don't need to ask how you spent the last week."

Wondering why he'd closed down, I shrugged. "Being the new kid on the block sucks. Thought I'd get a heads up."

"Very noble." His smile was back—genuine, mesmerizing. I noticed the faintest dimple in his right cheek. He leaned across to check the title on the top book, brushing my arm in the process and I held my breath, surprised by how much I liked the momentary illicit contact.

Seemingly oblivious to my rigid posture, he flipped the book around. "This one's crap." He slid it to one side and sifted through the others. "Here, try this one."

"Thanks."

I exhaled as he straightened, a soft wistful sigh, practically inaudible. But as he stood, his hand brushed mine, a mischievous smile curving his lips. "You're coming tonight, right?"

"Uh-huh."

I held my breath again as he winked. "It's a date."

For the second time, I watched him walk away, my head a confused jumble.

Considering my lack of social life at Wolfebane High, it was no great surprise I wasn't a party animal. I never wore makeup beyond the occasional slick of gloss, I lived in jeans, and the only time I wore my hair out of a ponytail was in the shower.

Angry at myself for caring how I looked tonight, I brushed my hair ten times, slicked a sheer pink over my lips, and did a quick twirl in the mirror to check out my best jeans from behind.

Not good. My attitude, not the jeans.

With a resigned huff, I shimmied into a black T-shirt, slipped my feet into silver ballet flats, and barged out the door, slamming it behind me.

I knew where the mood came from. I hated being out of my comfort zone and that's exactly what would happen the moment I set foot inside Quinn's party.

I stomped down the corridor, headed outside and across a neat quadrangle toward the boys' dorms. I had no idea how many people would be there tonight or what the protocols were, let alone how to make small talk and pretend like I did this sort of thing all the time.

Since there were no door numbers, Quinn had hung a red scarf from his door handle, a move out of a bad B movie, and I smiled. I took a few deep breaths and huffed out some of my anxiety before knocking on the door.

It swung open immediately, and I almost staggered back from the cigarette smoke and thumping bass.

"You made it." Before I could respond Quinn tugged me inside and kicked the door shut. His smooth moves resulted in us both being momentarily off balance and me landing smack bang in his arms. Grinning, he hugged me tight. "Now this is what I call a party."

"Dick," I said, laughing as I wriggled out of his arms. Despite the semi-flirtation thing he had going on, it was too much too soon, and I was off-kilter enough without adding further complications.

He clutched his heart. "Ouch."

I rolled my eyes. "Your ego isn't that fragile. Get me a drink."

"What's your poison?"

Relenting after my abruptness a moment ago, I batted my eyelashes. "What have you got?"

He laughed, grabbed hold of my hand, and tugged me farther into the room. "See for yourself."

As we bumped and slid our way through the crowd of students, most of whom I recognized from the cafeteria or the library, I wondered what the attraction of parties was. Too many people crammed in a too-small space, the reek of cigarette smoke suspended in the air like a nuclear mushroom cloud, blaring bass so loud I couldn't hear my own thoughts, and—when we finally made it to the makeshift bar—enough alcohol to fuel a rocket ship.

Holding my hand aloft like we'd just traversed a Saks sale, he said, "What'll you have?"

I quickly scanned the bottles, recognizing vodka. "That, please."

"Coming right up." He sloshed vodka into a plastic cup and handed it to me, curling my fingers around the cup. "A toast?"

I sipped the vodka and hid a grimace as it burned a trail down my throat.

"To new friendships and new beginnings."

Corny, but sweet, and as I raised my cup to gently bump his, unease trickled through me. A cold clamminess that had little to do with the claustrophobic room and everything to do with an incoming vision.

I dropped my cup and Quinn froze. "What's wrong?"

"Nothing." Desperate for the door, I forced a smile. "I have to go."

He frowned. "But you only just got here."

My skin crawled, tiny zaps heightening my awareness of what was about to happen. "Sorry." I dashed for the door, forcing my way through the crowd.

I only just made it outside in time before darkness crashed upon me.

CHAPTER FIVE

A complex twist of dark, dingy tunnels opens into the cave with the altar.

The monster braces against the altar, chanting something in an eerie murmur.

A man flanks him.

The monster turns to him and nods once. "Bring her to me, now."

The man strides toward a crude archway in the far wall, reaches his arm through, and grabs something.

A long, low moan of torment fills the air, then is quickly cut off.

The man drags someone into the cave by the hair, feet fighting for purchase against the cold, hard stone. Scrabbling, twisting, writhing.

Mom!

I moaned as my eyelids fluttered open and I found myself crumpled against the wall outside Quinn's room, with him and Magenta Mohawk standing over me.

"You okay?"

Concern creased Quinn's brow and Magenta Mohawk stared, then kicked me in the ankle with her steel-capped boot. "Here's a tip. Stay off the booze."

She guffawed as I shot her a death glare.

"Lay off, Maisey."

"*Maisey?*" I managed a hoarse chuckle that quickly grew into full-blown giggles at the irony of a badass like Miss Mohawk having a sweet old-fashioned name like Maisey.

Maisey's eyes narrowed. "You laughing at me?"

My slightly hysterical laughter had more to do with the vision than a punk girl with a bad attitude. I desperately needed an outlet for the wild fear careening out of control and making me laugh like a hyena on an acid trip.

I'd just seen my mom being manhandled and brought to some monster like a sacrifice. For that's what that altar conjured up, some kind of spooky place for crazy rituals. And judging by the monster's cut-glass commands, I could imagine him going in for some seriously crazy stuff. On second thought, I didn't want to imagine. Seeing him in scary snippets was bad enough.

Trying to subdue my chuckles, I snorted a few times before finally sobering up enough to say, "'Course not. You could be called Daisy Duck for all I care."

She flipped me the finger, ignoring me as she started patting down her pockets with her other hand.

"No pot," Quinn said in a voice threaded with steel.

"Just great," Maisey muttered, her Mohawk bristling like an

angry porcupine as she glared at me like I'd told her to lay off the drugs.

"My room, my rules. If you're heading back into the party, stay off the dope."

Maisey stood toe-to-toe with Quinn, who didn't give an inch.

After a tense standoff that couldn't have lasted more than a few seconds, she said, "Fricking drug police." This time, she flipped us both the finger before flinging open the door, stomping back into Quinn's room, and slamming it shut.

"Nice company you keep."

Quinn shrugged, his smile bashful. "Chicks love me. What's a guy to do?"

I loved his confidence and lighthearted banter, but now that we were alone, the enormity of what had just happened crashed over me again.

My mom was in the hands of a monster.

While she wasn't my favorite person and never would be, I broke into a cold sweat at the thought of her being tortured or abused. She didn't deserve that, even if a small part of me would have liked to torment her myself for abandoning me.

I rolled my tense shoulders and tried to unwind. But all the exercises in the world wouldn't relax me if I couldn't wipe the vision from my mind.

Quinn's smile faded. "Want to talk about it?"

I shook my head, needing time to process what I'd seen and the implications for my mom before I articulated it to anyone, let alone I guy I liked. "I'll head back to my room."

"Sure? Maybe the best way to handle this stuff is forget it for a while? Party on?"

He made some weird sign with his thumb and pinkie I'd seen on an old Hawaiian Elvis movie once and I couldn't help but wish I could be the type of girl who'd do exactly that: forget what had just happened, go back to the party, and have a good time. But I wasn't, and the sooner I got back to my room, back to my comfort zone, the sooner I could start analyzing what all this meant.

"Sorry, maybe another time?"

"Party pooper."

Before I could move, he slid an arm around my waist and hauled me close. Close enough to smell bourbon on his breath, close enough to see a tiny scar below the cleft in his chin, close enough to make me uncomfortable. For a second I was tempted to just lay my head on his shoulder and forget everything.

Slipping out of his semi-hug, I forced a smile. "See you tomorrow."

"Okay."

This time, he watched me walk away, and as I glanced over my shoulder at the end of the long corridor and he raised his hand in a wave, I could've sworn I saw my soul-deep yearning to share my problems with someone else reflected in his face.

I didn't head back to my room. As I left the boys' dorms and the fresh air hit me, I immediately felt better, so I decided to take a stroll around the grounds. Probably not the smartest move late at night when I was already seriously spooked by that vision, but hey, it wasn't as if the visions could become a reality. At least, I hoped not.

The grounds were deserted; not surprising, considering most of the student body was jammed into Quinn's room. As I rounded the corner of the main building and saw the river glistening in the distance, I knew where I was headed.

I loved the water. I loved the fact that Nan's cottage was nestled on the shores of Lake Wolfe and I had a view of all that pristine blue every morning I opened my eyes. I'd grown up paddling and canoeing on the lake, and more recently had spent hours curled up on the sandy bank re-reading favorite childhood books. Nan had known how much I loved the lake and had known my shifting moods by how often I went or how long I spent down there.

Picking up the pace again, I pinched the bridge of my nose to stave off tears. Thinking of Nan, of home, made me maudlin. I called the hospital every day to check on her progress. The generic "sorry, no change" reports did little for the part of me yearning to be back in her kitchen, gobbling her infamous chicken pot pie.

"No more," I'd told her a million times, yet she still forced a huge slice on me every time.

"Packed with protein, good for you, young lady," she'd say with her patient smile and I'd fork a little more into my mouth, despite my skinny jeans busting at the seams.

We went through this ritual often, for while Nan never spoke of Pop, who'd died a few years after they'd married an eon ago, she always made chicken pot pie, his favorite, when she heard a song that reminded her of him. Lucky for me, because that pie was seriously good, and she made it often.

A loud hoot made me jump and I glanced up in time to see an owl spread its wings and take flight, majestic as it swooped down on its prey.

Prey …

Gulping, I tried to eradicate the instant image of that monster ordering his lackey to drag Mom into the cave by her hair. Barbaric, chauvinistic bastard.

And that's when the futility of the situation hit me like a sucker punch to the gut. I sank to me knees, oblivious to the damp soil, and clutched my stomach.

I had no idea if any of this was real.

Maybe the visions were the warped product of my conscience, denied the truth of my mom's disappearance for so long? Maybe I wanted to believe she'd been abducted by some monster to avoid facing the uglier truth: that she didn't give a crap about me, hadn't loved me enough to stick around, hadn't wanted me in the first place.

I watched the owl grasp a helpless mouse in its claws.

No freaking way would I ever be that vulnerable.

CHAPTER SIX

Even when I didn't have visions, I was still a freak. That was the only explanation for the fact that I was up, dressed, and raring to go on my first day of lessons. There was something about new classes, new books, new subjects, that made me edgy with anticipation. I liked to learn, to fill my head with facts, to memorize fascinating stuff.

Total freak.

After snagging my messenger bag, I opened the door to find Quinn standing there with his fist raised to knock.

"Hey, you look great."

"Thanks." I preened at his compliment before I registered his poorly hidden worry. He'd expected to find a blathering idiot after last night. I eased out into the corridor, not wanting to talk about the vision. I'd self-analyzed myself into a coma afterward.

"Ready for today?"

I shrugged. "First days are the same everywhere. Big time suckage."

He laughed. "Can't fool me. A girl who spent the last week poring over texts in the library would be itching to sit in the front row."

"Asshole."

We grinned at each other. He pushed the dorm's outer door open, and I stepped through it and under the stone archways that covered most paths in the school.

As I walked past the first arch, the sun hit me in the face, momentarily blinding me. I blinked several times, confused by the scorching heat that spread from my face down. My arms tingled. I shook them out, but that did nothing for my burning body and jelly-like legs. I stumbled, reached out to the nearest stone, and blindly slammed my palms against it. Unable to get a hold on the rigid stone, I slid down, burning from the inside out. My eyelids slammed shut and my body curled inward, protecting me from the debilitating heat.

As the burning slowly receded, I swiped a hand across my eyes and opened them.

And screamed.

"What the … ?"

Nan always said talking to yourself was the first sign of madness. If what I was seeing was anything to go by, I'd bypassed an entire highway of signs and arrived straight at the nuthouse.

The bright lights of New York City in the distance cast a gray glow on a murky sky, creating that weird, permanent half-light that mega cities had. Cities like Tokyo and Singapore and London, cities that appeared constantly awake because of that strange, undeviating light that clung like a pall.

I saw a large parkland dotted with makeshift housing in rows, fringed by dilapidated, squat apartment buildings. And trees, millions of trees, some surrounded by food and incense and votive candles.

A few people wandered the dirt pathways between the roughly constructed houses, some tending to the bizarre offerings beneath the trees. They appeared normal enough—no antennae, no multiple limbs, no green complexions—which meant I was having a run-of-the-mill dream. Delusion. Whatever. Or maybe heat exhaustion. That had to be it, what with the bizarre heat that had flushed my face and felt like it had blistered my lips. I closed my eyes, took a deep breath, and re-opened them.

To the same scene.

If being shipped off to C.U.L.T. hadn't been bad enough, now that'd I'd been here a while, maybe I'd ended up with a one-way ticket to Crazy-Town.

"About time you showed up."

I jumped at the derisive voice too close behind me and whirled around, off-balance, off-kilter, just plain off. What I saw didn't help. A boy with startling blue eyes, dark brown hair curling around his collar, and enough muscle to make a superhero jealous. Though a surly sneer ruined the overall sexy thing he had going on.

Annoyed by his unwarranted antagonism, I eyeballed him.

"Well, I would've shown up sooner, but I guess my invitation got lost."

Something akin to amusement shifted in his eyes before he eradicated it with a deliberate blink. "You'll need that sense of humor around here, Holly."

He knew my name. Just like that, my bravado vanished. I tried to speak, but fear clogged my throat.

"It's okay. You're safe. For now."

I didn't like his addendum any more than I liked being in this freaky dream. "Who the hell are you and what's with all the cryptic crap—"

"That's enough."

Rude jerk. His frown deepened; his social skills were on par with mine: not good. Could his rigid posture and grim expression make it any more obvious he didn't want to be near me?

He couldn't have been much older than me, but the awareness in those too-blue eyes, like he'd seen what the world had to offer and had come back for seconds, made me feel gauche and awkward and naïve. Nan would've called him worldly and promptly warned me off guys like him. I probably would've listened. I didn't go in for the whole bad boy thing, the palpable danger that emanated off brooding guys like him.

While I'd always hated being tall, standing around five-eight in my ballet flats, he was dauntingly taller, towering over me by at least a head. As he continued to study me with those hypnotic eyes, my stomach flip-flopped. Maybe it was fear, maybe it was hormones, but I'd never felt such an instant connection with a guy before; just my luck it had to happen in a dream. A million hyperactive butterflies slammed against my ribcage, leaving me breathless as I racked my brain for something witty to say.

"Joss." Grudgingly, he held out his hand, and after staring at it longer than polite, I shook it. My palm tingled with the same heat that made my face feel like it was on fire. *Joss.* Impressive name. Matched the guy. Shame about the personality.

I released his hand and flexed my fingers, wishing the buzzing would stop. If his handshake rattled me, it had nothing on his reluctant smile as the heat from my hand spread through my body and, embarrassingly, stuck in my cheeks.

"The heat? The tingling? It's normal."

"Yeah, if you're a freak." Great, I'd finally found my voice, only to sound like a total loser.

"You're confused." He took a step toward me, and those damn butterflies started breakdancing on my heart. "Let me simplify this. I'm here to protect you."

Flinging my ponytail over my shoulder while silently cursing my grungy jeans, faded cherry "I Heart Reading" T-shirt, and navy striped hoodie, I gave him my best don't-jerk-me-around glare. "Don't need protection. I'm a big girl, so thanks but no thanks." Under my breath, I added, "Some dream."

"It's not a dream."

I raised an eyebrow, begging to differ.

"You've teleported."

My jaw sagged. None of this made sense. Weren't hot guys in dreams supposed to make you feel good, not confuse the hell out of you?

"You astral traveled. Transferred to another plane. Eiros."

"*Where?*"

"New York's Innerworld."

"Right, well, that clears up my geographical confusion."

He chuckled, a low, smooth sound that warmed me better than Nan's hot chocolate. But the thought of Nan made my eyes sting and I blinked rapidly, determined not to cry. Mistaking the reason behind my tears, he touched my arm and *wham*, more of that scorching heat.

"Hey, don't cry."

"I'm not!" Which, of course, served to bring on the waterworks in a big way.

"Let me explain."

I didn't want an explanation. I wanted to wake up back at school. Or better, back at Nan's, in my old room surrounded by my books, my fifteen pairs of jeans, and the only photo of the mother who'd abandoned me six months after I was born.

I stood almost toe-to-toe with laugh-a-minute Joss, rolling on the balls of my feet, wanting to punch something. "Explanations are a waste of time. I'm going to snap out of this dream or whatever any second, so save it for someone who cares."

The corner of his mouth twitched, and some of my resentment dissipated. Leaning against a nearby tree, arms folded, biceps bulging nicely, thank you very much, he reminded me of James

Dean, that rebel dude in one of Nan's old movies. Nan said he'd been hot in his day. Joss had the same sense of coiled tension, of inner restraint, ready to snap at any second.

"You're special, Holly, more than you know."

Now he was trying a line on me?

"It's not a line."

My jaw sagged for the second time in as many minutes. "How did you do that?"

"The protection thing? Means we're connected. I can read your mind."

Dream Boy was psychic? Could this get any weirder?

"So go easy on the nicknames like Dream Boy."

Blushing, I plucked at the edge of my T-shirt before pinching myself, hard, trying to wake up or snap out of this heatstroke. It hurt like the devil, but did little. I was still here.

"We've been waiting for you."

We? Was he using the "royal we" or referring to a load of other figments of my imagination?

"The Sorority of the Sun."

I hated the mind reading thing. Couldn't a girl have a little privacy in her own dream? "Sororities suck."

His lips thinned in an unimpressed line. "Not this one. Trust me."

"I don't even know you."

"Easily rectified." He pushed off the tree, invading my personal space and I gulped, more from his serious hotness than fear. I wasn't used to guys hanging around me, let alone standing this close, and no matter how hard I honed my tough-girl exterior, inside I was a bundle of confusion and edginess and hopeful hormones.

Joss was the type of guy I'd admire from afar. An untouchable. Someone way out of my league. Which didn't mean I couldn't look and dream, right?

Guys like him didn't give girls like me a second glance—I should know. Been there, done that, pined over a yearbook picture of the hottest jock at Wolfebane High for an embarrassing two years before snapping out of it.

As he leaned forward, the faintest waft of sunshine and apple orchards washed over me, tempting me to bury my nose in the crook of his neck and inhale deeply. When he lingered near my ear, close enough that if I turned my head slightly our lips would be inches apart, I nearly passed out from the anticipation.

"We've got all the time in the world to get to know each other before this thing is through."

His soft breath feathered my ear and sent another tingle shimmying down my spine. I didn't dare move, no matter how much I wanted to, afraid I'd shatter the moment, afraid I'd read too much into this encounter, real or otherwise, and that I would make an absolute idiot of myself.

When he straightened, I exhaled in relief—and disappointment. What did I expect, for Dream Boy to kiss me after knowing me ten seconds?

He didn't touch me. He didn't have to. His voice, his eyes, his body, all screamed knowledge of me, and an intimacy I didn't understand. But I wanted to. Despite my false bravado, I wanted to know why I was having such a vivid dream and why a guy like Joss was scrutinizing me like I was the only girl who existed on the planet.

He acted like he knew me, *really* knew me. Impossible, considering I didn't know myself. I preferred not to overanalyze, because digging deep could reveal stuff I'd rather not know. Like the real reason Mom abandoned me.

And why I'd recently started having freaky visions.

"Sorry to disappoint, but this *thing* is all in your imagination." Shaking my head, I held up my palms, backing away. "Or mine, actually. Your protection jargon and getting to know each other? Wrong girl, wrong dream."

"I know it's a lot to take in—"

"You're full of it. Teleporting isn't real. Your ridiculous *Innerworld* isn't real. I'm not really here. So you can take your protection and your stupid sun sorority, whatever that means, and stick it." If I *had* teleported, they would've heard me all the way back in Wolfebane, I was that loud.

"You'll see. This is just the beginning."

Like hell. If he thought I'd be having another dream like this in a hurry, he was sorely mistaken. I folded my arms and glared. How *did* you get through to a stubborn figment of your imagination? "You're seriously pissing me off with the aloof, cool act and all the crap you're spouting."

He shrugged, like whatever I said meant jack. "You're rebelling. Understandable. But our bond is real, whether you like it or not."

He touched the center of my forehead with a fingertip and traced a spiral pattern. The blinding pressure from that light touch made my knees wobble and something indefinably scary explode in my chest like a fireball.

I staggered and would've fallen if he hadn't grabbed me and set me back on my feet. When he touched me, I felt some kind of connection that made me feel safe, rather than terrified. After the initial shock wore off, the heat and the pressure felt strangely comforting, like he'd wrapped me in my favorite duvet, sat me down next to a blazing fire, and plied me with hot chocolate. I was that toasty, that secure, and so freaking out of my mind I was starting to buy into his whole "we're connected" crap.

I wanted to move, wanted him to release me, but when his hands started stroking my upper arms in a soothing rhythm, my potential freak-out faded and I swear I sighed like a lovestruck goof-off.

"I didn't expect our bond to be so powerful."

His eyes widened until I could see my reflection in all that gorgeous blue. I didn't like what I saw. A girl in serious danger of believing in a fantasy that wasn't real.

I shrugged off his hands and took a step back. "What did you do?"

"Tested our bond."

"You're a freak," I muttered, fearing I was more of a freak than I'd realized. "This can't be happening."

"You must learn to control it."

"I would if I knew what *it* was."

"Your teleportation gift." Joss raised an eyebrow in disbelief. "I already told you."

"Yeah, but that doesn't make it real." I thrust my chin up, daring him to deny it.

He smirked. "It's real. All of it. You'll come to know that in time. But for now, it's not safe for you here. Cadifor's gaining power. The gray Eiros sky is a pale imitation of its former brightness, hovering between Cadifor's darkness and the light."

"Cadifor?"

His voice dropped to a conspiratorial whisper. "The Lord of Darkness."

Okay, now I'd seriously crossed into fantasyland. "You're making this up."

"He's evil."

"So is half the world's population. Get over it."

He shook his head, glaring at me like I was a problem child. "This isn't a joke."

I quirked an eyebrow and pretended to study my chewed nails as if I didn't have a care in the world. "Do I look like I'm laughing?" Realizing how bad my nails were, I thrust my hands into my pockets. "I'm over this dream. So if you could kindly wake me up—"

"Listen, Cadifor is a monster and he needs Arwen to regain control. If Cadifor finds Arwen, he obliterates our world."

"Liv Tyler's in on the dream too?"

He frowned and I rolled my eyes. "Lord of the Rings movie? Liv as Arwen? Get it?"

Annoyed my smartass comment didn't elicit a glimmer of a smile, I glared right back, trying to pretend his reference to a monster, hot on the heels of my visions, didn't scare me as much as the wild gleam in his eyes.

Feigning indifference, I shrugged. "Fine, I'll humor you for whatever time is left in this freaky dream."

The corners of his mouth twitched. Yeah, as if grumpy Dream Boy would crack a smile. He was so focused on all this evil-lord-of-darkness crap that he couldn't be any tenser if he tried.

"Though don't you find all this stuff a tad overdramatic?"

His eyes narrowed, not diminishing the beautiful blue one iota. "You said you'd listen."

With an exaggerated huff, I said, "Fine." I gestured around us. "When you say 'our world,' you mean this place?"

"You've never studied the druids in history?"

Unimpressed, I blew out an exasperated puff of air aimed at my bangs. "Do you think I would've asked if I knew?"

Unfazed, he thrust his hands into his pockets, seriously distracting me for a moment with the way his biceps flexed. "The original druids were based in Ireland. Thanks to the Irish settling in New York many moons ago, much of the Innerworld is based on Celtic mythology. Ever heard of Newgrange?"

I shook my head, more intrigued by his impromptu history lesson than I cared to admit.

"Newgrange, *An Liamh Greine,* means Cave of the Sun. Basically, it's an underground grave complex made from stones. We have something similar here."

I quaked at the mention of an underground grave, my visions fresh in my mind.

"It has a long, narrow entryway with a high shaft at one end. For about a week before and after the winter solstice, around December twenty-first, sunlight enters the shaft, travels along the passageway, and ends at a stone block decorated with spirals." He seemed reluctant to go on. "It's believed the stone was originally an altar used for human sacrifice."

I usually loved spooky stories—give me anything from wizards to vampires to zombies and I was in fantasy heaven—but real-life historical stuff like this? Too creepy.

I wanted to bolt, but he rushed on. "Eiros worships the sun as a god, which is where you come in."

"Me?"

"You're bound to Belenus, the sun god." He cleared his throat, as if his revelations were somewhat uncomfortable. "You're the Scion."

"What's that?"

"By definition, the youngest member of the family." He shrugged. "In your case, you're the sun's progeny. An heiress of powers." He sighed, as if the thought of me being the heiress of anything made him supremely uncomfortable. "You're the most important member of our culture."

His low, steady tone willed me to believe, but all I could think about was how my life could have gotten so crazy.

"The Innerworld is real. Think of New York City with a veil around it. Eiros is the extra layer behind the veil. We exist on a different plane, but run concurrently to the present, kind of like a parallel to the Outerworld. We're fringe-dwellers, caught between the city and the druid history that binds us."

I was a little intrigued as he continued. "Belenus created the veil initially, establishing Eiros as a place for his gifted descendants to reside comfortably without being made to feel like freaks. Anyone with special powers is welcome, but you must believe in Bel and his solar reign."

"Guess that counts me out, then."

"Not really. Most of the inhabitants were born in Eiros, but those who are gifted non-believers can cross between the Inner and Outer worlds. Like you." His smirk irked me. "Think of us as New Jersey. On the outskirts of NYC with an interesting population."

I shook my head and glared at him in disbelief. "You honestly expect me to believe this crap—"

"Eiros is where you belong. You're one of us."

His calm, his conviction, almost made me believe him.

"Who *are* you?" I whispered, caught up in the magic of his story and the otherworldly sense of this place despite my reticence.

But before he could answer, I heard a footfall, and he stiffened, his head snapping up. "Someone's coming." If Joss was a warrior, every muscle in his body screamed he was ready to do battle as he held a finger up to silence me.

"Joss is behaving strangely again. Guilt, perhaps?"

He paled at the nearby voice, and before I had time to ask what he'd done to be guilty of, he hissed, "Go. Now."

He placed three fingers on my forehead, the heat licking along my skin and erupting in a fireball. Panicked, I squeezed my eyes shut, my stomach churning until I thought I'd barf, but thankfully it faded quicker this time, only to be replaced by a cold clamminess I knew all too well.

The images started, fragments on fast forward, flashing before my eyes, making little sense.

Dark cave. Altar. Circle of stones.

I willed more to come, focusing so hard a sharp pain cleaved my brain. But I persisted, desperate to control this, to make sense of it.

Some kind of offering. Daintily arranged within the stones. The monster steps forward to the altar, holds out his hand to a nearby figure.

A faceless shadow whispers, "I'm right here, Cadifor."

Hand reaches out, accepts his, sets a match to the offering.

The flames illuminate them standing hand in hand, very much together, very much a couple.

They peer into the flames, their heads so close they touch.

The shadow isn't faceless anymore as she watches Cadifor in adoration.

Mom, how could you ...

I moaned, a low, guttural sound ripped from deep within.

Then nothing.

Blackness. A terrible, empty void that left me gasping and clutching my stomach, wishing for more, yet terrified it would come.

When I opened my eyes, I was crumpled in a heap outside the dorm door, with Quinn's arm around my shoulder, his expression one of fear and confusion.

That's when the waterworks started, because the last thing I needed now was for one of the few friends I had in this place to think I was nuts.

"Shh ... I'm here." Quinn wiped away the tears streaming down my face and smoothed my back while I sobbed, helpless and frustrated.

I wasn't a weak person. I'd been through worse as a kid, had wallowed in the pits of despair when everyone around me at school had the perfect families, the perfect moms who helped in the classroom and baked cookies and hand squeezed lemonade. I had tried to be stoic for Nan, had determinedly studied hard with a single-mindedness no one could understand.

Yet seeing my mom happily holding hands with a monster who abused the crap out of her ripped a hole through my bravado and left me vulnerable. As for me being a Scion and being able to teleport? Didn't help my susceptibility.

When the last sob faded to a hiccup, I stood, embarrassed, and stepped away from Quinn to establish some distance. He didn't say anything, and for that alone I could've hugged him back, but when I finally raised my reluctant gaze to his, I knew why.

He'd seen my horror, my rage, my helplessness. All of it was reflected in those expressive green eyes, focused unswervingly on me, sending me a silent message that everything was going to be okay.

After what I'd just seen?

Like hell.

CHAPTER SEVEN

I paced Brigit's office like a caged raccoon on speed. I hadn't wanted to see her, but Quinn insisted, his cool, rational arguments no match for the blubbering mess I'd been after the last vision.

I didn't understand why they were coming so frequently now, couldn't comprehend if they were real or present or future. Whatever they were, I couldn't ignore them any longer. Seeing my mom and the monster as BFFs left me no option.

I needed help, pronto.

"Thanks, Quinn. I'll take it from here."

Brigit waved toward the door, but Quinn didn't move. He waited, concern creasing his brow.

Touched by the way he'd stood by me during my semi-freak-outs—at the party and this morning—I forced a smile. "I'll be fine."

"Sure?"

"Uh-huh. And thanks."

With a funny half-salute at me, he nodded at Brigit and left me alone with the woman I now had to rely on.

I didn't like relying on anyone. I loved Nan but had shielded her: from my emptiness, from my alienation, from my desire to demand answers to questions I'd had since I was a toddler. I'd never felt close to anyone but Nan, and thanks to an understanding guy who accepted me for who I was, visions and all, I felt closer to Quinn than I had to anyone at Wolfebane High. Maybe it was all the weird stuff happening to me, but I felt strangely vulnerable. I could use a friendly face in what would come.

Brigit slammed the door and I jumped. Her expression bordered on maniacal as she faced me. "What happened?"

"I had another vision."

She squinted at me, carefully assessing. "Quinn said it was more than that."

I wanted to tell her everything, wanted to blurt the entire crazy truth, but something held me back, a paranoid fear that saying it out loud would make it more real.

When I didn't respond, she shook her head and squashed into a chair next to me. "He said you blacked out before the vision. And when he touched you, you were burning up."

I nodded, giving her that much.

"Did you black out under an archway when the sun hit your forehead?"

I stiffened, spooked by her fanatical grin as she grabbed my hand, squeezing way too tight.

"You're *the one*."

Wriggling my hand out of hers on the pretext of smuggling a tissue out of my pocket to swipe my nose, I couldn't shake my increasing foreboding. First Joss, now her. I couldn't be *the one* anything. I was too ordinary, the girl nobody noticed, the girl nobody cared about. Being *the one* implied I was special, and that was so far from the realms of reality that it was laughable.

"There's been a mistake. I—"

"No mistake." Brigit leaped from the chair, no mean feat considering her butt had been wedged a second ago, and started pacing. "I've been waiting for years, and now you're finally here."

She stopped and considered me like I was Santa Claus, the Easter Bunny, and the Tooth Fairy all rolled into one, and I didn't like it. Those things were fictitious for a reason; they didn't exist, just like Joss and Eiros and some make-believe monster called Cadifor.

"Arwen is within reach. ... " She sighed, then bestowed an ecstatic smile on me.

I still hadn't figured out exactly what Arwen was. Too busy bad-mouthing Dream Boy and his ludicrous proclamations instead of asking questions. Proclamations now being echoed by my principal, proclamations becoming more real by the minute.

"You teleported, didn't you? To Eiros?"

"How did you know?" The words were out before I could stop

them. I'd been doing fine up until now, letting her do all the talking, trying to make sense of it. But something in her conviction, in the way she rattled off Arwen and Eiros as if they were facts, unnerved me. As long as I believed teleporting was a dream, I could handle it. If it became real ... if I really could move between worlds, behind some creepy *veil* ... no way, I couldn't think about it.

Having the visions made me feel like enough of a freak. Add teleporting to the mix and I was likely to go off the deep end.

"You're the Scion. Part of a legend."

"I can't be."

"Ah, but you are." She wriggled into the seat again, staring at my forehead until I squirmed. "I've been waiting for a descendant of Bel to walk through these doors. The stones in some of the archways are aligned a certain way, so when the sun hits your third eye—" She pointed at my forehead. "—the Scion will be teleported to Eiros, home to the Cave of the Sun."

Bel ... Belenus. Cave of the Sun. She positively beamed while I made the connection. "Belenus, the sun god. Your family *geis* binds you to him."

Every time she said something to echo Dream Boy, it made this uncanny situation all the more real. "Geis?"

"An unbreakable bond."

I shook my head, refusing to process any of this.

"Let me explain."

I knew I wouldn't like what she was about to say, not one bit.

"You're part of an ancient druid culture. Druids were keen

observers and recognized that a child born in a certain season would develop certain abilities."

Unfortunately, I was beginning to see exactly what *abilities* she was talking about.

"When's your birthday?"

"August first."

She nodded and gave me another ear-splitting grin. "Lammas, Celtic Lugnasad."

I had no idea what she was raving on about but had a feeling I'd soon find out.

"Our calendar is different from the norm. It's based on solar equinoxes and sabbat cross quarter festivals." She pointed at me. "Even your name ... among Celtic tree astrology, Holly has regal status. Those born under the Holly sign take on positions of leadership and power ... you're seldom defeated. ... "

Her body quivered with excitement like a giant mound of Jell-O. "We'll have to add extra subjects to your study load." She scribbled down a few additions to my schedule on a manila folder and handed it to me.

Unfortunately, lithology, semantics, and dendrology didn't make any more sense than the rest of what she'd said. Smiling at my confusion, she ticked the subjects off on her fingers. "Lithology is the study of rock structure and composition. Semantics is the study of signs and symbols. Dendrology the study of trees. All valuable knowledge for your quest."

"To find Arwen and save the world," I mumbled under my breath. "Yeah, yeah, so I've been told."

"You found your warrior already?"

I had two choices here: play dumb, learn nothing, and end up in a nuthouse for sure, or cooperate and hopefully understand the upheaval turning my life upside down.

Resistant to the end, I slouched and folded my arms. "All I know is when I walked along the corridor outside the dorm a little while ago, the sun poked through one of those holes in an arch. I got all hot and woke up in that Eiros place you mentioned. Some guy Joss said I was bound to him and a sorority had been expecting me."

I hesitated, not wanting to tell her the rest for fear she'd think I was on some weird power trip. "He mentioned I was the Scion and that Arwen thingy would save the world."

"Anything else?"

I twisted my hands, indecisive, and she slammed her palms on the desk. "This isn't some game. Your worst nightmare is about to come true if you can't do this."

I didn't like the obsessive glint in her eyes or her stupid scare tactics. Maybe Drake had been right? With her angry frown and compressed lips and crazy eyes, she certainly channeled psycho.

"Listen up. You've heard of Armageddon? The end of the world?"

I shrugged. Who hadn't?

By her glower, she didn't appreciate my silent sullenness, but she didn't scare me. I had scarier stuff to face than one edgy principal, like that monster in the cave if this Scion stuff was true.

"If Cadifor finds Arwen before you do, he'll reunite with Mider,

Lord of the Underworld, and Nemain, Lord of Panic and War, and resurrect every underworld creature to cause a great war, the last for humankind. Demons, zombies, the undead, you name it, the Dark Trio will use it to battle humans, who don't stand a chance against immortals."

The corner of her right eye twitched. Nerves? Lies?

"Once they have total domination of the Inner and Outer worlds, darkness will prevail forever."

She paused, and I half expected her to say, "Do you want to be responsible for all that?"

Like a guilt trip would work.

When I deliberately stayed silent, she continued, "In a huge battle many suns ago, Bel triumphed over the trio. Mider and Nemain vanished. Cadifor renounced the light, so Bel banished him to exist underground, powerless. Arwen is the only thing that can help him rise to full status again."

She paused, her sideways glance shifty. "Your mother is underground too, you said, in your visions?"

She knew. Damn it.

On the walk over here I'd already started piecing together the coincidences of my mom being in an underground cave with a monster that just so happened to sound like this lord of darkness. What were the odds of my mom abandoning me in favor of a monster? And how much of a freaking sad case did that make me?

Not wanting to talk about the connection I'd already made between Mom and Cadifor yet, I stalled for time. "What's Arwen?"

"A powerful biokinetic icon. It uses kinetic energy to rearrange or control genes in the body. If mastered, genetic reprogramming could produce superhumans."

Brigit's fanaticism made me want to rub the goosebumps off my arms. "Or in the wrong hands, Arwen has the power to produce indestructibility. Immortality."

My doubt must've shown, as her fervor increased. "This isn't fiction. There've been a lot of strange phenomena lately, indicating Cadifor is closer to finding Arwen. If that happens ... "

She didn't need to elaborate. Even a novice-to-Weirdsville like me could figure out what the lord of darkness could do with an icon to create his own version of immortals.

Brigit fixed me with an intimidating stare. "You're the only one who can stop him."

"Me?" I squeaked past the growing lump of dread in my throat.

Brigit nodded, her expression solemn. "Druid legend says the Scion, a priestess, a descendant of Bel, will have the power to find Arwen."

A chill skittered down my spine as she touched my forehead, the exact opposite of what had happened when Joss touched me there.

"And don't forget, in doing so, you'll find your mother."

She didn't play fair. I didn't want any of this. This responsibility, this angst, this mindless panic—it was all some huge cosmic mistake. But having Mom tied in. ... Did I have a choice?

If I found her, I'd finally get a chance to ask all those questions ... to get closure ... to find peace ...

"You don't have a choice."

Her holier-than-thou tone made me bristle. "I do—"

"Breaking a geis can set in motion a chain of reactionary events. It will lead to misfortune, and in most cases, death."

I'd initially thought my visions had to be karmic payback, the great cosmos giving me the finger. Now I had to accept the rest of this legend or face impending death too? "What if I refuse?"

Brigit stood so abruptly her chair slammed against the polished wooden boards and I jumped, startled by the flicker of fury in her eyes. She blinked, her usual benevolence in place when she picked up her chair and resettled it.

"You can't. You're the only one who can stop him."

Some freaking responsibility, a responsibility I hadn't asked for, a responsibility I definitely didn't want, but if there was no way out of this, I'd have to feel the fear and do it anyway.

Glancing at her watch, she tsked. "I have a class to run. Help yourself to the Arwen texts over there. We'll talk more as soon as I'm done." She pointed to one of the floor-to-ceiling bookcases, softening her brisk tone with a fake smile that creeped me out as much as the ridiculous fairytale she'd told. "I know this is a lot to take in and you're scared. But you won't be alone. I'll help you every step of the way."

Her offer didn't reassure me as she swept out of the room, paisley caftan billowing behind her like a witch's cloak.

I had to save the world or die.

CHAPTER EIGHT

No principal should ever trust a student to be left alone in their office, yet there I was, surrounded by all this stuff. Then again, Brigit probably had supernatural eyes in the back of her head and would come swooping in on her broom the second I touched anything other than her precious texts.

I crossed to the bookshelf behind Brigit's desk. My hand skimmed the spines. I adored books, and Brigit's were fascinating. My fingers trailed along *Esoteric Traditions of the Innerworld*, *Celtic Gods and Goddesses*, and *Druid Bewitching Seasons*, before finally settling on *The History of Arwen*.

I slid the book out and laid it on the desk, surprised by the normalcy of it. Considering the month I'd had, I half expected the book to glow red, sprout horns, or emit puffs of green smoke. The simple black cover and gold embossed title didn't inspire me to read it, but the moment I flicked open to the first page and saw the sunburst, the same one I'd seen on the medallion hanging around that girl's neck in my vision, I was hooked.

It was the only time I'd seen her, during that vision in Brigit's office on my first day here. I wished I'd seen the girl more clearly, but she'd been in shadows.

Usually a methodical reader, I shrugged off my usual reserve and started flicking past pages. Chapter headings caught my eye: *The Battle of Belenus, The Fall of Cadifor, Dark Trio of the Underworld, Arwen's Triple Flame.*

Something inside me wobbled as I speed-read the text: *The Druids are a spiritual elite within Celtic society. They are poets, doctors, astronomers, philosophers, and magicians. They pass on necessary knowledge in oral rhymes. Historians say it took an individual Druid twenty years to learn them all. The most important of these rhymes is the legend of Arwen, an icon that brings great power to the one who possesses it.*

Only a female descendant of Belenus has the power to find Arwen. She will be the Scion and have an affinity for heat, able to move between the Inner and Outer worlds as an extension of her clairsentience. Initially manifesting as visions, or psychic knowing, this clairsentience will develop into astral travel through the manufacture of intense temperatures via the third eye.

The necessary high temperatures to travel will be invoked by the accurate pinpointing of heat onto the psychic eye via the sun's rays through ancient megaliths, the pyrokinesis of a warrior, or the use of a trans-channeling crystal in the sun. Another reported travel method is the Arwen symbol coming into contact with the psychic eye, assumed to produce instant high heat and enable spontaneous teleportation.

Horrified yet unable to stop, I read on.

Once the rift is opened between the Inner and Outer worlds, the Scion will come. Through the acquisition of Arwen she will restore Eiros to its former glory.

Following the Battle of Eiros, when Belenus banished Cadifor to the Underworld and ascended to the sun to take his permanent immortal place, Eiros—meaning 'bright' in Celtic—filled with light.

However, if Cadifor's powers increase and the Lord of Darkness breaches the divide to enter Eiros through nefarious means, a gray pall will settle over Eiros, indicating the imminent rising of the Underworld and the ultimate obliteration of all worlds.

When Eiros oscillates between darkness and light, time is of the essence as Cadifor is close to acquiring Arwen, and the Scion must master a series of tasks in order to fulfill the prophecy of finding Arwen and saving all worlds from the last Great War and permanent darkness.

My head spun with the implications of what I'd just read. Seeing it in print, bound in a book, made this all the more real and inescapable. I continued to skim, skipping paragraphs, reading others, the enormity of my so-called fate consuming me until the letters blurred.

I'd had enough reality checks for one day. I stuffed the book into my bag and headed for the door, the hardcover of my destiny banging against my hip as a reminder of what I had to do. Reading Brigit's texts on Arwen cleared up the last of my preconceptions that maybe if I ignored all this, it would go away. Seeing it in print made it more real than anything Joss or Brigit had said. I was tied to this sun-god-defeating-darkness tale, and the sooner I learned everything I could, the sooner I'd start to feel more in command.

The lack of control pissed me off, like all these different worlds were spinning around me and depending on the moon or the sun or whatever other orbit chose to affect me today, I might end up on any one of them.

Time to take back control. Time for me to call the shots. That meant another visit to Eiros This time, I wouldn't let Dream Boy send me scuttling back with a blast of heat from his fingertips. This time, I wasn't coming back until I had answers to the million questions stabbing my brain.

I glimpsed a thick cloud cover out the window. How would I get back to Eiros? As much as I didn't want to approach Brigit after her strangely manic behavior, I had no choice. She'd have the answers I needed.

I yanked open the door and found Quinn and Raven silently arguing with hand gestures and comic miming. They stopped the second they caught sight of me.

"Looking for me?"

Raven stared like she expected I'd spontaneously combust. "Quinn told me what happened."

Sheepish yet adorable, he shrugged. "We wanted to see if you were okay."

Their concern touched me, and the enormity of the truth teetered on the tip of my tongue. Maybe if I told them it would make absorbing the bizarreness of all this easier to accept. They'd probably understand.

I dismissed the thought in a second; I'd finally made friends for the first time in my life and I didn't want to jeopardize that. Right now, two of us shared average run-of-the-mill telemetric skills, while Quinn was blissfully normal, a fact I liked in my increasingly topsy-turvy world. Mention my teleportation and world savior crap, and who knew what they would think? What if they didn't believe me and thought I was some crazy attention-seeking liar? Would they think I was trying to go one up? Be the best? Suck up to Brigit for outstanding grades?

I knew what that was like, kids thinking I was a suck up. I'd been through it every school year. But I didn't want that to happen here. I didn't want to alienate Quinn or Raven. I liked them. Besides, I'd probably need them before this thing was through.

"I'm fine." I closed the door to Brigit's office and glanced at my watch. "Aren't you two supposed to be in class?"

Raven raised an eyebrow. "Could say the same about you."

I jerked a thumb over my shoulder at Brigit's office and grimaced. "Had to stay in there 'til I was feeling better."

"Wanna ditch for the morning?" Raven suggested.

I laughed at Quinn's horrified expression before he quickly masked it.

"Something tells me our learned friend here doesn't want to miss classes first day of a new term."

Quinn flashed me a grateful smile while Raven rolled her eyes. "He's so desperate to swap crystallomancy for algebra it's pathetic."

"It's my first day. Guess I should show up at a class or two," I said, leaping to Quinn's defense and earning a wink for my troubles.

"Lameasses," Raven muttered, shaking her head. "I'll make you a deal. One quick coffee, then we'll head to class."

"Deal," Quinn said. "You in?"

"Sure." I nodded, forcing a smile. If I didn't want my friends learning the truth, I had to start acting normal. As we fell into step, I ignored the tiny voice inside my head that said *"Acting normal? Waaay too late for that."*

CHAPTER NINE

Raven received a text as we rounded the first corner that sent her scuttling to her room, saying she'd catch up with us soon, and no amount of teasing or prying from Quinn could get anything out of her.

While Raven went off on her mysterious text jaunt, Quinn kept up a steady flow of chatter as we headed to the dining hall. I loved that, *the dining hall*. No plain old cafeteria for C.U.L.T.

"Did Brigit help?"

"With … ?"

"What happened earlier?"

"Yeah, she clarified a few things." Like how I should be a good little girl and do as I was told—or die.

"Good. I bet it's scary when all that weird stuff starts happening to you."

I wondered if he was patronizing me, but his guileless green eyes made me want to trust him.

"Bet a tough guy like you wouldn't be scared."

The green darkened to moss as something dark and painful shifted.

"It pays to be scared."

Before I could probe further, he smiled, his momentary seriousness gone. "You know what? Screw coffee. I'm starving. Time for an early lunch."

The round antique wall clock over his left shoulder read ten-thirty. "You're nuts."

"Matter of opinion." Grinning, he jerked his thumb in the direction of the serving line. "Besides, I skipped breakfast."

I sent a few *oinks* his way as I followed him. The crazy thing was, as soon as I smelled the food, my stomach rumbled. I hadn't had anything to eat since last night. I grabbed a tray and started loading it.

While the dining hall itself looked like something out of Harry Potter, all long tables, high ceilings and chandeliers, the food on offer was surprisingly tame. I piled a wholegrain turkey sub, a strawberry yogurt, and an apple on my tray and followed Quinn to a nearby table.

I hesitated, unsure which seat to take, not wanting to make a social gaffe. Sensing my discomfort, Quinn pointed at an empty chair and sat next to me. "Relax. Everyone's been where you are right now."

"In this seat?"

He grinned. "You're thawing enough to crack jokes. Good."

"I'm not frozen."

"I guess not."

Well aware he was referring to my burn-up session earlier, I shuffled in my seat and picked at a strand of lettuce hanging out of the sub. "Can we not talk about before—"

"Forgotten." He focused on his giant burrito doused in chili, but not before I'd glimpsed his raging curiosity.

"You really going to eat that at this hour?"

In response, he forked a giant clump of avocado, refried beans, and chili into his mouth, chewed quickly, and followed with a soda chaser. "Does that answer your question?"

Wrinkling my nose, I laughed, the happy sound strangely foreign.

He stabbed his fork in the direction of my sub. "Besides, it beats boring old turkey any day."

Yep, that was me, boring. Boring wardrobe. Boring taste. Boring social life.

My forehead tingled, making a mockery of my pity party for one, reminding me exactly how un-boring I'd become. "Any other newbies apart from Raven?"

"The rest have been here a while, six months or longer." He waved his fork at the tables around us, scattered with groups of students. "That's why they're hanging around here rather than in class. Seniors have different schedules and loads more free time. And even juniors get to set their own schedule to a certain extent. Makes for small class sizes and quicker learning potential, apparently."

Glancing around the huge hall, I noticed the general rowdiness of a normal cafeteria was not there. Instead, a muted hum filled the room like a low buzz from a million bees. Maybe the kids here didn't like talking as much as other kids? Considering why some of them were here, I didn't blame them.

Jerking my thumb toward a corner where an African-American kid was surreptitiously toasting his bagel with fire from his fingertips, I lowered my voice. "The normal kids are okay with watching weird stuff?"

"Yeah, they wouldn't be here if they weren't into all that New Age jargon, so nothing's a secret here."

I couldn't distinguish any particular groups beyond the popular girls fussing over manicures. No nerds with heads buried in books while they absentmindedly shoved food in their mouths, no geeks sharing megabyte data as they huddled over the latest technology. Here in Weirdsville, kids just mingled, moving between tables, comfortable in their own skin.

I envied them that, big time.

"Wonder if we'll ever fit in like that?" Quinn nodded at a group of laughing kids playing around with tarot, his uncertainty echoing my own.

"Seems like you already do."

His mouth curved into a laid-back smile that was becoming oddly familiar. "My mom calls me a chameleon. Always adapting to my surroundings."

"Good trait to have." Wish I had it, so I could blend in and hide from obsessive principals and hot warriors and lords of darkness.

He took another gulp of soda and set the can down. "What about your mom? Is she happy you're here?"

My hand stilled halfway to my mouth, my appetite instantly vanishing. I replaced the sub on the plate. "What's with the twenty questions?"

"Just making a little friendly conversation." He folded his forearms, rested them on the table, and leaned forward, creating an intimacy that made me uncomfortable. "Don't know about you, but I could use all the friends I can get in this place."

Quinn had a gift, one that was just as valuable as anything supernatural: putting people at ease. Other guys would've bristled at my defensiveness, lost their temper, or slouched off, calling me names under their breath. He, on the other hand, knew the right thing to say.

"My mom vanished when I was a baby. My Nan raised me … " I hesitated. "Mom's part of the visions I've been having. It's seriously weird."

He searched my face and then nodded, satisfied that I'd told the truth. And I had. Just not all of it.

"Do you think the visions will help you find her?"

"Not sure I want to."

His jaw sagged slightly. "O-kay then."

"It's complicated."

"Aren't all parents?"

Latching onto a quick deflection of attention, I said, "What's your story?"

He shrugged and took another slug of his soda, but not before I glimpsed a flicker of guilt in his eyes. "The usual. Dad ran off before I was born, Mom worked two jobs to make ends meet. I had a high IQ, which made me stand out at high school when I wanted to blend in. Then Aunt Brigit pressured Mom into sending me here to see if I'd develop any latent talents, and Mom, who's big on psychic phooey, jumped at the chance."

He tried to sound blasé, but I knew better. Being different sucked, but at least I had a reason for boarding here with the rest of the freaks.

"How close are you to your aunt?"

He screwed up his nose. "Honestly? I barely know her. She turned up at our place out of the blue a few years ago, Dad's long-lost sister apparently. Mom never doubted who she was, but ... "

I raised an eyebrow, sensing a story.

"It's kinda weird, you know, having someone you don't know act all friendly and offering you a place at school and watching you on the off chance you'll develop a talent other than blitzing algebra and impressing women."

I bit my bottom lip to stop from laughing out loud.

"You and Raven are the only ones who know Brigit's my aunt. The rest think I'm some teacher's pet suck up."

"Harsh."

He shrugged. "Who gives a rat's ass? I grew up surrounded by my mom's New Age crap, so I guess I'd be lying if I said I didn't hope something would come of my incarceration here." He chugged back the rest of his soda, crushed the empty can, and lobbed it into the trash. "Who knows? Maybe I'll outsmart you and Miss Moving Objects?"

Whatever talent Quinn might or might not develop, it'd have to be pretty damn spectacular to beat my *gift*.

"Do you miss your old school? Your mom? The city?"

He smiled, tiny laugh lines fanning out from the corner of his mouth, reminding me how seriously cute he was. "Now who's playing twenty questions?"

Sheepish, I toyed with the rest of my sub before ditching it. "Nan always said I was too curious for my own good."

"Your Nan's cool with you being here?"

"Nan's in a coma."

Tears burned, but I'd be damned if I cried in front of him. I'd learned to hide my true feelings from a young age, a handy trait for someone like me.

"Hey, you okay?"

He reached out and touched the back of my hand. I snatched it away, hating feeling so vulnerable. I was used to keeping everything locked inside, putting on a brave face for Nan, pretending like everything was okay.

Did Nan know about me from the start?

Did Mom know?

Is that why she left?

Did the possibility of having a freak for a daughter send her running?

"Holly, if you don't want to talk—"

"Hey, Psycho Man, move over." Raven teasingly bumped shoulders with Quinn as she sat on his other side, and I exhaled in relief. I didn't want to talk. What I wanted was answers and there was only one way to get them.

Find my mom.

I picked up my tray and stood. "I have to go." Raven's face fell and I forced a smile to put her at ease. "Psycho Man?"

"Psycho, short for psychometric. Our friend here is very touchy-feely, so I reckon he could be psychometric, able to read people by touching them." Raven placed the tips of her fingers against her temples, and leaned into Quinn. "I think I'm getting something. A vibe." She winked at me. "Nope, sorry, no vibe, just a vain hope for asking out one of the Movers and Shakers."

Quinn scooted away from her with a death glare. "You're a riot."

"Movers and Shakers?"

Raven took a bite of her chicken sandwich and waved at Quinn to answer.

"The telekinetic crowd, like our resident clown here, who move things." He jerked a thumb in Raven's direction, who continued to munch into her sandwich while flipping him the bird.

Their antics soothed my fear so I lingered a little longer. "Let me get this straight. Psychos are the psychometrics, Movers and Shakers are telekinetics. Any other group I should know about?"

Raven held up the fingers on one hand and ticked them off one by one. "The Cogs are your average post-cognitive and precognitive dudes, the Firestarters are the pyrokinetics, the Crybabies are the empathics, the Zeldas are the clairvoyants, and the MindReaders are the telepaths."

I gaped as she pushed down her last finger, not sure what confused me more, the nicknames or the range of abilities people here had.

"You've bamboozled her." Quinn shook his head. "Precogs have visions, like you, pyrokinetics produce heat or fire, empathics gain knowledge by touching an object or person, clairvoyants predict the future, and telepaths are a mix of precog and clairvoyant."

"Clear as mud," I mumbled as Raven crooked her finger at me and I leaned forward.

"Just so you know, those names aren't public knowledge."

I liked these two, I really did, but I had more pressing things to do than stick around and swap banter, like find Brigit and ask how the hell I could get back to Eiros and start searching for Mom— oh, and her precious Arwen.

"I have to go catch up with Brigit before I eventually make it to class. Maybe later?"

"Yeah, sure," Raven said, her disappointment audible. Quinn did a funny half-salute thing that made me smile as I picked up my bag and slung it over my shoulder. I took two steps before I realized something. At Wolfebane High, no one had cared whether I left the lunch table early. Quinn and Raven made me feel something I'd never thought I'd ever feel at school.

Like I belonged.

CHAPTER TEN

I caught a glimpse of Brigit striding across the grounds toward her office as I left the dining hall. I hurried after her, needing answers to the questions raised by her text. It had mentioned something about a crystal being able to teleport me when combined with the sun. Hopefully Brigit could elaborate.

My footsteps pounded the pavement and Brigit stopped, her initial frown easing, replaced by a benevolent smile that didn't soothe my anxiety for a second. "I was just coming back to see how you were getting on. I suppose you have loads of questions."

"Only a few hundred or so."

"Well then, let's head back to my office and see if I can answer some of them."

"I'd rather get the answers firsthand. From the people involved," I added, as if she wouldn't know who I was talking about if her little spiel about waiting *years* for the chosen one to walk through her school was any indication.

She rubbed her hands together at my apparent enthusiasm to return to Eiros.

"Come with me."

She led me down a neatly trimmed path winding through towering oaks before stopping near the river. I saw an old stone shed nearby.

"Did you read up on teleportation?"

I shook my head, feeling every bit the slacker student under the principal's watchful eye. "Only the basics." What with Arwen and the geis and impending death hanging over my head.

"You need to understand the science behind astral travel if this is going to work."

I nodded, wishing she'd hurry up. Clouds churned and shifted overhead. If that shed nearby was made of stone, I'd bet the roof had some of those weird holes. Holes plus sun plus some stupid legend binding me to Bel equaled instant teleportation.

Holding up a finger, she said, "Concentrate. Empty your mind. Focus. Tell me what you see."

My inner smartass wanted to say a finger but this was too important to muck up. I stared at her finger, deliberately blanking my mind, half-expecting sparks to fly out the end. Instead, a thick white band appeared, shimmering around her finger like the ring around Saturn. I didn't blink, too afraid it would disappear, and was surprised when the ring turned golden.

I risked a blink and refocused on her finger, thrilled when the golden ring was still there. A small victory, minute in the grand scheme of things, but it felt good—great, in fact—to make something happen.

"You see it, don't you?"

Brigit's voice quivered with excitement, and I nodded, blinking several times to ease the dryness in my eyes. The golden band disappeared.

"The energy field around objects is the etheric plane. All objects are part of a physical plane, and a portal is a wormhole of energy within the light matrix of a physical plane."

My attention started to wander and she smiled. "There is so much for you to learn. Ultimately, you will have to create your own portal to travel to and from Eiros, using heat and your third eye." Her finger pointed at the spot on my forehead. "So far, you've been able to psychically teleport only, which means your psyche instantaneously traveled to Eiros."

"Does that mean my psyche can teleport to other places too?"

"No, you're bound to Belenus, so your geis ties you to Eiros only."

I swiped my brow in an exaggerated show of relief, but she didn't smile.

"For you to find Arwen, you'll need to master the art of extensive teleportation, when your body and spirit move as one." Fixing me with a serious glare that meant business, she lowered her voice. "The only way to dodge an attack is to use this method. Otherwise ... " She shook her head. "Your psyche can teleport to escape a battle, but if your body is left behind ... "

I got the picture. Dead body meant my spirit would spend eternity ... what? Floating around haunting the jerks at Wolfebane High who'd made my life a misery? Not such a bad option, but for now, I wanted to live. I wanted to discover what made me special enough to be the Scion. I wanted to explore my friendship with Quinn and Raven. I wanted to experience the highs and lows of a first boyfriend, first kiss, first love. Then there was Nan's homecoming and my graduation and college.

I had a lot to live for.

Brigit's fingers dug into my skin like claws, her touch anything but soothing. The more obsessed she acted, the more I dwelled on Drake's warning. My gut instinct wouldn't let up, insisting there was more behind her eagerness to find Arwen. I'd rather take my chances returning to Eiros without her overzealous help by slipping into the shed and waiting for the sun about to break through the cloud cover.

"My head's spinning with information overload. Think I'll study those texts some more, and we can concentrate on the lessons later?"

She pinned me with a suspicious glare that elicited a ripple of unease. I tried to appear suitably exhausted. "Fine. Continue reading and meet me at the end of the day for follow up."

"Thanks, will do." I forced a brittle smile, sagging in relief when she strode away.

Rubbing my arms to get rid of the goosebumps, I wandered toward the stone shed down by the river. As I neared it, I tilted my head to one side to check out the roof's design. No doubt about it:

those stones were aligned in the same odd pattern as the arches covering every walkway in the school. This place would be perfect for practicing a little astral travel, newbie-style.

My hand rested on the door handle, my sense of apprehension growing.

I wrenched the handle. The door creaked open, and taking a deep breath, I peeked inside the dingy shed. Inside, slouched in a tatty armchair, was Maisey, holding up a crystal and squinting through it. I wondered if it was too late to make a run for it.

"Are you planning on standing there like an idiot all day? Come in and shut the door before you get us both expelled."

"Like you'd care." I forced one foot in front of the other and stepped inside. The door slammed shut, effectively trapping me in the shabby shed with the scariest freak at school.

She dropped the crystal into a small purple velvet sack on her lap and motioned me forward. "The thing is, I do care, because no way in hell I'm leaving this place 'til I figure out what that crazy psycho did to Drake."

Clueless, I waited, hoping she'd elaborate if I stayed silent.

Sniggering, she tossed the velvet bag from hand to hand. "You better watch out. Our illustrious leader loves *nurturing* newbies for her own agenda."

Trepidation shimmied through me. "You're just trying to scare me."

"Scare you?" Maisey leaped from the chair. I stumbled backward, and my knees collided with a crate. "If I really wanted to scare you, I'd tell you how Drake and I were dragged into Brigit's *otherworld* experiments. I'd tell you how I chickened out the first night when my dreams were invaded by the meanest friggin' demons you've ever seen. I'd tell you that Drake helped that psycho and ended up brain dead for a week, mumbling *rift* over and over. Before he left here without looking back."

Rift? No way. My knees knocked together, my mind swirling with the implications of Brigit somehow using Drake to open the rift between the worlds and potentially letting loose a monster. "Why didn't you go with him?"

She rolled her eyes. "Already told you, lamebrain, I'm going to discover what her parapsychological mumbo-jumbo did to Drake if it kills me. He wasn't the same when he left."

I could've sworn her bottom lip wobbled for an instant. Then the iron bar threaded through it straightened as she sneered. "I want my dude back, same as he was before that crazy psycho messed with his head."

I had no idea what to do or say until I focused on the velvet pouch in Maisey's hand.

I pointed to the pouch. "What are those for?"

"Drake gave me the bag before he left, so I figured it was part of the last experiment, the one that sent him … " She made loopy circles at her temple with a finger. "I've played around with the crystals, but I can't conjure up anything."

Asking a rebellious cow like Maisey for the bag would ensure she'd shove it into her pocket and slouch out of there. I needed a different approach.

"You're a pyrokinetic like Drake, right?"

"So?"

"Maybe Brigit did something to those crystals so neither of you could reproduce her experiment? Maybe she's scared you'd acquire some new power? Maybe someone else should try? That way, they'd face all the danger and you'd get your answers."

She regarded me with something akin to admiration before she tossed me the velvet pouch. "Knock yourself out."

"You think I should do this?"

She shrugged. "Whatever. I'm outta here. Let me know if you meet a demon or two while playing with those."

Maisey pushed past me, deliberately bumping me with her shoulder, and slammed the door. A cold gust of wind hit me in the face.

Rift.

On shaky legs, I stumbled to the armchair and sank into it, my hands tearing at my messenger bag to slip the Arwen text out. Careful to not damage the precious book, I flipped pages until I found what I was searching for.

Once the rift is opened between the Inner and Outer worlds, the Scion will come.

I closed my eyes, the significance of what I'd read earlier taking on new meaning following Maisey's revelation. I'd assumed Cadifor had opened the rift between the worlds, desperate to get his evil hands on Arwen. But if what Maisey said was correct, and she had no reason to lie, *Brigit* had opened the rift.

A wave of dread prickled my skin. There could be a perfectly logical explanation for this. Brigit wanted to stop Cadifor and his evil buddies from annihilating the world. Her intentions were altruistic.

But if Brigit couldn't be trusted, what was really going on at this boarding school?

I focused on the teleportation paragraph.

The necessary high temperatures to travel will be invoked by the accurate pinpointing of heat onto the psychic eye via the sun's rays through ancient megaliths, the pyrokinesis of a warrior, or the use of a trans-channeling crystal in the sun.

The crystals … I flipped through the book to see if there was a chapter on crystals and came up blank. I eased the book back into my bag and pulled at the drawstring of the pouch, sliding the contents into my palm.

The crystals were of various shapes, sizes, and colors, and as I held one up to my forehead, I remembered conducting my very own "sun through a magnifying glass" experiments as a kid, and the results: fried ants.

Hell.

If I was going to do this, it'd be trial and error, a matter of holding each one up to my forehead and waiting for the sun to poke through the stone roof.

I juggled them in my hand for a moment, contemplating the wisdom of trying to teleport on my own. But if I didn't try this, who would I turn to for help? Brigit? Not likely. Besides, the sooner I learned how to do this, the sooner I would get answers to the endless questions pinging through my head.

With a resigned sigh, I sat there, holding different crystals up to my forehead and waiting for the sun to peek through the clouds and through the hole-pebbled roof. When it finally did, I repeated the process, slower this time, hoping my brains wouldn't get fried if I stumbled across the right one.

On the fifth attempt, my forehead flared and I squeezed my eyes tight. The blistering heat spread through my body at lightning speed, pooling in my stomach, my lower back, my throat, and my head, pounding in time with my heart that was leaping and jerking like it was being defibrillated with paddles.

Nauseated, I waited until the urge to puke passed and the heat faded before I opened my eyes.

And found myself surrounded by three strangers—and Joss.

CHAPTER ELEVEN

"This isn't the best time for you to be here," Joss said, his frown reflected in the three other faces lined up like a firing squad alongside him.

I didn't like the way they were staring at me, like I was a juicy bug and they were ravenous spiders. I glared right back, hoping they couldn't read the fear in my eyes.

"The way I see it, there's never going to be a good time for me to be here. But I'm here now and I'm not leaving 'til I have answers."

My attempt to appear undaunted must've worked, for the only girl among them smiled. "Don't mind Joss. He takes his duties very seriously."

"Must be that warrior geis thing I've heard about."

Joss stiffened, obviously affronted I'd dare make light of it.

Before he could speak, the smallest of the trio stepped forward, a young guy with curly dark hair and twinkling brown eyes. "Joss is right, this isn't the safest time for your introduction to Eiros, but we're glad to finally meet you." He held up his hand, fingers and thumb spread wide. "I'm Mack."

The girl leaned forward, her whisper loud enough for everyone to hear. "He's the boss, being a direct descendant of Bel and all, but don't let his whole 'son of a king' routine fool you. He's really a pushover."

Mack smiled, a genuine "I'm happy to meet you" smile that eased some of my tension.

"I'm Maeve, by the way." She pointed at Mack's upright hand. "That's our greeting. You're supposed to place your palm flat against his, fingers and thumb spread to symbolize the sun's rays."

"Oh, right," I said, embarrassed I'd already made my first mistake. Not that I could've had a clue about their greeting. I had a feeling it would be the first of many things I'd learn here. I raised my hand and tried not to slap it against Mack's in a mistaken high-five. There was something strangely intimate about our splayed hands pressed together, in much more than a brief handshake, and I was grateful when he dropped his hand.

"And Mr. Happy over here is Oscar."

I bit back a smile at Maeve's apt irony. The guy with the short wavy chestnut hair and hazel eyes could've been cute, if he lost the scowl.

"Hey," he said, raising his hand in a laconic wave that confused the hell out of me, as I thought it was another sun greeting and lifted my hand only to find it hovering embarrassingly in mid-air when he quickly lowered his.

"The Sorority is pleased to welcome you. Come." Mack looked like a laid-back sprite, but a hint of steel underlined his voice, making it a definite command and not a request.

They surrounded me like four compass points: Joss on my right, Mack leading, Maeve on my left, and Oscar behind me. I didn't like the grouchy one having my back.

As we moved toward the dilapidated houses, I felt like a million pairs of unseen eyes were trained on me, assessing, finding me lacking as their *Scion*.

Would they inspect the tall blonde in the skinny jeans and black hoodie and scream *fraud*? Would their judgmental expectations fall flat the moment I botched my first ceremony or initiation or whatever other freaky event I'd have to attend to prove my worth? Would they see through me and sneer at my deep-seated fears that I'd never be good enough, that I'd fail spectacularly at the tasks I'd need to master and be responsible for an apocalypse?

That was my greatest fear: that if I was this so-called Scion, I was nowhere near ready for the responsibility. In trying to prove myself, I could lose more than my limited self-esteem.

I'd end up losing the world.

"She'll be safer inside," Joss said, halting outside a whitewashed cottage with black-trimmed wooden windows and a terracotta roof.

It was like something out of the Hansel and Gretel fairytale I'd loved as a kid. Nan used to read it to me and make killer gingerbread afterward ...

A pang of longing, so sharp, so painful, sliced through me, and I winced.

"Holly's had a rough trip. She needs to rest."

I could've hugged Joss for his intuition. His mouth quirked at the corners. Why did he have to read my mind for that stuff?

Nobody spoke, all deferring to Mack. I could barely see two feet in front of myself; shadows from the surrounding trees blanketed everything. As Mack turned toward me, his solemn expression sent a quiver of foreboding through me.

"There are others you need to meet. I'd prefer we toured the community before we confer privately. Is this agreeable to you?"

Once again, I had the impression this was a command, so I glanced at Joss for guidance. Far from happy, his lips compressed into a thin line as he exchanged frowns with Oscar. I barely knew these people, but even I could sense the strong undercurrent of tension running among them.

"Give us five minutes. She needs a drink, at least."

Joss squared his broad shoulders as if daring Mack to argue. After a tense moment, the leader nodded. "We'll wait here. Don't be long."

I managed a sarcastic smile of thanks, and followed Joss into the cottage, not having much time to notice my surroundings as he whisked me through a small lounge and into a kitchen.

"What—"

"Are you okay?"

He stopped so abruptly I slammed into him, and he steadied me, his hands spanning my waist. A delicious thrill shot through me at his protectiveness. I was used to taking care of myself, and while it was nice having Nan dote on me occasionally, having Joss fuss made me feel cherished in a way I never had before.

"I'm fine."

A tiny crease appeared between his brows, not detracting from his gorgeousness one bit. "You didn't look it back there."

"Overwhelmed, I guess."

To my mortification, my voice wobbled. His grip on my hips tightened, as if he could hold on tight enough to anchor me and stop the events swirling beyond my control.

"It's a lot to take in—"

"I can handle it."

"Good, because it only gets tougher from here."

"I figured."

As his grasp eased, I became acutely aware of how close we were and how his hands felt pressed against my hips. Solid and warm, his fingers splayed and dipped below my waist, an inch away from sliding between the gap of my T-shirt and jeans and encountering bare skin.

My pulse skittered as I wondered what it would feel like to have his hands on me. Would his touch be soft and gentle, or hard and commanding? Or an intriguing combination of both, a combination that encapsulated my warrior?

Ridiculous, as the only reason he had his hands on me was to steady me after I'd almost bowled him over, but as I chanced a glance at his face and our eyes locked, it was like I'd been electrocuted. I'd never had a guy regard me like that before:

a heady mix of brazen, confused need mingled with overprotectiveness. The longer I stared into those intense blue eyes, the easier it was to believe a guy like Joss could want more than to protect a girl like me.

When it seemed like we'd been staring at each other forever, Joss blinked and his expression hardened. "Our time's up."

He scowled and released me so quickly I stumbled, but this time he didn't touch me. He'd already headed for the sink where he was busy filling a glass of water, leaving me convinced I'd imagined that whole tension-filled episode a moment ago. "Here, drink this, then we have to go."

"Yes, sir."

My mock salute elicited a glower as I downed the water and handed him the glass. My admiration raised another notch when he rinsed it and propped it on the sink sideboard to dry. "Is this your place?"

His shuttered expression and quick shake of the head didn't invite further questions, which only served to raise my curiosity. "Safe house."

"And you need a safe house because ... ?"

"You'll find out," he murmured, a moment before the door flung open and Oscar loomed, grouchier than ever.

"Ready?"

Joss nodded. I huffed, hating all the secrecy.

When we appeared, they took compass positions around me again, and Mack said, "Come, we will begin."

His formal speech patterns seemed incongruous for a guy his

105

age. Then again, what did I know? The guy was royalty—and if I had my jumbled thoughts straight, probably some kind of distant family, with Bel being our common link.

Feeling increasingly uncomfortable with their treating me like the president needing Special Services protection, I fell into step, my head craning every which way as I got my first real look at Eiros.

For some crazy Innerworld inhabited by bad guys, the place appeared surprisingly cool. Like someone had scooped up Central Park and dumped it at the edge of suburbia. We were surrounded by lovely greenery and eclectic houses. But in contrast to the real park, if I squinted, I could make out grimy apartment buildings that thinned out as high-rises gave way to squat, ugly housing.

Most of the houses looked like they'd been slapped together by kiddie carpenters, though some had been carefully constructed from large, rectangular stone blocks the same charcoal color as the spooky archways back at school. A few had garish white roofs, dotting the landscape like tufts of cotton. The distant lights of New York City cast an eerie glow along the horizon, highlighting a hulking stone monstrosity that covered a hill as far as I could see, like a bizarre mix of urban grunge and jolly old England.

This old-world stuff didn't do it for me, and along with their formal way of speaking I was beginning to wonder if I'd done more than just teleported. "Have I time traveled?"

Oscar shot me an incredulous glare. "What do you think this is, a novel?"

A nervous frown creased Maeve's brow as she glanced at Oscar, then at me. "No time travel involved. It'd be so much easier if you could … " She trailed off and this time they all frowned at her. "What?" Defiant, she ignored them and focused on me. "If you could travel back you could meet Bel, discover the exact whereabouts of Arwen, and Cadifor wouldn't be a problem anymore."

"Good point."

"Do you know *anything* about Eiros?" Oscar asked.

Ignoring his audible derision, I nodded. "A little. Though I'd know more if you spent less time giving me attitude and more time treating me like I had half a brain."

Oscar snorted and Maeve chuckled. "Don't mind him; he hasn't had his rowan-berries fix today."

I raised an eyebrow, increasingly clueless and hating the feeling. Guess my high IQ meant jack in this place.

"Fruit of the quicken trees, what you probably know as ash trees. The berries are sacred, said to hold a magic for eternal youth."

Oscar snarled. "Quit babbling. She needs to know more important stuff than that."

Maeve smirked and poked her tongue out. "Like how you're a warrior but haven't guarded anything since you were out of diapers?"

I stiffened, caught in the crossfire as animosity rolled off Oscar in palpable waves. But before he could respond, Mack held up a hand. "Holly needs to meet Dyfan."

Whoever this Dyfan dude was, he held enough power to shut

the squabbling duo up. Mack led us up a garden path bordered by herbs and knocked at a wooden door inlaid with a weird symbol of five overlapping circles.

Joss caught me staring and reached out to trace the symbol with a fingertip. "The five-fold represents balance. The four outer circles symbolize the four elements: earth, air, fire, water. While this one—" His finger lingered on the inner circle, as if reluctant to break contact. "—unites all the elements to reach perfect balance between energies."

"Who's Dyfan? And why is this symbol on his door?" And why were they taking me on some grand tour when I wanted to ask questions?

Before anyone could answer me, the door swung open to reveal an older guy with long hair, a goatee, and some serious fashion issues, judging by his funky white PJs. They looked like pajamas, but on closer inspection resembled a long tunic and flowing trousers.

"Welcome, children. Come in."

As Mack led the way into the small cottage with a brief nod in Dyfan's direction while the others barely acknowledged him, I had an instant glimpse into the group dynamics.

Dyfan deliberately spoke down to Mack. Baiting him? Mack had to be in his mid-twenties, so lumping him in with the rest of us was a slap in the face. What I wanted to know was why.

"Dyfan is our philosopher-cum-head-priest." Mack wandered over to an overflowing bookcase and trailed his hand over the leather spines. "He presides over our rites at the Temple of Grian, the sun temple."

The philosopher stiffened at Mack's offhand tone, confirming my earlier suspicion. No love lost between those two.

"What our illustrious leader failed to mention is that I'm also his chief advisor." Dyfan's fake smile grated as he turned his attention to me.

"That's not your primary role, though, is it?"

"We call him our jack of all trades, don't we, Dyf?" In what I was fast recognizing as typical Maeve fashion, the bubbly redhead diffused the situation.

"You're too kind, Maeve." Dyfan nodded at her. "But I'm sure our guest has questions she'd like to ask."

Where to start? "What does a philosopher do?"

Oscar snickered as I belatedly realized the smartass response would be *philosophizing.*

Thankfully, Dyfan didn't mock me. "Please, sit. Then we'll talk. Drink?"

"Some rowan-berry juice might kick-start proceedings," I said, my nerves making me blab the first inane thing that popped into my head.

Mack grinned, Maeve chortled, and Joss shook his head, but the corners of his mouth twitched. Even Oscar the grouch managed a semi-smile.

Dyfan peered around the room, confused, which only served to widen Mack's grin.

Mack indicated we should sit around the table. "A Sorority joke. You know how it is."

Judging by the frown creasing Dyfan's brow, he didn't, and that pissed him off royally.

While Dyfan placed a tray of wooden goblets on the table, we sat. The guys perched on the edges of their seats, too big for the small round table. Maeve and I squeezed onto a bench for two.

"The Druids of Eiros are divided into three orders: The druidh, the filidh, and the baird." Tapping his chest, Dyfan puffed up with pride. "I'm a druidh. We're the teachers, philosophers, physicians, high priests of our community."

"Impressive," I said, gaining a beaming smile for my trouble. Oscar covered a snicker with a fake sneeze.

Ignoring Oscar, Dyfan swept his arms wide in a theatrical flourish. "We mediate disputes, try cases, and set penalties for criminal acts—"

"Dyfan's main role is to provide guidance to those who want it," Mack interrupted, sounding like the last person who'd seek out the druidh for advice.

Bowing his head in Mack's direction, Dyfan continued. "It is the druidh's place in the Innerworld to provide assistance to the reigning deity." He paused, his grin oily. "Particularly when that deity is so young."

And inexperienced. He didn't have to say it; his condescending tone was enough to make Mack bristle.

"Tell me about the others you mentioned."

Dyfan slipped into haughty teacher mode easily. "Filidh are

seers, soothsayers, gifted in divination."

When I frowned in confusion, Mack said, "They predict the future."

How convenient. Wish they could predict mine. Like whether I'd be any good at searching for Arwen. Whether I'd find my mom. Whether I'd get the answers I craved. And most of all, whether I'd survive this outlandish quest.

"The baird are poets and singers." He pronounced it like they cleaned toilets, and I waited for one of the Sorority to interject.

They didn't disappoint. "What our illustrious druidh has failed to mention is the baird are also known for their wisdom, often beyond that of other druid orders." Oscar tempered his snide explanation with a patronizing smile, taunting Dyfan to respond.

I didn't understand the politics of this place, but it didn't take a genius to figure out the group dynamics here sucked. If no one respected the chief advisor, where did that leave the community?

"But I'm sure the real reason the Sorority brought you to me tonight is to discuss the tasks you must master."

"Get on with it," Oscar muttered.

Dyfan held up his hand, fingers and thumb extended. "Firstly, you must master the art of traveling between worlds."

Mack winked at me. "Safe to say she's blitzed that one, considering she's here."

I shot him a grateful smile, thinking *if only he knew*. I hadn't mastered anything yet, fluking my latest teleporting effort courtesy of a nameless crystal.

Dyfan pushed down his index finger. "Next, you must gain

control over your clairsentience and use your visions to follow your gut."

Easy for him to say. Right then my gut wanted to rehash the last meal I'd eaten, which was too long ago.

His third finger flexed. "Become proficient at scrying." He pushed down his fourth finger. "You must face and banish one of the Underworld's lesser creatures."

Maeve patted my hand and murmured, "Banshees aren't so bad."

Easy for Little Miss Optimism to say.

Dyfan lowered his pinkie. "And lastly, you must become one with the Arwen Triple Flame to use it."

Once again, I had no idea what that meant. I nodded, relieved when Mack stood and beckoned the rest of us to follow suit. "Thanks for the enlightening chat, Dyfan. Holly has a lot of ground to cover tonight, so we'll take it from here."

"Thanks," I echoed, not surprised when the others merely grunted.

"My pleasure." Dyfan's quaint little bow made me want to giggle despite the churning in my stomach. "Remember, you need to master all tasks to stand any chance of facing Cadifor." His mention of my adversary made the blood drain from my face. "I'm happy to assist you in whatever capacity you need."

Joss touched my arm. Leaning down on the pretext of unlatching the door, he whispered in my ear, "You'll be fine."

I managed a brief nod, clamping down on the sudden urge to bawl. And trying to ignore how darn wonderful his warm breath felt against the sensitive skin behind my ear.

When he made to move away, I snagged his arm. "You know that mind-reading thing? Can you do it all the time?"

His lips curved into a smile that made me forget who I was, why I was here, and what any of this meant. "Why? Worried?"

"'Course not. Just curious."

"Bull," he said, the spark in his eyes alerting me to the fact I wouldn't like his answer, but would be powerless to do anything about it.

He was hot, and having him here, near me, made this whole crappy thing bearable.

He gently tapped the side of my temple. "Let me see. I'm getting a read right now that you're more than curious. You're downright petrified I can read every single one of your thoughts."

"Don't be a dick," I said, holding my breath when his finger stopped tapping my temple and slowly traced an invisible line down my cheek, lingering on my jaw before fading away.

Bending down, he whispered in my ear, "You also think this geis thing binding us isn't half bad."

"Screw you," I said, without a hint of malice, my voice embarrassingly shaky as his breath tickled my ear again.

"Relax. Because we're new at this, getting a read on your thoughts is like tuning into a shoddy radio. Intermittent and shaky at best."

"Really?"

"Yeah, you're off the hook." He touched me behind the ear where his breath had fanned me a moment ago—a brief, barely-there brush of his fingertips that short-circuited my brain and fired tingles through my body.

"For now."

We stared at each other for a long, drawn-out moment, a moment that signaled I could fall a little bit in love with my warrior if I wasn't careful.

I opened my mouth to say something, a smartass comment to shake me out of the stupor he created simply by looking at me, but he studied my lips before slowly, tantalizingly sweeping back to meet my eyes, and I almost melted on the spot.

"Don't say anything."

He pressed a finger against my mouth, and I clamped my lips shut before doing something incredibly out of character.

Staring into my eyes, he murmured, "I get it."

I was glad someone did, because at that moment, with my heart hammering and bucking like a wild thing, my skin prickling with hyperawareness and my soul yearning for a little romance, I didn't get a freaking thing.

"You're scared. But you can do this."

Oh. He'd misread my held breath and wide eyes as fear of what I faced. Disappointment filtered through me, for during that one, long, heart-stopping moment when we'd connected, I thought he actually *got* it, that I was fast developing a crush on my reluctant warrior.

Before I could say anything, he swung open the door, stony expression back in place as the others joined us. I slipped into my position as compass center, far from ready to face my next foray into life at Eiros.

"That went well," Maeve chirped, her constant optimism a tad annoying.

"As well as can be expected." Mack shrugged.

"Dyfan can be unpredictable," Oscar said, glancing over his shoulder as if he expected the philosopher to come swooping down any second. "And unpredictability is dangerous."

"We don't trust him," Maeve added, her expression surprisingly solemn. "He's tried to use his role as Mack's advisor to twist things to suit himself."

Mack nodded. "Dyfan is irrelevant in your quest, but when you start formal lessons here, he'll be one of your teachers, so it's best you're aware of his hidden agendas."

I focused on one thing. "Formal lessons?"

My voice came out an embarrassing squeak and Mack eased into a grin. "There is so much you need to know, so much you need to learn to help you on your quest, and here is the best place for that."

"But what about C.U.L.T.?"

"You'll need to split your time, weekdays there, weekends here. Combine theoretical and practical lessons across both worlds." Mack shrugged, as if my new seven-day schedule meant little. "You need to immerse yourself in your new culture if we're to succeed."

Oh, he was good, honing in on my feeling isolated, including me in their group, using *we* to show I was part of them. All very well, but I barely knew these people, and I was expected to trust them with my life.

Joss touched my hand. "You have to do this." My hand burned where his skin touched mine, a scorching heat that comforted. "Don't worry. You'll never be alone."

I don't know what freaked me out the most: the fact I'd be studying 24/7, the fact my life wasn't my own anymore, or the fact I liked Joss's touch way too much to be good for me. Accepting he could read my mind was freaky enough; crushing on him was beyond crazy.

Needing to string coherent words together, I faced Mack. "Do I get a say in any of this?"

"A feisty one," Oscar muttered, his grudging respect a surprise.

Mack shot him a quick frown before focusing on me. "You're overwhelmed. We understand. But time is running out and we need to get you up to speed as soon as possible."

I froze. "What do you mean, running out?"

He pointed upwards. "You've seen the sky?"

I nodded, some of what Joss had told me and the Arwen text I'd read coalescing.

"That permanent grayness is a sign that Cadifor is gaining strength." Mack's low voice sent a ripple of unease through the group, who stepped closer to me as one. "If Cadifor's confidence is increasing, he's getting closer to finding Arwen. And if that happens … "

He didn't need to spell it out. Even I knew the consequences if the lord of darkness ascended to power again.

Guess I didn't have a choice, and glancing around at the motley faces surrounding me—Mack skeptical, Oscar resentful, Maeve hopeful, and Joss stoic—I knew what I had to do.

"When do I start?"

CHAPTER TWELVE

Brigit didn't have a problem with my expanded schedule. Why would she, if I was merely an adjunct to her finding Arwen and gaining parapsychological notoriety? Or worse, if Maisey was to be believed.

While Raven would probably understand my newest abilities, what with her telekinetic talent, I didn't want to tell Quinn. Not that he wouldn't understand—he'd seen enough at this school to blow any preconceptions of normal sky high. On the contrary, he'd probably offer to help and I didn't want that. Quinn was my touchstone to reality, blissfully normal in a world where I didn't know what to believe anymore. I needed that normality more than ever.

Raven slid into the chair next to me, dumping a stack of books on the desk between us. "Divination first thing. Hope you brought your crystal ball."

"Sorry, left it at the cleaners."

She laughed, her open friendliness a stab at my conscience. It was good seeing a familiar face at my first divination lesson, but hanging out with Raven and Quinn made me increasingly guilty I couldn't tell my new friends everything.

"Where's Quinn?"

"No idea." Raven rolled her eyes. "Probably off on secret guys' business."

Wish I could ditch divination and delve into the many secrets plaguing me.

"Did Brigit give you a hard time yesterday? We didn't see you at dinner." Raven slouched into her chair, her kohl-rimmed eyes free of suspicion, which made lying to her even harder.

Feigning great interest in unpacking my bag, I mumbled, "Nah, she was okay. I was beat by the end of it, though, so I hid away in my room."

"Don't blame you. Not your average hole in the wall with a desk and bed, huh?"

Understatement of the year. My room at Nan's cottage could've fit into my dorm room four times over. "I kinda like that aspect of things around here."

She wriggled more books out of her backpack and plonked them on the desk. "We're treated like we're special and not some freak science experiment."

I nodded, thoughtful. "I hadn't thought of it like that, you're right."

Raven picked at the fraying spine on her copy of *Mastering Your Inner Scryer.* "Were you scared when you first arrived here?"

Surprised, I glanced at her to see if she knew anything and was subtly prying. But she appeared guileless, her expression uncomfortable, like she hated admitting any weakness.

"Honestly? I was petrified."

Her face eased into a smile. "Me too. I had no idea what I'd be in for. Like I wasn't feeling ridiculous enough anyway, what with the … " She waved her hand beneath the desk, pointing at my pen and levitating it towards my hand. It landed when I reached for it, and I laughed.

"When did you first discover you could do that?"

She screwed up her nose at the memory. "On a date with Randall Silverson. Down by Escanaba River, near Lake Michigan, where I'm from."

She flushed and glanced away, focusing on her stack of books. "I'd liked him for ages but we never hung out. Then we got partnered on a science experiment and he finally started to notice me, you know?" She waved a hand at her clothes. "It felt like he could see past all this, really see me. I kinda liked it."

I knew exactly what she meant. I'd felt the same way when Chad Holmesworth, jock extraordinaire at Wolfebane High, had started chatting to me around the time of the Spring Dance. I'd been stunned into immobility, but went along with it, curious to see why he was paying attention to me. The friendlier he got, the higher my hopes he'd ask me to go with him. He asked me, all right—for a year's worth of English lit essays so he wouldn't flunk and have that affect his college choices later.

"We started studying together, hanging out on weekends, that kind of thing. Then he asked me out. I couldn't believe it." She plucked at her bottom lip, her eyes hazy with remembrance. "We had pizza, and the crazy thing? I remember every topping on it, how it smelled, how he smelled ... "

My heart ached for her.

"After we ate, he held my hand and wanted to take a walk down by the river. Pretty romantic, huh?" Melancholy darkened her eyes. "The ass-wipe wouldn't take no for an answer and I was fending him off, wishing all the time something would land on his head and knock him out."

"And?"

She shrugged. "It did."

"Tree branch?"

"A rock. From the riverbed. Twenty feet away."

"Wow," I murmured, imagining how scared she must've been, fighting off a horny jerk and then discovering she could make things move just by thinking about it.

"I didn't believe it at first. Thought someone must've been spying on us and wanted to do the right thing." She paused, her strange smirk confusing me. "So I tried again later that night in my room. Draped my skinny jeans over the lampshade after I'd dumped them on the floor. Made books spin on top of my to-be-read pile. Rearranged my wardrobe. All while lying on my bed just thinking about it."

"Did you tell anyone?"

"Waited a month, then called my folks, asked them to transfer me to a different boarding school. Here."

A bitter undertone made me tread with caution. "How did you—"

"I searched 'moving stuff with your mind' on the Internet. Came up with loads of links to Brigit and her parapsychology crap. Found this place, so here I am." She toyed with the edges of her book, folding the corners into little triangles, and from her shuttered expression, I knew it couldn't have been as easy as she made out. "That Randall thing was a nightmare, but in a way I'm grateful. Maybe if it hadn't happened, I wouldn't have discovered the telekinesis."

"You like it? Being different from everyone?"

"Don't you?"

"Jury's still out."

She squared her shoulders. "I think it's cool and I love being here. Beats the dropkicks at my old school."

She had a point.

We didn't have time to talk further as a teacher breezed into the room. He made straight for the front desk, barely giving us a second glance. "Turn to page twenty-one of your *Divination for Beginners* text and start assembling the tephramancy experiment," he snapped.

His deep voice, extreme pallor, scraggly black hair, and head-to-

toe ebony clothes—shirt, trousers, overcoat—made him look like a caricature of every fictional baddie I'd ever read.

Raven must've thought the same, because she muttered something that sounded suspiciously like "Hogwarts" and I giggled.

"Do you have something to share with the rest of the class, Miss Burton?"

My grin faded. I shook my head. My cheeks burned as I quickly opened my textbook to the appropriate page.

"Don't let Crane intimidate you. He thinks he's a badass, but I bet he's a marshmallow," Raven whispered, as she ducked down to pick up a pencil she'd deliberately dropped on the floor.

"Okay, thanks." I smiled. Until I saw the first line of our first lab.

"Tephramancy is the art of foretelling the future by burning tree bark and reading signs in the ashes."

A memory of Cadifor leaning over a stone altar, lighting a match to an offering that closely resembled a bunch of twigs, flashed across my mind, and I clutched the text to my chest in fear.

"This is so lame," Raven muttered, pulling a bag of bark from her bag along with a small stone vessel.

"Was I supposed to—"

"Nope, I read ahead."

She blushed, and her diligence endeared her to me. Nothing wrong with being prepared. Unless you were the only conscientious one in a class of slackers at Wolfebane High. I liked that we had that in common. Interesting how I felt closer to Raven in a short space of time than to any of my classmates at Wolfebane High over the years.

She shook out a small pile of bark into the vessel and handed me the matches. "Here, you do the honors."

My fingers fumbled with the matches, and I muttered, "klutz," so Raven would mistake my trembling hands for anything but the fear snaking through my body. Having seen Cadifor doing this experiment in a vision did not make me like it. In fact, I would've rather been anywhere else, doing anything else, than striking a match and lighting bark.

Bracing, I touched the match to the bark, the tiny hiss and sizzle masking my sharp indrawn breath.

Crane paced between the desks, grunting his approval here and there, a perpetual frown on his face. He couldn't have been more than thirty, but with the dorky side-parted hair, long sideburns, and shaving rash, he could've passed for twenty.

Raven waved her hands over the twigs and closed her eyes. "I predict if you don't make this pile of crap catch in the next ten seconds, our sorry asses will be in detention for the next week."

With a nervous chuckle I blew on the twigs and bark gently, watching them catch and burn and smolder down to the ashes that would supposedly reveal the future.

Raven peered into the gray ash, tilting her head this way and that, her dubious smirk telling me more than the ashes. "Only thing that pile of cinders revealed is that I'm going to flunk divination."

Reluctant, I pulled the vessel towards me. "Here, let me try."

Brave words, considering the last thing I wanted to do was peer into the ash and see my future. Considering the track my visions were heading down, I was guaranteed to see something horrendous—like my mom and Cadifor doing more than holding hands.

Leaning forward, I peered into the embers, wondering if this was like the tea leaf thing Nan used to do to make me feel good about potentially scary stuff: first day starting school, first time away at camp, first trip to the dentist.

Nothing.

I observed harder. Blew on the ash a little, stirring the wispy fragments into miniature tornadoes. Still nothing.

Holding about as much faith in reading tree bark ash as I did in my visions, I nudged the vessel away. That's when I saw it. I blinked, squinted, but the image remained: a baby curled in a crib, next to another crib, empty, a faint blurry outline among the ash.

Then the baby in the crib opened its eyes, strange golden eyes, and stared straight at me.

Maybe it was a trick of the light? A shadow created when I moved the stone vessel?

"You see something?" Raven's curious voice broke the spell and I shook my head, not surprised that when I glanced back the ashes were just that: a pile of burnt bark.

"Thought I did, guess I was trying too hard." I wanted to mention what I'd seen, but it didn't make sense, and no way did I want Crane psychoanalyzing me.

Raven jerked a thumb towards the table next to us. "We're

in for a little one on one."

Crane swooped down on us, looming like a crow, studying our faces more than our pile of ash. His gaze flicked over Raven, dismissive, but when he peered at me, I felt a jolt all the way down to my toes.

He knew.

I held my breath as I focused on my text.

After what seemed like an eternity, he said, "Carry on," and moved on to the next desk, leaving me more shaken than I cared to admit.

The way he'd scrutinized me ... like he could see all the way down to my soul. Probably just a figment of my overactive imagination, but given what people could do in this place, not out of the realm of possibility.

If he could read me, why hadn't he called me on what I'd seen? Questioned me? Pushed me for answers like the rest of the uptight teachers I'd had before? That made me uneasier than anything. I didn't like games, and hated teachers playing them more. As he cast a quick glance over his shoulder at me, I sucked in a nervous breath. When a nerd at the front asked a question and distracted Crane, I sighed in relief.

Raven muttered, "He's spooky," before slouching in her chair and flicking through the rest of the text. "When do we get to the good stuff? Bet I see heaps in crystallomancy."

I raised an eyebrow.

She grinned. "And you thought the old crystal ball gazing was a fallacy."

We didn't have much more time for chitchat as Crane strode to the front of the class and started expounding on the best methods for divination.

I was glad. I had a lot to think about, starting with making sense of what I'd seen and how it fit into the crazy jigsaw puzzle my life had become. If tephramancy told the future, what did the baby with golden eyes have in store for me? And worse, how could something so innocent possibly be tied to Cadifor's evil?

CHAPTER THIRTEEN

After surviving my first divination lesson, I sat through semantics and parapsychology with Raven and Quinn, who made the lessons bearable. Well, semi-bearable. Whenever a teacher droned on about esoteric traditions or imbuing charms or channeling your inner urban warrior, my brain would fog—not from lack of interest, but this stuff was all so new to me. I didn't like lagging behind the rest of the class. I'd been a brainiac at Wolfebane High, but C.U.L.T. gave me a severe case of brain overload.

Symbols and planetary alignments and ancient parapsychological experiments spun around my head until I was dizzy. Meeting my spirit guide might be kind of useful in my quest, but sitting in a classroom of sleepy zombies staring at individual candles while barely able to breathe from the dense incense fog didn't do much for me. I didn't see a blue light approaching me from a distance, I didn't see it take on a human form, I didn't get to invite her to sit with me and discuss what problems I had—and boy, could I have done with that chat.

Maybe I didn't have a guardian angel or maybe I was spiritless; either way, I sucked at the labs. Ironic; my initial fear of not fitting in at a school for freaks, because I couldn't control my gift, was superseded by my fear of flunking.

Soon I had to head back to Eiros and act like I was cool with weekend lessons. Assume responsibility for finding Arwen. Be part of a sorority that was fractured at best.

"Concentrate." Quinn nudged me with his elbow and pointed at the text lying open between us. "If we don't get this assignment on auras out of the way, we'll have to spend the whole night doing it." With a wicked smile, he leaned closer and murmured, "Or maybe that's your plan, huh? You want to get me alone so you can take advantage of me?"

I gulped at his proximity, at the way his lips curved temptingly in the corners, and at the thought of spending some one-on-one time with him. I liked being around Quinn. He made me feel good, and anyone who could do that amid all the crazy stuff was welcome to flirt with me anytime. "In your dreams."

His moss-green eyes sparkled. "You have no idea."

I elbowed him back, hoping I wasn't blushing like an idiot, and yanked the textbook closer. Not that I didn't enjoy his flirting; it just made me a little uncomfortable after the buzz I had going on with Joss. Strange thing was, when I was with Joss, I didn't give Quinn a second thought, and when I was with Quinn, Joss faded to the furthest recesses of my memory.

"How about it? You and me, doing some study tonight?"

Brownie points for persistence, but even if I had wanted to hang out with Quinn, I couldn't.

"Can't."

"Hot date?"

His voice had an edge I didn't like and I shot him a glare. "Visiting my Nan."

Sheepish, he shrugged. "Sorry."

Not wanting to talk about Nan, I flipped to the next page. "Which means we need to get this done now. Ready?"

He nodded and picked up his pen, tapping it against his notebook like a conductor's baton. "Go."

I led in with an easy question. "Define aura."

His eyebrows shot up. "Come on, you can do better than that."

"This is my pop quiz. I'll ask the questions." I tapped his nose and he laughed. "Answer before the buzzer, please."

We grinned at each other and it struck me how easy being with him was. No hassles, no pressure, just two friends helping each other out. Trading banter with Quinn made me wish life was as easy as this: studying with a cute guy, enjoying the challenge of learning new stuff with my hardest task being absorbing new lessons, and not saving the world. For an all-too-brief time, with him flirting and teasing and making me laugh, I could forget my responsibilities.

"Sometime this century would be good," I said, and he rolled his eyes.

"The literal translation of aura is breath. Apparently Zeus turned Aura, the companion of the goddess Artemis, into a spring, and she embodies mild breezes, literally a cool breath from water."

I drew a check mark in the air and he threw up his arms and mouthed "score" complete with fake audience cheering.

Laughing, I glanced at the page for my next question. "Okay, wiseass, what's the parapsychology definition of aura?"

"Too easy." He interlocked his fingers and stretched forward. "A collaboration of expressing one's life force and in response someone skilled perceiving it. Basically, the emanation of a person's emotional state made visible to certain psychics."

"You sure you didn't swallow this text for breakfast?"

"Just smart, I guess."

"Smartass more like it," I muttered, earning another heart-stopping grin that had my insides fluttering.

I flipped the pages faster, trying to come up with a question to challenge him and distract me from his all-round appeal.

"Okay, to win the car, answer this question: Can auras be photographed?"

He screwed up his eyes and pretended to think, then snapped them open in a fake light bulb moment that had me wanting to hug him, he was that cute.

"Yep, they can. A Ukrainian dude, Kirlian, accidentally discovered he could photograph auras, known as the corona effect, in nineteen thirty-nine while fixing medical machinery. A person's body part subjected to a high-voltage electric field against a photographic plate creates an aura image on the plate. Then, according to the color, a diagnosis can be made." He leaned toward me and tried to sneak a peek at the textbook. "So, how'd I do?"

"You're a nerd."

I closed the book and threw it on the desk, secretly pleased he was so smart. Looks were important, as was a sense of humor, but give me a guy with a brain and I was hooked.

He tapped his head. "Up here for thinking," he said, and wiggled his feet. "Down there for dancing."

I snorted. "Do those lame lines usually work for you?"

The laugh lines around his mouth crinkled adorably as he crooked a finger at me, beckoning me closer. "You tell me."

Rolling my eyes, I said, "So not working."

He shrugged and his smile widened. "Just means I'll have to keep trying."

Poking out my tongue, I silently cheered when the teacher, Miss Morris, demanded the class's attention again.

I didn't want to encourage Quinn; it felt lousy I couldn't be completely honest with him.

Not yet.

Visiting Nan broke my heart, and using her as an excuse for my absences from school only served to increase the constant guilt that I'd put her here. The only woman I truly loved in this world was in a coma because of me. She'd devoted her life to raising me, and how had I repaid her? By freaking her out so badly she'd had a stroke. Rubbing the ache centered in my chest at the thought, I headed for the nurse's station.

"Go on in, Holly. I'm sure Rose would love a visit."

I gave the nurse a tight smile along with an "are you for real" glare. How could that plump, perky twenty-something possibly know what my comatose Nan would want? Unless she had a gift for reading minds along with a gift for patronizing relatives.

I held my breath as I walked down the long corridor, but some of the nasty odors still managed to seep into my nose: bland mushy food, antiseptic, industrial detergent, and musty old people. And something else I didn't want to acknowledge: the cloying smell of death.

Outside Nan's room, the last on the right, I smoothed a hand over my face, hoping to wipe away my horrified expression at being here. Though Nan couldn't see me, I felt like a traitor walking into her room with doom and gloom written all over my face.

Knocking from years of manners she'd instilled in me, I eased open the door, squared my shoulders, and stepped into the sterile room, only to slump as if an invisible opponent had sucker punched me. Seeing my vibrant, bossy, quirky Nan lying in that bed, hooked up to machines monitoring her every breath, snatched away mine.

I edged closer to the bed, the frail, pale, white-haired old woman not equating with my Nan. My Nan who loved long walks around the lake, tending her herb garden and giving me a hard time about preferring books to real dates. My Nan, whose kooky predictions rarely came true but were close enough to unsettle me, whose adoration of fossils like Frank Sinatra and Sean Connery gave me good teasing fodder, whose love of knitting kept me in enough scarves and gloves to keep the next millennium of freezing Wolfebane winters at bay.

She'd always insisted I wear a new scarf every winter and I did to please her. Even the time she'd unwittingly knitted a bright, glary number in rainbow colors. I'd valiantly worn it out of the cottage as far as the end of the street before yanking it off and stuffing it into my bag. About two seconds too late since the biggest gossip in school had seen it. I'd borne the brunt of tasteless gay jokes that day and the next, but because of the loving twinkle it had put in Nan's eyes to see me wear it, I wore that thing out of the cottage every morning for the entire winter.

Struggling to hold back tears, I blinked rapidly and tiptoed toward the bed, my fear increasing the closer I got. She'd lost more weight, her gaunt face almost skeletal. I placed my hand over hers on the bedclothes, wishing I could infuse some of my warmth into her.

"Hey Nan, it's me. How you doing?"

I cringed at my stupidity. Like she could answer. The nurses had said to act completely normal, maintain a normal conversation; sometimes coma patients could hear every word spoken even though they couldn't respond. I'd tried the few times I'd visited, but my monologues were on par with my teleportation skills: below average at best.

Determined to try harder, I squeezed her hand. "I've survived my classes at C.U.L.T. Made some new friends. Loving my dorm." I carefully avoided any mention of my gift, considering my revelation had resulted in her current state. "You'd like Raven. She pretends to be this goth chick, but she's funny and smart and nice. And Quinn is cool."

I paused, knowing she'd grill me down to height and weight if I mentioned a boy. "Cute, too. Taller than me, amazing green eyes, kind. And smart? The guy's a brainiac. Funny, he's a nerd just like me. And he laughs all the time. And makes other people around him smile, which is really great. We've been hanging out, studying together, they've been great ... " That made my deception even harder. Raven and Quinn were my only true friends I had in this topsy-turvy world, yet I consistently had to lie to them. They thought I was spending the weekend with Nan, cleaning the cottage and sleeping at the nursing home.

Little did they know.

"I'm studying really hard. But you'd know that, right?"

What she didn't know was the subject matter and how I totally sucked at everything. In subjects like algebra and English and chem, my brain rocked. Give it a hint of otherworldly stuff and I was a dunce with a big fat *D*, sitting in the corner with my pointy hat. As for the start of my formal lessons in Eiros this weekend, I wouldn't go there. I could just imagine Oscar's disdain and Mack's disappointment when they got a whiff of my failure in all things Innerworld.

Though visiting Eiros wouldn't be all bad. *Joss* ...

I had to admit, he was the one bright spot in all of this, and a small part of me was excited to be heading back to Eiros for the simple pleasure of seeing him again.

Knowing Nan would get a real kick out of my crush, I moved my chair closer to the bed. "Want to know a secret, Nan? Quinn's cool and I like hanging out with him, but I like another boy. He's hot. Smoking, burn-your-fingers-if-you're-brave-enough-to-touch-him hot, hotter than that amazing chocolate fudge sauce you make. He's strong, super confident, and really tall, about a head taller than me. And his eyes … bluer than the lake on a summer's day, the color of that old dude you crush on all the time, Frank Sinatra."

I wished with all my heart I'd hear a faint chuckle, see her eyelids flutter, some sign she could hear me. Staring at the face I loved, I willed it to happen, focusing my meager power.

Nothing.

Emotion clogged my throat and I swallowed, then continued. "Though I'm on to you. I see the way you perv on George Clooney." I forced a laugh. "Careful, Nan, your friends down at the Rec Hall will start calling you a cougar."

Not a flicker, her face remained perfectly serene and motionless.

I couldn't stand it a second longer. "Anyway, I have to get back to school. I'll visit again next weekend, okay?"

Swiping away the tears trickling down my cheeks, I bent over and kissed her forehead. After a last glimpse at the only person I truly trusted in this world, I headed out the door for my date with destiny.

CHAPTER FOURTEEN

"Glad you're back." Joss couldn't appear less glad if he tried. He frowned and folded his arms, glaring at me like I'd mucked up before starting. "You've mastered teleporting?"

"No," I blurted, not sure which annoyed me more. The fact I still used Maisey's crystals to get here but had no idea how they worked, or the fact Joss could read my mind. "I'm having trouble with all things ... odd."

No matter how many times I evaluated this situation logically, I came to the same conclusion: This was nuts. An average girl from innocuous Wolfebane, New Hampshire, was the *Scion*. I never even got picked to be on the track team, so how the hell did I wind up being chosen for a quest this monumental? Handling the visions was bad enough, but throw in the expectation I master those Eiros tasks against a ticking clock and I was starting to panic, big time.

I glared at Joss like it was all his fault. "But I guess you already know that, right?"

His lips thinned in an unimpressed line. "I don't always hear your thoughts, remember?"

"Just when it's convenient?"

He studied me as though trying to read my mind, and I held my breath, wondering what he'd say, but as his frown deepened I sighed in relief. He hadn't been able to get a read on my thoughts.

"Stop doubting yourself. You're a descendant of Bel, You have his gifts in you, otherwise you wouldn't be here in the first place. You'll finesse teleportation and master the rest."

"You really have that much faith in me?"

"I have to," he said, and as he glanced over his shoulder toward the housing nearby, I only just caught his muttered, "I have no choice."

He was talking about the geis, but for a moment his latent resentment scared me, like he didn't want to protect me, but was being forced into it.

"Where am I staying?" I couldn't help sounding abrupt, my awkwardness at misreading our entire relationship making me want to run and hide.

For the first time since I'd met him he appeared less than confident, his gaze fixed on an elm behind my left shoulder. "With my mom."

My mouth dropped.

"I'll bunk at Oscar's."

"Lucky you," I muttered, grateful we wouldn't be under the same roof.

"Mom's cool. You'll be okay. Just don't believe everything she tells you." He shuffled his feet and glanced down. "About me, that is," he clarified, his bashful embarrassment as adorable as the rest of him.

There was something so utterly appealing about a big strong guy nervous about the revealing stuff his mom would say. And the fact he cared what I might think. Delighting in his tortured expression, I rubbed my hands together. "Bet she'll show me all your baby photos."

He winced. "No bet. Just don't check out the ... "

"Naked ones?"

His blush made me want to tease him more. Clutching an imaginary pen, I held up my other hand as a notebook, I said, "Note to self. First task of the weekend. Check out naked pics of warrior."

"Stop that," he said, grabbing my hands and lowering them. Our laughter tumbled over us, mingling like mist on the crisp morning air.

Our smiles faded as we stood less than two feet apart, holding hands, caught up in something indefinable and inexplicable and magical.

"Are there any pics of you I *can* peek at?"

"Only the ones of me winning the annual axe throwing contest."

Incredulous, I searched his face for signs he was teasing. "Axe throwing? What are you, part warrior, part Neanderthal?"

"And part crazy," he murmured, his thumbs caressing the pulse points of my wrists, sending bolts of electricity shooting up my arms. "Though I'll let you in on a little secret." He leaned closer and I held my breath. "I lied about the axe throwing."

He released my hands and I whacked him playfully on the chest, wishing I could linger and explore the hard ridges lightly outlined beneath his T-shirt. His eyes darkened to midnight, but all he said was, "Come on. Uriel's dying to meet you."

I didn't know what freaked me out more, the thought of staying with his mom or the fact he had such a great relationship with her he used her first name. As I lengthened my strides to keep up with his long legs, I glanced around, hating the permanent grayness, but seeing nothing out of the ordinary. It was all so ... so ... normal.

"It's a peaceful community, but appearances can be deceiving."

Casting him a sidelong glance, I said, "Now you're back to the mind reading thing."

His eyes clouded, as if he wasn't entirely comfortable with knowing my innermost thoughts. "Sometimes I can't help it. When your thoughts are particularly loud or forceful or opinionated, it's like you're inside my head."

Another note to self: When thinking how hot he is, make it subtle.

His fleeting grin had me silently cursing my inability to do anything right when it came to all this psychic crap. Determined to divert attention from my pathetic crush, I pointed to the rows of trees.

"Why are the trees lined up like that?"

"You haven't read up on ogham yet?"

I shook my head. "Think it's on my study list but I haven't started yet."

He beckoned me toward the nearest tree and caressed its leaves with a tenderness that made my breath catch. "Ogham is an ancient Celtic alphabet of twenty characters, each character represented by downward or upward strokes, and each of these symbols represents a sacred tree." He squatted, picked up a stick, and beckoned me to kneel next to him.

"This is the ogham symbol for holly." He drew a vertical line downwards, with three horizontal strokes on the left, sort of like a backward E. "In English, this would represent the letter T. Its ogham name is Tinne."

Intrigued, I traced the letter in the dirt with my fingertip. "What does it mean?"

"Action, assertiveness, objectivity."

Three of the least likely adjectives I'd use to describe myself.

"Don't do that. Don't undersell yourself."

"Don't do that. Don't intrude into my head."

He shrugged, his smile making me forgive him anything. "Occupational hazard."

"Warrior geis is a bitch," I muttered, earning another grin.

"What's your symbol?"

"Ash."

He drew a vertical line with five horizontal lines to the right. "Nion." Before I could ask, he added, "Means connection, wisdom, surrender."

He'd drawn the symbols back to back, and as I scrutinized them, a cold clamminess spread over my skin and I squeezed my eyes shut. I hadn't had a vision all week, had been grateful for the reprieve considering the bombardment of new information my brain had to cope with. Now I resented it, resented the intrusion when I was getting in some serious bonding time with my warrior.

My blood chilled as the image in my mind shimmered and coalesced.

Cadifor meeting with the same man as last time in a cave. Issuing inaudible orders.

The man stands on Cadifor's right, his rigid posture and clenched fists indicating barely restrained violence, rocking on the balls of his feet, itching for a fight.

He strides out of the cave, leaving Cadifor peering into a steel bowl of black liquid.

Seeing the Sorority.

Maeve, gorgeous in a flowing white gown, dancing with Mack, the smile on her face pure joy.

Oscar, playing a fiddle, his serene expression at startling odds with his usual scowl.

Joss, standing beneath an oak tree, wary, as he watches something or someone among the revelers.

Revelers at a festival.

Dancing, singing, happy crowds.

Oblivious to the faceless man walking among them, a shadow of death ...

I gasped and clawed at my throat for air, sweat trickling down the back of my neck and into my hoodie. I couldn't breathe; the fear clogged my throat, a rancid burn that extended down into my stomach and left me wanting to puke.

Cadifor had sent that guy to harm the Sorority or someone in that crowd, there was no doubt in my mind. Suppressed violence had shimmered off him like the auras I'd learned about at C.U.L.T., and whoever he'd set his sights on didn't stand a chance.

Or did they?

For the first time since the visions had started, I wasn't resentful or annoyed. I was glad that I now had the power to do something about Cadifor and his merry band of monsters sent to do his dirty work. Mastering my visions—my clairsentience—was on my to-do list on the way to facing off with Cadifor, and if I really got a hold on it, maybe I could foretell and therefore prevent bad stuff from happening.

As my fear subsided, my throat relaxed enough for air to gush into my lungs and I gasped. I blinked several times, fragments of the lingering images overriding Joss's concerned face before he eventually glimmered into view.

"How bad?"

I grimaced, pushing up into a sitting position when I realized I lay sprawled in the dirt. So much for my knight in warrior armor protecting me.

"It's best not to touch a person having a precognitive episode. It may interfere with the vision."

"Right," I said, feeling uncharitable and a tad bruised where I'd landed on my elbow. Bending it several times, I waited for a wave of nausea to subside before I tried to articulate what I'd seen.

"Does Cadifor have a minion? A right hand man he trusts?"

Joss nodded. "Keenan. He's Cadifor's main man. Does his dirty work."

"They're planning something," I blurted, rubbing the sudden goosebumps on my arms. "They were gawking at a bowl of black stuff, watching the Sorority at some festival."

He stiffened, glanced over his shoulder. "Are you sure?"

I raised an eyebrow at his skepticism and he quickly amended, "What I mean is, is there anything else?"

"That was pretty much it."

He leaped to his feet, started pacing. "This isn't good."

I'd never seen him anything but cool, so to see my big, brave warrior rattled? Not good.

"You know what the festival is?"

He stopped pacing and nodded. "Beltane. Next weekend. It's Bel's official feast day, when all fires are extinguished and relit from Bel's fire at the Temple of Grian."

He wasn't telling me everything. I could tell by his evasive, generic retelling of a festival I could've gotten out of a textbook.

"And?

Respect gleamed in his eyes, making me feel like I'd finally done something right.

"And it's to be your official welcome into the Sorority. Kind of like a baptism."

"Baptism by fire. How poetic."

He didn't smile. "In your vision, did Cadifor see you in the scrying bowl, or only the Sorority?"

I dredged up the recent images, and they clarified. "Only you guys." *Thank goodness.* Cadifor scared the bejeezus out of me. It was bad enough having to battle him for this Arwen thingy, but to have him know about me before I mastered all my tasks would ensure I was doomed from the start.

"Good; he doesn't know about your role at the festival. Yet."

I could've done without that final little add on.

"We need to keep it that way."

"I'm all for that plan." I gave him two thumbs up and he finally cracked a smile.

"Did you see anything else that might give us a clue as to when Keenan will strike?"

"Don't think so."

I closed my eyes and swallowed the instant fear that bubbled up. It wasn't like I'd hurl headlong into another vision; guess I should be thankful I usually got some warning with that cold clammy crap. But the darkness behind my eyelids was reminiscent of the darkness in that cave, of the darkness that clung to Cadifor and Keenan and everything associated with evil.

Determinedly ignoring the numbness building from the base of my spine, I concentrated. "I told you. Cadifor issuing orders I couldn't hear, that rough dude Keenan leaving. Cadifor staring into the bowl, seeing Maeve and Mack dancing, Oscar fiddling, you watching the crowd—"

"He's going to wait 'til after the ceremony to strike."

My eyes flew open, my heart thudding with trepidation at the hint of alarm in his low tone. "So what I saw helped?"

His expression softened. "You did great."

Gnawing on my bottom lip I nodded, at a loss for some smartass comeback for once. I could barely comprehend the enormity of what I was facing, and all I wanted to do right then was go someplace else and fill my head with anything other than the visions of Cadifor playing on rerun like a bad movie in my mind.

Sensing my need to do something—or reading my mind, I didn't really care this time—Joss gestured for me to lead the way.

"We need to get you settled, formalize your lessons for this weekend, and prep you for Beltane. Ready?"

Was he kidding? I'd never be ready. But I guess I had to start somewhere.

CHAPTER FIFTEEN

I followed Joss to the last house in a long grove, admiring the way he walked, long easy strides of a guy comfortable in his own skin. I loved his quiet inner confidence that extended to everyone around him. I felt safe when I was around him; handy, considering he was my warrior and I had to trust him implicitly. He had a presence, an aura. ... I mentally winced, remembering studying auras with Quinn, how laid back and cool he'd been, how *normal*, while being with Joss accentuated everything about me that wasn't.

Joss represented everything in my life I didn't want to acknowledge at the moment, while Quinn ... well, Quinn made me remember how I used to be before any of this crap started. I wanted to hang on to that feeling, wanted to remember Nan healthy and Sundays at the cottage and reading by the lake, all perfectly safe, uncomplicated things that encompassed my life not that long ago.

While Quinn didn't make me feel half as flustered as Joss, I wanted to be close to him for the simple fact I needed to hang onto my sanity, that last, tiny, remaining piece of me deep inside insisting I was still normal despite everything.

I pointed to the abundant fruit hanging from every tree in the house yards. "Apple?"

Preoccupied with glancing around—seemed like my vision freaked him out a little and he'd taken his warrior role to extremes—he nodded. "When you meet my mom, you'll know why we live in the apple grove."

"What's the meaning behind apple?"

"Beauty, love, generosity."

"That's nice."

"That's my mom."

My heart did a weird little skip thing. Did he have any idea how amazingly appealing it was to hear a macho guy talk about his mom like that? I wondered what the ogham symbol was for abandonment, selfish, traitor? Probably some obnoxious weed. That's where I'd find *my* mom.

Joss held a gate open for me—manners too, wow—and as I stepped onto the path leading to his front door, a strange sense of déjà vu washed over me.

Uriel's herb garden could've been Nan's, transposed. It held the same profusion of lavender, thyme, sage, oregano, and basil. As I closed my eyes and breathed deep, I was transported back to a time when Nan was clipping herbs and I read under a tree.

Nan had this habit of snipping off large bunches and then grumbling about it while I'd nod and smile, totally distracted by my book. Though I did like hearing her talk about the herbs and what they were useful for. Maybe it was the nerd in me hungry for facts, but when Nan used to drone on about lavender and its relaxation properties or the hundred and one uses for basil, I'd lower my book and really listen, soothed by her gentle voice.

Nan had been like that with me always: patient, comforting, reliable. That I couldn't turn to her at a time like this left me lonelier than I'd ever been in my life.

"Memories are important. They give us strength to face the future."

I managed a tight smile. Another thing I liked about Joss: his ability to say the right thing.

We'd barely made it halfway up the path when the front door flew open. Uriel was nothing like I expected. Petite and curvy, with frizzy blonde hair, pale skin, and brown eyes bordering on black, she was the opposite of Joss in every way. There was not even a glimmer of resemblance. The religious pendant she wore captured my attention and my surprise shot into the stratosphere.

"Welcome, Holly, I'm so glad to meet you."

"Same here, Mrs. ... " Belatedly, I realized I didn't know Joss's surname.

"Call me Uriel, please." She clasped my hands, her skin warm and rough, the fingertips callused. "Come in."

Joss was enjoying my shock. I could see it in the wry gleam in his eyes, the upward curve of his lips he fought.

I surreptitiously pointed at the gold cross hanging around his mom's neck and prominently embroidered on her tunic. I lowered my voice. "You didn't tell me your mom was Christian."

"Does it matter?" He ushered me into his home. "My mom died when I was three, my dad a few years later. Uriel was my nanny. She's been here ever since."

An apology seemed too trite, but I had to say something; if I could speak past the lump stuck in my throat, that is. "I'm sorry, about your folks."

"I am too." He stared into the distance, his jaw rigid, a vein pulsing beneath the skin over his temple. When he finally refocused on me, the bleakness in his eyes made me want to hug him.

Glancing away before I embarrassed us both, I realized the house was set away from the others, the last in the grove, and it suddenly made sense. "The community doesn't accept her?"

"The Innerworld reflects New York culture, so we're cosmopolitan." He paused, choosing his words carefully. "You know, Eiros is based on an ancient druid culture. People are still wary of those who aren't solely Bel worshippers."

"Does that prejudice toward Uriel extend to you, even though you're part of the Sorority?"

His eye roll didn't make sense, not when he was such a vital part of that tight-knit foursome. What could be more important than being the warrior of the *Scion*?

"My father was a warrior, a direct descendant from the Red Branch, the highest order of warriors in Eiros. No one can take that away from me."

No matter how hard they tried. He didn't say it, but I could see it in the despondency blurring his proud features and I instantly hated the entire prejudiced community for hurting the guy I cared about. "You're bound by all this ancient legend. But what about Uriel? Why does she stick around?"

He blushed and I knew the answer before he spoke. "Because of me."

She loved him that much. Something I could understand the more time I spent with him. Before I could think, I touched his arm. "You don't like that?"

He glanced at my hand, his remote expression softening for a moment before he shrugged it off. "I think she'd be happier elsewhere, but she's here for me, and that makes me responsible."

"You can't be responsible for everybody."

His withering glare told me he could.

"Why don't they accept her fully?"

His frown deepened. "Because most are descendants from the Druids. If you're not ... " He glanced across at the house and his pained expression made me want to gather him and Uriel in a group hug. "It's nothing overt, and she has good friends here, but there's this undercurrent that reeks of old-school hierarchy I can't stand even for her sake."

"Does she mind?"

He held a finger up to his lips as footsteps headed toward us.

Uriel waved us inside. "Joss, where are your manners? Show our guest around."

His softening expression banished the shadows of non-acceptance by a cliquey society, the hint of little boy adoring his mom making me melt all over again.

"Your room's ready, Holly. Joss can show you, then you can join me in the kitchen for a snack."

"Thanks."

Please don't let me be sleeping in his old room, the sane part of me silently begged, while another part pleaded, *Please let me be in his old room so I can snoop around and discover everything I can about him.*

I didn't know whether to smile in relief or cringe in disappointment when he said, "You're in the guest room."

I followed him down a long, narrow hallway before as he flung open a door. "Here you go. Clothes in the wardrobe. Girly stuff in the bathroom across the hall."

"Girly stuff?"

"Makeup and soap and crap," he said, blushing, reminding me no matter how manly he acted, he couldn't be more than a few years older than me.

"How old—"

"Eighteen," he said, his disgust making it sound like he was ten. "Mack's twenty-five, Oscar's twenty." Being the youngest in a pack of alpha males explained his disgust.

Personally, I thought it was beyond cool he was eighteen.

Crushing on an older dude would've been beyond pathetic. I'd seen unrequited love with classmates at Wolfebane High having the hots for older brothers, college guys, and it always ended in tears. I'd been there myself, with that moron Colt, of all people. Ogling him from my prime viewing spot several branches up our oldest oak when he went swimming in the lake in summer, hanging around in the garden when I knew he was due home, leaving my bedroom window open at night so I could hear the music he liked to listen to as I drifted off to sleep.

Thankfully, spending time with him in his family home after Nan's stroke had dispelled whatever delusions of love I'd ever harbored. Colt was a dick.

While Joss … he was a guy I could definitely fall for. Crazy, since I still didn't understand how this whole Innerworld and Outerworld thing worked, but a girl had to have a little fun daydreaming while figuring out how to save the world.

Thankfully, he kept silent for once, and I kept my head down and entered the room. Small and neat, with a bed covered in a handmade quilt, a dresser, and a chair, totally unremarkable in every way but for the symbols engraved on the wooden panels covering the walls and ceiling.

"Wow."

I turned around, tilting my head back to inspect overhead until I got a crick.

"Many of these symbols offer protection."

Ah … so that's why I was staying here.

"What do they all mean?"

He pointed to the first, a sign that looked like three legs running. "Triskelion stands for competition and man's progress." His finger moved to a triangular shape next. "Triquetra, a holy symbol for spirit, nature, the cosmos."

He traced the outline of three interlinked spirals. "The Triple Spiral represents the three powers of maiden, mother, and crone. It's a sign for female power, especially through transition and growth."

Boy, did I need that one. Maybe I should start wearing it, though I'd never gone in for jewelry. "What's the single spiral next to it mean?"

"Ethereal energy. Also symbolizes birth, growth, expanding of consciousness."

I'd already seen the five-fold on Dyfan's door, and the cross was familiar to almost everyone in the universe, but the next symbol I couldn't recognize.

Joss had already turned away and was heading for the door when I laid a hand on his arm. "You missed one."

He faltered, cluing me in that his omission was deliberate.

After staring at my hand for a moment, he eventually dragged his gaze upward to meet mine, and what I saw sent a jolt of alarm through me.

Bone-chilling fear.

In the time I'd spent with him, I'd seen many emotions in those expressive blue eyes, but never fear. What could be frightening enough to make my valiant warrior scared?

"You'll spend your life coming to understand that symbol and what it means for you, for Eiros."

I released his arm, trying to hide my growing panic as I pointed to the symbol he hadn't named yet. "All very profound, but what is that?"

His solemnity scared me more than his earlier avoidance.

"The Three Rays. Celtic symbol of the Triple Flame. Arwen."

I gawked at the three vertical lines that angled toward each other at one end. How could anything so simple, so innocuous, be my destiny? Shouldn't it be larger, bolder, and more dramatic?

I half expected a miracle to happen, but the symbol remained unchanged, as did I. No prickling, no heat, not even a hint, and I let out a little huff of relief while a small part of me, the part that still doubted my place in all this, was disappointed.

According to Dyfan, one of my tasks was to become one with the Triple Flame. Staring at the small, inoffensive symbol, I couldn't imagine how this thing could be so important in my quest.

"That's what I'm supposed to find?"

He shook his head. "This is merely a symbol of Arwen. No one knows what the icon actually looks like."

"So it's just a symbol like the rest?"

He nodded. "It all traces back to Bel. The sun produced heat, and ultimately, fire. Ancient Celts were aware of the fire's spiritually transformative properties, so they placed the Three Flames on the faces of their clansmen and women."

He held up three fingers, folding the middle one in half. "The flames were drawn in lines upward and outward on the subject's forehead, the base of the three lines meeting at the bridge of the nose."

He held up his fingers over my forehead but not touching, and even with a few inches separating us, I could feel the prickle of heat in the middle of my forehead.

"The motif is symbolic of Arwen, a Celtic concept of enlightenment, inspiration, and unification of polarities."

He'd lost me with all the psychobabble, but I sure could do with a healthy dose of enlightenment. As for the inspiration, I already had that. I was looking straight at him. "Huh?"

"It means a calm balance struck between opposites, like male and female, physical and ethereal."

I focused on the symbol tied to my destiny, surprisingly numb. Surely I should feel something? Some kind of buzz, a link?

"When the time is right, you'll feel it, become one with it," he said, heading for the door. "Mom's probably dying of curiosity by now. Let's go put her out of her misery."

Nodding, I followed him, glancing over my shoulder at the symbols scattered across the walls like stars on a wizard's cape. For a second I could've sworn Arwen glowed, but when I blinked it was as lifeless as the rest. Dismissing it as a trick of the pale morning grayness filtering through a small, high window, I headed for another interesting meeting with the inhabitants of Eiros.

Word must've spread of my first official morning in Eiros, because when I stepped into the light-filled kitchen, the six-seater table was crammed to capacity.

"Good to see you, Holly." Mack waved, his smile genuinely welcoming.

"Ditto," said Maeve, bouncing in her seat like a hyperactive toddler. "Can't wait to show you more stuff today."

Oscar lifted a hand in a half-hearted wave.

I didn't know the next person, a woman who stood and waved me over to the vacant chair next to her. "Come child, sit by me."

I bristled at the *child* tag but did as I was told, sensing the group held their collective breaths, waiting for me to blow a fuse. I sat and mustered a smile. "I'm Holly."

"I know, dear."

I didn't like the hint of condescension in her tone. There was something about her I couldn't put my finger on, an aloofness that bordered on scorn, like she'd sized me up as the chosen one and found me sadly lacking.

Up close, she had the most bizarre eyes I'd ever seen: violet, with tiny gold flecks making them sparkle. "I'm Bedelia. My friends call me Lia."

"Lia's our chief healer," Mack said, slightly starry-eyed as Lia beamed at him.

Ah ... so it was like that.

"Medicine woman," Maeve chirped up, also gawking at Lia with blatant admiration.

"Witch," Oscar muttered, earning a beatific smile from the ash-blonde woman.

"Thank you for acknowledging my Wiccan powers among my more human talents, Oscar."

While her words were harmless enough, her exaggerated saccharine-sweet tone wasn't, and I inadvertently leaned away from her. I didn't believe in witches or wizards unless they graced the pages of my favorite books. Then again, I'd never believed in mystical sun gods or lords of darkness or teleporting before.

"Lia's a good friend of mine," Uriel said, placing a huge batch of warm lavender cookies in the middle of the table alongside apple cider, pumpkin scones, and tea cake. "She popped around to meet you before formalities commence."

Joss stood by the window, his back rigid, taking his protective role seriously. I'd wondered about his silence whenever the Sorority was together, and after learning his family's story I wondered if some of that stemmed from insecurity, like he didn't feel like he truly belonged. He'd said he felt responsible for tying Uriel to Eiros, but did he have any idea how much she loved him, how her mouth eased into a small smile every time she glanced his way?

Funny thing was, I knew exactly how he was feeling. I'd often wondered if I was holding Nan back somehow, if she would've lived her life differently if she hadn't had the responsibility of raising me—a responsibility she hadn't asked for, but had been dumped with when my flaky mom took off.

Mack offered me a cookie and I took one, hoping the lavender would relax me. I nibbled on it, the churning in my stomach not easing a bit.

"By formalities, Lia means your structured lessons this morning." Mack clasped his fingers tighter, placed them on the table, and leaned forward. "We'll start with the basics, move on to cultural studies, and finish with some practical ogham."

I managed a mute nod, my brain already spinning into overload.

"Then this afternoon we'll take you to the Temple of Grian, and tomorrow, prepare for Beltane, which is next weekend."

Joss stiffened at the mention of the festival, and I expected him to interject and tell them of my vision. His silence surprised me, so I kept silent too, trusting him more than the rest of them put together.

Lia startled me by taking hold of my hand and shoving some kind of bracelet onto it. My momentary struggle ceased when I saw the rest of them grinning. Except Oscar, of course, whose face would crack if he ever dared smile, and Joss, who continued to stare out the window, posture rigid.

"This is why I'm here today, to initiate you into the magic of our forefathers." Muttering some kind of incantation under her breath, she waved her fingers over the bracelet, some kind of braided fabric the color of mud, about an inch thick.

If I ever went in for jewelry, I'd definitely pick something a lot less ugly than the bracelet, but the eager expressions on the faces around me quelled my urge to rip the thing off.

After a few more seconds of chanting nonsense, Lia touched a fingertip to the bracelet. "I have placed a powerful protection spell into the rushes used to weave this bracelet. Wear it at all times."

"Thanks," I muttered, increasingly daunted by the obsession about my protection. The symbols in the room, the bracelet, my very own warrior ...

Standing, Lia did a funny little bow. "My work here is done." Touching the pentagram pendant nestled in her cleavage, she muttered something else I couldn't understand before performing the ritual open-palm, fingers-spread greeting with Mack. "Stay warm, Sorority."

Was "stay warm" the equivalent of "stay safe" around here? I caught Joss's imperceptible nod a moment before he held the door open for Lia, who swept through it in a flurry of long white layered skirts and an emerald cloak that touched the floor.

Uriel touched my shoulder, her smile gentle. "Don't be intimidated, dear. Lia is a force of nature, but she'll do the right thing by you, always."

"Uh-huh," was all I managed before the Sorority descended on the food like a plague of locusts.

I remained silent, nibbling on my lavender cookie, content to listen to the conversation drifting over me. Topics ranged from a reforestation project in the birch grove to ordering new ritual robes for the Sorority. Joss rarely spoke, offering his opinion when asked, while Uriel buzzed around like a doting mother hen, refilling glasses, topping up plates.

It would've been a cozy scene, a casual chat over food, if not for the constant nagging feeling something wasn't right.

If Cadifor was on the verge of finding Arwen, and I was

working against the clock to catch up, where was the urgency? They were so laid back they were almost horizontal. Or was this part of some great plan they had, to lull me into a false sense of security, to build my confidence, before revealing the true extent of what I faced?

Regardless, I couldn't bear another moment of inanity when so much was at stake.

I pushed back from the table and stood. "Thanks for the snack, Uriel, but I need to start my lessons."

My gracious hostess didn't blink at my abruptness, but merely smiled and started gathering dishes. "Of course, dear. Joss will give you a key to come and go as you please. I'll be out for most of the weekend in preparation for Beltane."

The gold cross embroidered over her left breast drew my gaze, and I wondered how Uriel fit into the sun-worshipping community.

Sensing my curiosity, she said, "When I became part of Joss's family, I took on the Eiros customs." She touched the cross. "Incorporated my original faith. My parents both teleported to Eiros when I was young. They were gifted. I wasn't. But I was allowed to stay because of them."

"I didn't mean to pry—"

"You didn't." She patted my shoulder in an affectionate gesture so reminiscent of Nan I almost burst into tears. "Now, off you go, all of you. Prepare Holly for what she'll face."

Uriel shooed us out amid a flurry of thanks and groans from full tummies while her last words echoed in my head.

What she'll face … what she'll face …

The lone cookie I'd managed to eat threatened to come back up. As if having Cadifor's crony coming after me, finding my mom, mastering impossible tasks, searching for Arwen, and facing a potential battle against the lord of darkness with the fate of the world hanging in the balance wasn't bad enough, I also had to face my friends with the truth, face my true feelings for Joss, and face the possibility that Nan might not pull through. It was enough to have me surreptitiously rubbing my stomach and focusing on anything but my urge to hurl.

I couldn't stomach evil, yet the impending battle I would have to win would be steeped in it. Time to toughen up. Starting now.

CHAPTER SIXTEEN

My first Saturday morning of formal lessons at Eiros tightened the noose of responsibility, strangling me. From the tense expressions of the Sorority as they divulged each new gem of wisdom, expectations were high. Failure wasn't an option. Lucky me.

While I lapped up the facts the same way I did in English and chem, it was the constant surveillance that wore me down. With every fact imparted, one of the Sorority would scan my face, checking how I was coping, how I was absorbing vital details. It was exhausting.

Now they'd sprung my first pop quiz. After half a day? Did they think I was a freaking brainiac? Discounting the fact that the information was new to me, the lessons sounded like they were in another language most of the time, and the content was beyond crazy.

"How did our civilization begin?"

I rolled my eyes at Mack. *Bring it on, Leader.*

"With equal sharing of light and dark. But Cadifor got greedy, became jealous of Bel because people were happier in sunlight, and bad things happened under the cloak of darkness so people resented and blamed him."

I rested on my outstretched arms, settling into the story I thought was cool. "In an effort to control and punish them further, Cadifor staged a battle. Bel won and banished him to permanent darkness underground, along with his loyal consorts."

This is the part that scared the crap out of me—that I was the only one who could stop Cadifor. If Bel was all-powerful and such a clever sun god, why did he place the future of the world in one descendant's shaky hands? Surely he could've dumped this responsibility on some other poor sucker's head? But no, I happened to be the lucky female descendant with a freaky sun affinity and the hopes of an NYC-wannabe community hanging over me like a storm cloud. *Holly Burton, come on down.*

"Bel's spell is powerful, but can be broken if Cadifor gains control of Arwen, rejoins forces with Mider and Nemain, and brings about the last great war to end civilization."

Mack nodded, glancing down at his book for the next question. "Good. Next question: describe our religion."

Another easy one. "Based on the ancient druids, a system of Neo-paganism worshipping Belenus, the sun god, with the main goal being to return to a peaceful existence in the golden age." It all sounded very hippie and New Age to me, but hey, who was I to question their idealism? I didn't know what I believed in anymore.

Mack ticked another question off his exhaustive list, which I'd caught a glimpse of when he flipped the cover of his notebook. "Lifestyle?"

Another cinch. Maybe they were softening me up for the tough stuff to come? "The emphasis at Eiros is tree crops, reforestation, and organic gardening. Main areas of interest for those living here include ecology, astronomy, astrology, and sacred building construction." Which I found funny, for the bulk of the housing appeared roughshod at best, like a ghetto had been transported out here along with Central Park. A few of the houses, like Uriel's, were well kept, but combined with the sky's gray pall, the rest seemed grimy and depressing.

Suitably impressed by my rote learning, if his proud smile was any indication, Mack moved down his list. "Describe the role of warriors in Eiros society."

A subject close to my heart, and I risked a quick glance at Joss, who'd appeared impassive during my morning lessons, his indifference spurring me on to prove myself. While I liked the guy, he also had the ability to seriously piss me off.

"Warriors are born into the role of protectors. They police Eiros, maintaining the peace, enforcing laws, ensuring safety. They enter formal training at ten years of age and move into the apartments on the community fringe. Along with earning a high school diploma, they study all aspects of combat and hone their psychic powers."

I shot Joss another glance, but he kept his back turned, and I wondered how he'd coped with being thrust into a warrior's life so early. He'd lost both his parents, then he'd probably had to deal with leaving Uriel too, while still a kid, only to be indoctrinated into fighting and protecting while getting a grip on algebra and English. Way too heavy. Was that the reason for his worldliness? He had a maturity most guys in their twenties didn't possess; maybe dealing with all that loss so young and being forced to grow up quickly during training did that to a guy.

Maeve fired off a quickie. "Why are we called a sorority when we have male members?"

I bit back a smile as Maeve stuck out her tongue at Oscar, the grumpiest male member, who scowled. "Because Belenus was the first leader and he designed the Sorority to be a mix of sexes, empowering both males and females with his light. Which also explains why he didn't label it a fraternity, implying a male brotherhood only."

Mack scanned his list for the next question when Oscar held up his hand, permanent scowl grimmer than ever. "This is a waste of time." He jerked a thumb in my direction. "She can obviously recite facts back to us for the next decade. Let's test her on the important stuff, like her role during Beltane next weekend."

Mack glanced up from his list and nodded. "Why don't we head over to the temple now, run through the ritual there?"

Oscar leaped to his feet. "Action at last," he muttered, while the rest of us ignored him.

Maeve bounced ahead, exuberant as ever, while Joss held out his hand and helped pull me to my feet. Shame old-world manners had gone out of fashion. I kinda liked it.

Mack took a step, stopped, and turned to face me. "You're doing well, Holly. Much better than any of us could've hoped."

"Thanks. I think."

He smiled and headed off in Maeve's direction, while Joss released my hand, his blue eyes as intense as ever.

"He's right. You're a sponge for facts."

I shrugged, his praise meaning far more than anyone else's. "Why don't you call me a nerd and be done with it?"

A hint of a smile flickered across his face. "I'd like to call you many things, Holly Burton, but nerd wouldn't be one of them."

Mortified Joss had the power to make me blush so easily, I followed the others, his silent strength beside me a comfort.

I watched Maeve stroll ahead, Mack's long strides, Oscar slouching along beside him, and it hit me that apart from training me, I didn't actually know what the Sorority did.

"We ensure smooth running of the community, act as guidance counselors, stuff like that."

I had half a mind to think something really nasty and let Joss read that. Instead, I settled for the more mature approach of asking more questions. "So you've all been born and raised here? Schooling?"

"Home-schooled, and yeah, Sorority members are born and bred here."

Except me. What was I? Some no-name drifting between parallel existences, handy for the odd Arwen hunt but belonging nowhere? Story of my life, really.

"You don't do the self-pity thing well," he said, his voice steely, his expression unimpressed. "You belong here. You chose your destiny the moment you agreed to embark on this quest, so you're one of us now. Suck it up."

"What bit your ass?"

He dragged a hand through his hair. "Not all of us get a choice in what we do, but we have to stick with it and do our best."

"Yeah, or the world ends," I muttered, annoyed by his animosity. I was here, wasn't I? Filling my head with all these ridiculous facts about an ancient culture depending on a sixteen-year-old to save them? Getting a handle on some seriously spooky crap? "Believe me, I get it, I don't need you ramming it down my throat."

Interesting. He'd mentioned not everyone having a choice. Did Warrior Boy not want the job of protecting me and it was thrust upon him? "You didn't get a choice? Is that what this snit is about?"

His head jerked back as if I'd slapped him, his blue eyes blazing with bitterness. "Let's just say you're not the only one who has something to prove."

Unease slid through me. Had Joss mucked up in some way? Did he truly know what he was doing? I'd put my trust in him to protect me; what if he wasn't up to it? What then? Desperate to keep him talking and discover more, I made light of the situation. "Don't tell me. You're on probation?"

His expression twisted into a grimace. "Something like that," he said, defiant as he stared me down, silently challenging me to make something of his reluctant admission. "It doesn't mean I won't protect you with everything I can, even if it kills me."

Startled by his vehemence, my heart stalled.

"Holly? Come on, you guys." Maeve broke our silent deadlock when she called out. I silently cursed the bad timing. My warrior had some serious shit going on and I needed to know what it was. Before it got us both killed.

"Let's get moving," he snapped, before carefully, deliberately, wiping his expression.

"This isn't finished," I hissed under my breath, but he ignored me, raising a hand in the group's direction to signal our falling in.

As we followed the others, fear made my pulse skip in time with my steps as I analyzed everything he'd said. It sounded like protecting me was some kind of test for him, a job he had no choice about. What happened if he failed, and who had coerced him into this? And why was he moody and forbidding sometimes, and reluctantly caring others?

The weekend lessons at Eiros I could do without, but a chance to interrogate my mysterious warrior and discover the truth? I was so there.

Climbing down a steady decline through thick forest, I envisioned what the Temple of Grian would look like: a cross between the Acropolis, the Coliseum, and Stonehenge? When we finally stopped, my first glimpse far surpassed my imagination.

"The Temple of Grian," Mack announced unnecessarily, earning another scornful glare from Oscar.

Nestled into the bottom of the hill, the temple had eight towering stone columns covered in now-familiar symbols. Circular stone benches were arranged in concentric spirals toward the middle, where a stone altar took center stage. There was no roof; lush grass covered the floor, wildflowers spilled over the backs of benches in abundance, and bees buzzed in the background.

I didn't say a word, eager to explore, to take everything in. Thankfully, the others picked up on my reluctance to talk. The silence was peaceful, restful, at odds with the tense group dynamic.

"The temple is set out in a mandala design, oriented to nature, the four compass points, and positions of the stars and planets."

I glanced at Mack, not exasperated by the lesson for once. I wanted to know everything I could about this place. The second I'd seen it I felt something indescribable tugging at me, something I'd never experienced.

A feeling of coming home.

"It's beautiful."

Even Oscar lost his scowl at my declaration, the four of them flanking me as I picked my way down the hill toward the temple.

When my foot hit the first stone step leading toward the altar, I froze, overcome by the *rightness* of all this. It felt strange after my constant doubts about the validity of this quest, after the doubts that had plagued me my whole life.

Not being good enough for my mom to stick around.

Not being anything other than a burden, a responsibility my Nan couldn't shirk.

Not fitting in at school.

Not having friends like everyone else.

Not being cool enough or pretty enough or funky enough to be anything but a loner, a loser.

Yet all that faded as I focused on the altar, oblivious to everything and everyone bar the pale sun fighting its way through the omnipresent gray, bathing me in welcoming warmth and the certainty that every step I took would bring me closer to why I was here.

My ballet flats made soft scuffling sounds as I picked my way down the uneven stone path, but I didn't stumble. With shoulders squared, I marched toward the altar like I'd been born to do it, basking in the sense of power flooding through me.

For someone who'd always flown under the radar, I was so far over and beyond the radar right now it wasn't funny. But I wasn't scared by this inexplicable assuredness that being here was right. For the first time in my life, I felt like I'd found my place, a place I fit.

The Sorority hung back when I reached the altar, probably waiting to see what I'd do, whether I'd bungle this.

Driven by an inner certainty, I stepped behind the altar, confident I would find the source of my newfound confidence. I saw the flicker of flames within a cylindrical stone receptacle surrounded by a spiral of rocks, a fire without a wick or kindling of any kind, a fire that drew me for no other reason than I knew I had to be near it. I knelt and held out my hands to the flame to warm them, not surprised when my palms burned so intensely they could've blistered.

I sensed a presence next to me, and was relieved when Joss placed his hand on my shoulder before joining me on his knees.

"How did you know Bel's fire was here?"

I opened my mouth to speak, trying to articulate even half of what I was feeling. Inadequately, I settled for, "It called to me." I tapped my chest. "In here."

An inner confidence nothing could shake as long as I was there, near the flame, filled me. I remembered feeling the same serenity when sunbathing by Lake Wolfe, the sun caressing my skin making me feel warm and safe and happy, one of the few times in my life I didn't feel lonely. In that moment, standing by this tiny flame that reproduced the same security, I really, truly believed I could be bonded to some ancient sun god.

"Never doubt you're the Scion. *Never*, you hear me?" Joss's blatant approval was as dazzling as the flame that drew me.

"You know what you said earlier, about me doing my best?" I pointed to the flame. "When I'm near this, I feel I can."

The intense blue of his eyes rivaled a Wolfebane summer sky for brightness, but it was the expression in those beautiful eyes, a compassion that snatched my breath, that made me want to fling myself in his arms and cherish this surreal moment.

"I'll grant you Bel's fire is special, but you don't need it to be powerful." I stiffened as he reached out and traced a heart over my left breast. "You've had that power in here all along."

There was nothing remotely sleazy in his touch, his unwavering sincerity proof of that, but the instant he touched me there, fire of another kind raced through my body. "Tell me more," I murmured, unsure whether I was asking to hear more poetic reassurances or more facts about Bel.

A small part of me couldn't help but be disappointed when our intimacy shattered and he reverted to his typical aloofness. "Bel's fire never goes out; it's our sacred sign of him watching over us always."

I was glad we were back on familiar, offhand terms and my heart could return to its normal rate. "What happens at Beltane?"

"We formally welcome you into the community, celebrate the light."

He glanced at the Sorority and I immediately got the impression he was holding something back. I didn't want to push. For now, I wanted to bask in this feeling of rightness, wanted to hold on to it, no matter how intangible and fleeting.

"Here." Joss pulled a small bag of fruit from his pocket. "An offering. Lay it around the altar in a circle."

Maeve handed me a bag of flowers, Oscar gave me vegetables, and Mack passed me small branches from a tree I couldn't identify. When I'd laid the last apple, potato, sunflower, and twig, I stepped back, sure the flame burned brighter.

The Sorority raised their hands in the greeting sign, murmuring "Stay warm," and it felt the most natural thing in the world—and not lame at all—when I pressed palms with each of them.

CHAPTER SEVENTEEN

I've never been super brave. Confronting cheerleaders who'd snatched my books out of sheer bitchiness? Made me want to vomit. Reading my science paper on conduction in front of the class? I actually did vomit; later, thank goodness.

So when the first prickling coldness of a pending vision swept over me, I should've blabbed to the Sorority—loudly, to cover the knocking of my knees. Instead, I did the unthinkable for a coward like me. I asked them to leave. I asked for some private time to wander the temple, absorb the ambiance, and get connected.

They bought it, except Joss, who with the barest inclination of his head indicated he'd be waiting for me in the nearest grove.

Mouthing "thanks," I waited until they'd climbed the spiral path and disappeared from view before sinking onto the nearest stone bench and letting the fear overcome me. My stomach churned with unusual force and I clutched it in the hope of warding off the escalating queasiness. It didn't help as the roiling intensified until I could hardly breathe.

Hunched over, I sent a silent message to Joss. *"I'm okay, leave me be."* I knew he'd be down in a heartbeat if he picked up one iota of my distress.

Once I'd communicated to him, I let the vision come.

Cadifor towering over Keenan, pointing at an object hidden in the sleeve of his robe.

"The newcomer. Who is she?"

Keenan keeps his head bowed. "I don't know, my lord."

"Find out!"

The order, accompanied by a backhand, brings Keenan to his knees.

Cadifor yanks him roughly to his feet. "Do not return until you have her identity and something of hers I can use."

As Cadifor turns, the object tucked into his sleeve falls to the ground.

A photo.

Of me.

I came to with a whimper, fear coursing through me like a river of fractured glaciers, sharp and unrelenting and brutal, slicing through any delusions of power I may have had. I'd been a fool, high on the thrill of belonging, on the mysticism of the ancient temple, believing I could do this. The cold perspiration drenching my brow, the icy terror flowing through my veins, gave me the wakeup call I needed.

Cadifor was real. Cadifor was scary. Cadifor was hot on my trail.

One of Cadifor's consorts was out to identify me and take

something of mine. To *use*? Use for what?

In the aftermath of the vision, I'd forgotten to block my thoughts, or to at least try some semblance of the skill I'd been practicing to ensure privacy from curious warriors probing my mind.

Joss launched himself from the trees and flew towards me. He skidded to a stop when he saw I was in one piece. "What—"

"If I'm to master the tasks, I needed to do this on my own."

Sadness flickered across his face before he quickly masked it, confirming what I already knew. He cared behind the terseness, would do anything to protect me. It should've made me feel better. After what I'd just seen? It didn't.

"Vision?"

I nodded. "Cadifor and Keenan."

I wished I could save Joss the worry, but it was fruitless trying to hide anything from him. "What would Cadifor want with an item of someone's?"

He paled, deciphering my indirect question immediately. "He wants something of yours?"

I bit my lip so hard I tasted blood. I nodded, the panic I'd barely managed to subdue flaring in an instant. Joss hadn't answered my question; he didn't have to. His pallor spoke volumes. Cadifor's motivation for wanting something of mine couldn't be good. I thrust my hands into my pockets so he wouldn't see them trembling.

I tried to erase the residual terror from my mind. "He had a photo of me. Wants to know my identity. And wants something of mine he can use."

"For scrying."

"To see my future?"

Joss nodded, casting a nervous glance over my shoulder as if expecting Cadifor to materialize right this very second. "You're a newcomer here. He may have suspicions about who you are. Having something of yours will strengthen whatever scrying spell he uses."

He avoided my eyes, and I got the distinct impression he wasn't telling me everything. Hell, what could be worse than a monster wanting a personal item of mine? Revulsion made me quiver. Not that I had a lot. Clothes and books constituted the bulk of my worldly wealth and he could have my oldest hoodie. If he touched one of my books, though, I'd kill him.

Joss's palpable anxiety made my fear blossom as a horrible thought struck. "When you say something of mine, you mean like a hairbrush or a sweater, right?"

He paused, and I knew the answer before he spoke. "No, he needs something more personal. A hair, a fingernail, something of *you*."

"Gross." As if having the lord of darkness on my trail wasn't bad enough, I now had to watch out for some creepy stranger wanting a piece of me?

"Let's get out of here."

He grabbed my hand and tugged. I didn't move. "This telling

the future stuff? How accurate is it?"

"Depends." Taken aback by my question, he released my hand, started the pacing thing I'd come to recognize as his way of thinking, of dealing with stuff.

"Some are truly gifted scryers, others not so much."

"Is Cadifor—"

"I don't know."

I appreciated his blunt honesty. Appreciated it, but didn't like hearing the guy I trusted with my life had no clue whether Cadifor knew his scrying stuff or not. That was part of the relentless fear in all this, the not knowing. Every time I had a vision, it was supposedly a precognitive event, meaning it hadn't happened yet. But if the future was dependent on free choice, the choices we all had to make, couldn't it be changed? And if so, what did that mean for me? For Mom? For all of us?

"You're right, the future can always be changed by the choices we make, so no matter how many hairs he throws into the scrying bowl, what you do can alter the course of history."

"Wow, profound."

He shook his head, a smile tugging at his mouth. "You're either the bravest girl I've ever met or the dumbest."

"I'll take the first, thanks."

Jerking a thumb toward the forest, he said, "After the morning you've had, you've earned the afternoon off. We'll head back to my mom's and you can crash." I took a step. He held up a finger. "But whatever you do, don't leave the cottage, okay?"

"Yes, boss," I muttered, balking when he tried to grab me,

enjoying catching him unawares. I goofed off for a while, lunging and dodging and weaving, surprised when my uptight, serious warrior joined in, a nice way to blow off the tension of the last hour.

I'd survived my first morning's lessons at Eiros and finally controlled an incoming vision. Chalk up one to the Arwen hunter.

CHAPTER EIGHTEEN

When I'd agreed to Joss's caveat of not leaving the cottage all afternoon, I hadn't quite realized what I'd be letting myself in for.

Nothing. Absolutely nothing.

Even though he didn't live here, I hoped he might've left behind a few books. He had, but nothing cool; *Drawing the Short Sword* and *Mastering Your Inner Fire: Pyrokinesis for Beginners* didn't do it for me. There were no magazines, no TV, and no iPod. Even me, Geek Girl, would've killed for a *Teen Vogue* or a *Gossip Girl* rerun right about then.

With Uriel a no-show all afternoon and Joss on secret sorority business, I'd explored almost every inch of the place. The only rooms I hadn't explored were Uriel's bedroom and Joss's old room. Not that I wasn't tempted. Anything to relieve the unrelenting boredom and give me insight into the guy I couldn't stop thinking about.

He confused the hell out of me. He could be brash and abrupt and surly, yet other times he'd been caring and understanding and supportive. From his own admission it sounded like he'd been forced into protecting me, but that didn't make any sense if I believed all that geis and bound-together crap. Unless he hadn't wanted the job and had been blackmailed into it by the Sorority? Stupid conspiracy theories, but I was bored.

The thing was, whether Joss was grumpy or nice, I liked him. He wasn't like most of the guys I knew, guys I'd grown up with at school who, once they hit puberty, talked about nothing but themselves. Who scored the most touchdowns, who had the biggest car, the biggest allowance, the biggest dick. Ironic, as they all did. They were all big dicks the way I saw it.

Joss was nothing like that. In saying less, he said more, conveying so much in a few well-chosen words, in a fleeting touch. And whatever his motivation for protecting me, having him by my side made me feel a whole lot safer.

Even mooning around over Joss couldn't distract me enough. I'd cooked up a batch of vegetable soup. I'd wiped down the countertops. I'd even dusted, and I freaking hated dusting. I was about to throw a bunch of herbs into a stainless steel bowl and try to master scrying—if only to tell me when someone would return—when a noise at the window made me jump.

The sane thing would've been to back away from the window.

But this new me, fresh from accepting the challenge to find Arwen and master a bunch of psychic challenges and the liberating experience of connecting with Bel's fire, had me grabbing a knife for some meager protection and inching toward the window to peer out.

I flattened my back against the wall and edged toward the window, my heart thumping so loudly I could barely think past the noise pounding in my ears. I eased around the window frame, angling for a better view, peeking behind the gingham curtains ...

Slam! A rock crashed through the window, showering me with glass. I screamed as a hand reached through the gaping hole and yanked me by the hair. Yelping, I dropped the knife; my first instinct was to save myself from being dragged through the razor-edged window headfirst.

I clawed. Scratched. Writhed. Used my body weight to launch forward. Away from the window, despite the sheer agony of having my hair pulled out by the roots. It worked. I dragged my assailant's arms across the jagged glass in falling forward, resulting in sudden, welcome release.

Frantic to escape, I tried to stand, slipping on the glass fragments covering the floor, going down in a sprawling heap. I couldn't stay still, my hands and feet working in sync as I scuttled backward in a bizarre crab walk, desperate to get away from the gaping window. My throat, raw from screaming, convulsed as a leg appeared, hoisted over the windowsill and I glimpsed Keenan's evil face leering at me.

Propelled by terror and adrenalin, I surged to my feet, slipping and sliding but not stopping for anything. I bolted for the guest room, slammed the door, and leaned my head against the wall as my legs gave out. I slid down the wall and landed hard on my butt, praying to Bel or Jesus or whichever god was out there to save me.

Heavy footsteps thudded down the hallway and I scrambled to my feet, pressing my ear to the door, then backing away the closer they got. Whimpering, I rested my forehead against the wall, shocked at the familiar burning, the blistering heat, the stomach-tumbling freefall. When I opened my eyes, I'd never been so glad in my entire life to be slumped in the stone shed by the river at C.U.L.T.

Alone.

I'd fallen off the old armchair and lay sprawled against the wall, my legs shaking so much I couldn't have stood if I'd wanted to.

What the hell had just happened? One moment that lunatic Keenan had been chasing me, the next I woke up back at C.U.L.T.

My forehead throbbed and I tentatively probed it, surprised by its smoothness when it felt like a colony of worms wriggled beneath the skin. A residual heat lingered too, and I lowered my hand as realization hit.

I'd been powerless and petrified in that guest room in Uriel's cottage, my hands a bloodied mess and useless to defend myself. Defeated, I'd rested my forehead against the wall and ... the symbols. Hadn't Joss mentioned something about the guest room being a safe haven in that house because of the symbols? Obviously, my third eye had connected with one of them and I'd ended up back here, thank goodness.

But my relief was short-lived when I imagined Keenan hanging around the cottage, waiting for the return of Uriel. ... I tried to stand and pain sliced through my forehead, an agony so intense I saw stars for a few seconds.

I collapsed against the wall and dragged in deep breaths, waiting for my vision to clear.

I had to go back; there was no question. Uriel could be in danger. Plus Joss and the rest of the gang would seriously freak when they saw the carnage in the house and would assume the worst: that I'd been taken.

My bleeding hands throbbed, shredded by the glass fragments. Common sense insisted I fix them before attempting a return journey. As much as I wanted to press the crystal to my forehead and return instantly to help protect the people I'd grown to care about, I'd be useless to anyone until I could use my hands in some capacity.

I braced for the pain, taking deep breaths to steady my wobbly knees as I stood. Thankfully, the excruciating roar in my head subsided to a dull ache and I managed to stay upright as my feet touched the ground.

At least I had a clear plan: head back to the dorm, clean up, and get back here ASAP before the sun set and I lost my opportunity to do my crystal trick. All without running into anyone and arousing suspicion. Easy, right? However, like the rest of my life over the last few months, nothing was easy, and as I limped across the school grounds and slipped into the dorm, the first person I ran into was Raven.

"Uh-oh," I muttered, as she glanced at my hands, then my hair.

"Jeez, what happened to your hair?"

Trust Raven to make me laugh at a time like this.

"Your hands too," she added belatedly, with a wry smile. "Seriously? The blood I can put up with. Your hair?" Her hand wavered. "Not so much."

I needed to come up with an excuse, fast. Something I'd never been any good at, thinking on the spur of the moment. When I stood there like a dummy, she grabbed my hands and turned them palms up.

"You've got glass bits stuck in there. Want some help?"

I couldn't afford the time but accepting her offer made sense. Tweezing left handed would be tough and this way I'd be out of here faster. "Thanks."

I limped to my room, her constant sideways glances annoying the crap out of me. At least our silent walk down the corridor gave me time to invent an excuse.

As soon as we stepped into my room, I headed to the bathroom, calling over my shoulder. "I'm such a klutz. Wanted to master the next chapter in our scrying text to get Crane off my back, so I took stuff down to the river. I slipped, smashed the bowl on the rocks, snagged my hair in a tree branch, and ended up falling on top of everything."

She didn't believe me. I could see it in her slightly narrowed eyes, her thinly compressed lips. "You know scrying requires a steel bowl?"

Holding my cut hands up, I shrugged. "I do now."

She took pity on me despite my sheepish smile and lousy excuse, not pushing for answers. "Let's get you cleaned up." She followed me into the bathroom, got the first aid kit from behind the mirror, and pointed to the bathtub. "Sit."

I did as I was told, holding out my hands and holding my breath. One thing I hated more than a lord of darkness chasing my ass? Blood.

"This won't hurt a bit," she said, her tone teasingly gleeful as she took hold of my right hand and pressed the tweezers into my palm.

I gave a yelp and jerked back as the cold metal tip dug into my skin.

"Don't be a wuss," Raven said, holding my hand tighter. "What would Lissa do?"

I managed a small smile at her *Vampire Academy* reference as a distraction. "Considering she's a mortal vampire, she'd probably suck her own blood."

"Eeew!"

But Raven's question did the trick as we started debating the strength of Lissa and Christian's relationship, the whole Strigoi/Moroi thing, and how hot Dimitri was.

Every time the tip of the tweezers dug into my palm I flinched, biting back a host of words both of us had heard a million times before. Every time a fragment of glass dropped into the sink, I got angrier. Really angry. An anger I'd never felt before. An anger that served to fuel my hunger. My hunger to win.

What if Uriel had been at the cottage when Cadifor's groupie broke in to get me? Would she be considered collateral damage, eliminated?

The thought of Joss losing another mom made me want to puke.

Raven finally plucked out the last piece and handed me a glass of water. "Here, you've turned green."

"Thanks," I mumbled, gulping it down, forgetting how sore my throat had been from all the screaming.

"Could be worse," she said, dabbing cotton with antiseptic. "Lucky you were wearing shoes."

Glancing down, I wiggled my toes. If I hadn't been wearing my favorite ballet flats, I probably wouldn't be here. No way could I have run from that madman in bare feet; the glass would've hobbled me.

"So, would you do Harry Potter or Ron Weasley?"

I played along, bracing for the teeth-clenching sting of antiseptic.

"Harry in a heartbeat," I said, letting out an almighty yell as she dabbed at my palms.

"There, all done." She bandaged them, sat back, and dusted off her hands, admiring her handiwork. "Not too bad. You'll get a sympathy vote at dinner."

I slid off the bath rim and stood, glad I wasn't so wobbly

anymore. "I'm not coming to dinner."

"Why not?" Raven rinsed off her hands, her curious gaze meeting mine in the mirror.

"I need to go see Nan."

"On a Saturday night?"

"Uh-huh."

Raven grabbed a hand towel and spun around to face me. "Weren't you supposed to spend the whole weekend with her?"

I hated lying. Not that I'd done a lot of it, but the few times I'd spun Nan little white lies, I'd get so caught up in the web I couldn't escape without the whole thing unraveling. "Yeah, but I was feeling a bit overwhelmed by the new lessons and thought I'd do some catching up in private, so I stuck around here today."

"Cramming on a weekend when you could've escaped this place?" She shook her head and pointed at my hands. "Hopefully you've learned your lesson. No pun intended."

I smiled and started shifting from foot to foot, eager to return to Eiros, my guilt at lying to Raven stinging as much as my hands.

Picking up on my edginess, she headed for the door. "Anything else I can do?"

Waving my bandaged hands in the air, I said, "You've done enough. Thanks again."

She shrugged, suddenly bashful. "I guess if this telekinetic thing doesn't work out, I can always resort to nursing." She waved. "Later."

I gave her a ten-second head start before bolting out the door, my feet flying along the corridor, out of the dorm, and across the lawn toward the river. A bunch of juniors saw me and cast curious glances my way, focusing on my head, and I belatedly realized I hadn't done anything about my hair. I'd caught sight of it while Raven had fixed my hands. It wasn't pretty. Thin and wispy at its best, it now looked like I'd seen a ghost, sticking up in crazy clumps all over the place.

It was the least of my worries as I tumbled into the stone shed, fumbled for the crystal bag, and shook out a few, picking the one that worked. I sat against the far wall, the one where the sun poked through the holes in the roof just right, and held the crystal to my forehead, closed my eyes, and waited.

As the heat drained from my body, I opened my eyes to madness.

The front door to the cottage was wide open. Mack and Oscar were arguing, their voices ear splitting. Maeve alternated between wailing, knuckling tears, and shooting death glares at Joss, while Joss paced his mom's kitchen, his face pale, his expression blank and his lips compressed, like a guy who'd withdrawn and shut off from the world. But his eyes told a different story. They blazed with a fury that took my breath away and I knew exactly who he'd be angry with: himself, for thinking he hadn't done a good enough job protecting me.

Joss was the first to notice me as I stepped through the front door and all I could think when we locked gazes was *hold me*.

"Holly!" He flew across the room and bundled me in his arms, squeezing so tight I couldn't breathe. Not that I minded. He smelled of the outdoors and apples and crushed oak leaves, familiar, comforting, and oh so delicious.

He released me as the rest of the Sorority crowded around, assuming his stoic warrior face again. But I could see the emotion in his eyes, the muted anguish he'd gone through the last half hour, and now the relief.

Emboldened by my recent brush with evil, I touched his hand. *I'm okay. And really glad to see you.*

Before he could respond the others jostled me, hands urging me toward the dining table and pushing me to sit. Mack, Maeve, and Oscar wore matching expressions: shock, their mouths slack-jawed, repetitively blinking like they'd seen a ghost.

"Hey guys, lighten up. You think I'm that easy to grab?"

Their open-mouthed silence answered that particular question.

"How did you ... ?"

Mack trailed off and I filled in the blank.

Survive?

As I glanced around at their concerned faces—Maeve still sniffling and swiping tears, though this time in relief, Mack staring at me in wonder, Joss's tumultuous emotions barely hidden behind his warrior mask—I don't know what freaked me out the most: the fact that even Oscar seemed seriously glad to see me, or that everything had been cleaned up so quickly, like my struggle with the bad guy never happened.

The glass had vanished, the jagged edges protruding from the window had been removed, and there wasn't a rock in sight. I could've imagined the whole thing if it weren't for my throbbing hands and the residual adrenalin that had me twitchy as a bookaholic at the *Mockingjay* launch. I'd come back here to reassure the Sorority I was okay, to make sure Joss knew he hadn't failed, but being here, where that creep had tried to get me, had me jittery enough to want to go after him and beat the crap out of him myself.

"Give her a second," Joss said, standing close, protective. What I would've given to have him here thirty minutes ago.

"I'm fine," I said, flashing him a grateful smile, which he acknowledged by brushing his fingers across the back of my wrist. *Ooh ... nice.*

"I was following instructions, hanging out in here, when a rock crashed through the window and that guy tried to grab me." Touching my sore scalp, I winced. "I swear the creep ripped out half my hair. Anyway, he came in after me. I ran to my room and heard him coming down the hall."

Panic welled as I mentally relived the attack, but I subdued it. This wasn't the time to wallow. This was the time to get even.

"I was pretty much freaking out and was exhausted, so I leaned against the wall, and next thing I know, my forehead connected with the Arwen Triple Flame symbol and I woke up back at school."

Mack, astute as ever, pounced on one tiny detail.

"*That* guy? You knew him?"

Uh-oh, slip up number one. How many more would I make

before I saw this thing through? Not in the mood for judgment, I ducked my head. "Kind of."

Oscar shook his head. "What does that mean?"

Joss touched me again, a gentle nudge with his hand in the middle of my back, and that was all the encouragement I needed. I trusted him, and if he thought I should blab, I would. Truth time. "I saw him in a vision earlier today."

Mack frowned. "When?"

"At the temple. When I asked for some time alone."

Maeve's tears had dried and Oscar's frown had returned. So much for the sympathy vote. Not that I needed it, but it had been nice to have them view me like a vulnerable human for once instead of a freak of nature they needed to tolerate to further their own ends.

"I haven't had a vision all week; then, at the temple, I had one."

"Of?" Mack prompted, his skin drawn tight over his cheekbones, the tension aging him.

Before I could respond, Oscar jabbed a finger in Joss's direction. "You knew about this?"

Joss nodded, his jaw clenched, probably to stop from saying something he'd regret.

Oscar scowled. "And you didn't tell us because?"

"Because we all know visions aren't reliable. They could mean anything, be interpreted a hundred different ways," Maeve chirped up, assuming the peacemaker role as usual, and I shot her a grateful smile.

Oscar scowled. "He still should've told us. This isn't a one-man show."

Mack held up his hands, palms down, placating. "Let's get back to Holly's vision."

I held Joss's gaze for a long moment, hardly believing he could convey so much in a simple glance. *I'm fine, Oscar doesn't worry me, just tell the truth, I'm here for you.*

Buoyed by his silent support, I nodded and continued. "I saw Cadifor talking to this guy. His right hand man?"

"Keenan?" Mack asked, and Joss nodded.

"Cadifor was hiding something up his sleeve," I said.

Mack, Oscar, and Maeve leaned forward as one.

"He had my picture."

They relaxed—obviously they'd expected a knife or poison or something equally dastardly—but not for long.

"He knows who you are?" Oscar growled, shooting Mack an "I told you so" glare.

I shook my head. "Not yet. He asked Keenan to find out who I was."

"And?" Mack prodded gently, astute as always.

"He wanted something of mine."

They stiffened. Their simultaneous reactions would have been comical if not for the fact Cadifor now had exactly what he wanted: a piece of me. Several, judging by the gaping chunks of hair missing from my scalp.

Maeve pointed to my hair and winced. "That looks painful."

"Not as bad as these." I waved my bandaged hands around like war wounds, sucking in a breath when I accidentally bumped them together. False pride, Nan would've said, and clucked her tongue in a way that made me feel like a naughty five-year-old.

"That explains why the glass is gone." Mack jerked a thumb at the clean floor, then glanced at my bandages. "You cut your hands on the glass pieces?"

I nodded, flexing my fingers to show they still worked.

"Hell." Oscar slammed his palm on the table and everyone jumped.

Confused by their collective horrified expressions, I said, "What's wrong?"

Apart from the obvious, that Cadifor was one step closer to discovering my identity? And I had some serious bed-head going on.

Mack glanced at Joss, who nodded. Mack sighed. "Along with your hair, Keenan must've collected all the glass."

"So he's a clean freak? Big deal." Silence greeted my smartass response, a silence that grew.

They all glanced at Mack, so I did too. The longer they stretched this out, the higher my anxiety shot. On a scale of one to ten, my panic was a healthy eleven right about then. "Tell me what's going on."

Mack rubbed his temple, as if trying to stave off a blinder of a headache. "You cut your hands on the glass."

"Duh. Just say it—"

"He now has your blood."

Creepy, but not catastrophic on its own. It wasn't like he had a forensics lab down there or anything. "And that's bad because?"

"The more DNA he has of yours, the more powerful the divination spell he can use. With blood ... "

Oscar swore again. "Blood intensifies the potential of the divination a hundredfold."

Whatever blood I had left congealed in fright. "But Joss said you don't know if he's any good at scrying. Maybe the stuff he saw in the last vision was a lucky guess. Maybe using my DNA will show him nothing."

Joss stepped forward and laid a steadying hand on the small of my back, that small yet profound touch scaring me more than anything "Unlikely," he said. "Using someone's blood in a scrying spell is like examining them under a microscope."

I didn't like Maeve's palpable pity while Oscar glared, his expression solemn.

"So he'll know who I am?"

Mack nodded. "And he'll know why you're here."

"How? By getting a glimpse of me?" My voice rose, a tinge of hysteria audible.

"Keenan would've seen the symbols in that room, told him you'd vanished, and he'll know you're the one."

"Crap." It was creepy enough Cadifor had pieces of me and would soon know who I was, but to know who I *really* was? It was too soon. I needed time; time to learn every trick in the book to face off with a freak like him.

Mack rubbed his chin, thoughtful. "It's not all bad."

Oscar sniggered. "How do you figure that, Einstein?"

I managed a weak smile at Oscar's sarcasm.

Mack glanced at me, his admiration encouraging. "You've mastered another task, becoming one with the Arwen Triple Flame and using it."

Four expressions immediately lightened as I sagged in relief. "At least something good came out of my scalping and bloodletting."

"Better than good," Joss said, his tone warm with approval. "Being able to use the Triple Flame is hard to master. And if you used it to teleport … "

I'd discovered another way to move between the worlds. Way to go me. Speaking of tasks, something else occurred to me. "Hey, if I faced off one of Cadifor's baddies, isn't that another task?"

Maeve shook her head, gnawing her bottom lip. "No, you need to *banish* one of the Underworld's lesser creatures, not escape from it."

"There's a difference?" Surely escaping from that madman should've counted for something?

The Sorority nodded in unison. I didn't want to delve further into what *lesser creatures* I'd be facing in the not-too-distant future, not while I was still in a funk after escaping the clutches of Cadifor's crony.

"It's not safe for her to be here right now," Joss said, folding his arms and facing down the others.

Mack nodded. "Agreed."

"But what about tomorrow? Preparing for Beltane?" Predictably, Oscar wouldn't lose sight of the ultimate prize:

me finding Arwen before Cadifor did.

"Crash course via textbooks back at school. Then we'll do a quick run-through before the festival next week, okay?" Joss didn't budge from his protective stance, and I shot him a grateful smile.

Oscar scowled. "She needs more practical experience. Beltane's a big deal. She needs to be ready."

"She will be." Mack's steely tone brooked no argument. "We'll make do. We have to. We can't risk her … "

"Dying?" I helpfully supplied.

Joss rested his hand on my shoulder, solid and comforting. "We won't let that happen."

For once, I bit back my first words:

You almost did.

CHAPTER NINETEEN

As the gang filed out, leaving Joss to work his magic on my forehead, I knew what I had to do.

"Time to go."

I shook my head at Joss. "I need to do something first."

"What?"

"Visit Bel's fire."

"Are you insane?" He swept his arm wide. "You were attacked! Now you want to go traipsing through Eiros at night?"

I pointed at the darkening sky. "Honestly? Hard to tell the difference between night and day with that permanent grayness."

"That grayness is courtesy of Cadifor getting closer to finding Arwen. And in case you've forgotten, we need you alive to prevent that from happening."

"Good point." I gave him a moment to stew. "But I still need to see Bel's fire."

He folded his arms, his cold warrior face more intimidating than his mini-rant. "No way."

While I bristled at his bossy attitude, a small part of me melted at his obvious concern. For him to lose his cool meant he cared, and the thought warmed me all the way down to my quivering soul. Tilting my head to one side, I smirked. "Didn't you forget the part about *over my dead body*? Or is that in poor taste right about now?"

"You're pushing it." He jabbed a finger in my direction, trying another frown on for size, but not before I'd seen his lips twitch. "And no, just 'cause you think you can make me smile doesn't change my mind. We're not heading down there."

Bad move, taking the high road with me. I could out-stubborn Nan—and that's saying something. She held out on me getting a bellybutton ring for two years.

"You want me to find Arwen before Cadifor does, right?"

He clamped his lips tighter and nodded.

"I need to find out what he knows, and if we head to the temple, maybe I'll have another vision."

"I thought you couldn't control them yet."

"Technically, I can't, but when I felt that one coming on earlier today, I held it off until I got rid of all of you, then let it come. So my control is obviously increasing. Besides, I felt something down there." How could I make him understand without sounding like a total dork? "A kind of pull, a connection, like Bel is there, watching out for me, wanting me to succeed."

His stoic expression softened. "He is, but right now I'm the one entrusted with watching you. And I almost—"

He bit back the rest of his words and turned away. I snagged his arm and dragged him back to face me.

And it was all there, every conflicted feeling: confusion, excitement, fear, anticipation, all the emotions twisting my insides like a pretzel; they reflected in his gorgeous face, like he was going through the same thing. But he was doing his damndest to protect me from it, trying to be the valiant warrior, and it made me want to hug him all the more.

Unable to stop myself, I reached out and cupped his cheek, savoring the faintest prickle of stubble against my palm. "You didn't fail. You can't be with me twenty-four-seven."

Fleeting anguish darkened his eyes to indigo before he blinked, erasing it, covering my hand with his own, pressing it against his cheek. "But I have to be, can't you see that?"

"Why?" I whispered, afraid to break the intimate cocoon we'd created among all the madness.

"You know." He leaned forward ever so slightly and rested his forehead against mine, prolonging the sweetest moment of my life.

I closed my eyes, cherishing the moment, imprinting this incredible feeling on my heart to give me strength to face what was to come.

I don't know how long we stood there but the prickle of heat on my forehead scared me—no way in hell I wanted to teleport back to C.U.L.T. right now—so I reluctantly eased back.

"From now on, every second you're here, I'm going to be your shadow."

After what we'd just shared, not such a hardship. "In that case, stay close while I make a quick dash down to the temple."

His frown slashed a deep furrow between his eyebrows. "You're not going to give up on this, are you?"

"Nope."

With a resigned sigh, he glanced out the window. "The Sorority will kill me if anything happens to you, especially after the close call we had tonight."

Mentioning earlier events reminded me of something. "Why do you think Keenan came after me? In the bedroom? I mean, he had a good handful of hair, and the blood from the glass. Why chase me down?"

Joss's grim expression increased my apprehension. "Because a vial of blood would've been better than the droplets they'll distill off the glass."

My stomach clenched. "O-kay then, glad I asked."

"Don't you see? This is serious!"

I spun away from him, not wanting him to see the fear in my eyes. "You think I don't know that? I was the one who had to fend off that lunatic. I'm the one your precious Sorority expects miracles from. I'm the most ill-equipped person ever for this job, but I can't shirk the responsibility because so many people are depending on me. And I'm the one supposed to master all these tasks on a time limit, find this stupid icon, defeat evil, and save the freaking world."

I was shouting now, my chest heaving like I was going to puke. I turned back and jabbed him in the chest. Hard. "So don't you *dare* tell me how *serious* this is!"

I battled tears, swallowing the great embarrassing sobs rising in my throat, my hands shaking. I would've bolted, but he bundled me into his arms and held me tight. Not some half-assed hug, a real good squishy one. He rested his chin on the top of my head as I released some of the pent-up fear and frustration bubbling up inside. I didn't want to show weakness, didn't want to cry, but my tear ducts had other ideas. I drenched the front of his T-shirt in five seconds flat.

"Shh ... " He smoothed my hair, every straggly clump of it, the warmth from being in his arms slowly seeping into me, bringing calmness with it.

Eventually I stilled and he eased back, tilting my chin up. Mortified, I couldn't meet his eyes.

"Holly?"

"Uh hmm," I mumbled, staring at his chest.

"Look at me."

When I did, my throat clogged all over again.

He cared about me.

I could see it in the worry lines around his mouth, the genuine concern in his eyes.

Then his gaze dipped to my mouth, and I held my breath, caring replaced by something entirely different in those staggeringly beautiful blue eyes.

I waited. And waited. And waited.

For my first kiss.

I was a sad case, and that corny sweet-sixteen-and-never-been-kissed cliché? Totally applied to me.

My heart jumped around so much he had to have heard. With one hand around my waist, the other cradling my head, all he had to do was bring me a little closer and ...

"Fine. You have one hour at the temple, and I'll be right beside you the whole time."

My overheated body suddenly cooled as he released me. If I'd cried before, I really wanted to bawl now. Surely I hadn't misread the situation that much?

For the first time since all this craziness had begun, I wished he could read my mind all the time. Then he'd see how much I wanted him to kiss me, how much I wanted him, and how he'd just carved up my heart by rejecting me.

"Never cry over me," he said, his tone harsh. "We can't be together."

"Why not?"

Anguish contorted his mouth for a brief second before he shook his head. "Finding Arwen and defeating Cadifor is too important. No distractions."

"Maybe you should've thought of that before you almost kissed me?"

I could kill him. For being so high and mighty and in control, for having the sense to pull back from a kiss that would only complicate matters, for having a conscience, but most of all for being him and making me want him so damn much. "Let me guess.

There's some lame rule against warriors fraternizing with their charges."

He shook his head, his lips compressed in a stubborn line, as I mustered my best badass glare and flung open the door.

This was so not the time for him to be reading my mind, and as I stalked past him, he snagged my wrist and murmured, "There's too much at stake."

I couldn't agree with him more, my breakable heart being on top of the list.

The Temple of Grian pulsed with a faint glow the closer we got. Imposing in daylight, it was incandescent in the soft moonlight, the promise of magic and mayhem all the stronger as I stepped onto the path spiraling down towards the altar.

I could hear Joss's steady, dependable steps behind me, but I didn't stop. I was still mad as hell at him for that aborted kiss—and for making me like him in the first place.

With each step on the flagstones I relived every mortifying moment in excruciating detail. My mini-rant exposing some of my innermost fears, my blubbering all over him, my inviting that kiss … I stopped from making an L with my thumb and index and holding it against my forehead, just.

Besides, with my freaky forehead, who knew where I'd end up?

"You're not in this alone."

I stopped, silently counted to ten, and clenched and unclenched my hands a few times before turning to face Joss. Either that or deck him. But the minute I caught sight of his face, some of my anger dissipated. He wasn't playing games. He was too honorable for that, too damn noble. He genuinely believed finding Arwen and defeating Cadifor was all-important, even at the risk of ignoring the attraction buzzing between us.

I guess that's what made me so furious; deep down, I knew he was right. This wasn't some twisted game. This was real, every terrifying moment, despite my wishing the contrary.

Not intimidated by my don't-mess-with-me glare in the slightest, he shrugged. "I'm just saying."

"Don't. Say anything, that is."

If the guy didn't shut up now he had a death wish.

"I heard what you said earlier, about everyone depending on you. Yeah, it's true, but we're here to help. If you let that kind of responsibility eat away at you ... "

He understood. That's probably how he felt. I was his responsibility, and while being a warrior was his calling, it wouldn't ease the constant burden of being expected to succeed.

For once, he didn't say anything, but he knew I knew. It was there in the faint pink staining his cheeks, the defiant smirk, daring me to call him on it.

I went one better.

"You know why it sucks having this responsibility dumped on me?" I threw my arms wide, encompassing the temple. "Because I didn't ask for any of it. All I ever wanted my whole life was to be normal. To not stand out. To cruise along, doing the right thing. Good grades. Good granddaughter."

Thinking of Nan made my voice waver and I hurried on. "Then these stupid visions start messing with my head, my Nan ends up in a coma because of it, and I get dumped at some crazy boarding school. Normal?" I clicked my fingers. "Out the door, just like that."

"Normal is overrated."

I rolled my eyes. His serene expression got on my nerves. "Spoken like a true warrior who can read minds and produce heat to propel freaks like me through existence."

"Responsibility is tough, but have you ever considered it from another angle?" He spoke so coolly, so rationally, he piqued my curiosity. "It's nice to be needed." Back to his lecturing best, he continued, "I don't know about you, but I've spent my life going through the motions. Being a good kid for my dad when Mom died, welcoming Uriel, being there for her when Dad died, getting good grades, undergoing warrior training without knowing if I'd ever get to use any of it apart from the general policing stuff."

"But if we're bound, wouldn't you have known to expect me?"

He stiffened. "The rift could've been created at any time. You might've been too young and then ... "

He didn't have to spell it out. If Cadifor—or Brigit—had opened the rift between worlds too early, Cadifor would've probably succeeded in finding Arwen and annihilating both our worlds.

Tension emanated off him, and I didn't understand why. He

was trying to give me a pep talk; why would that make him visibly uncomfortable?

"I learned all that stuff from the text, but what does warrior training really involve?"

A perfectly innocuous question designed to get us back onto safe ground, but if anything, he seemed ready to clam up tighter. After a lengthy silence, he finally spoke. "Warriors are mostly born."

"Mostly?"

His evasive glance away as he nodded made me wonder. Had Joss *not* been born into this role? Did that explain his overprotectiveness? His obsessive dedication to doing a good job? His reluctance to pursue the spark between us?

Before I could ask, he rushed on. "Warriors in the Innerworld are like soldiers in the Outerworld. We're here if you need us, but active duty isn't a given. If people need protecting, like the Sorority, we do the job. Otherwise, we maintain general peace, keep watch for Cadifor's consorts, that kind of thing."

"How do you earn your stripes?"

I expected him to smirk at my corny army joke after his reference to soldiers. His back went rigid instead. "Like you must master tasks, we are given assignments."

"People to protect, you mean?"

"Yeah."

"Lucky for me I've got someone who probably earned his stripes at birth," I said, determined to show I had full confidence in him.

"Yeah, lucky." Rubbing a hand across his clenched jaw, he looked like a guy who didn't believe in luck. "Protecting you is like being called up to the big leagues. I screw up, we all lose."

He meant *we all die*. Like I needed reminding. "Is that why you're so antsy all the time?"

His face relaxed a smidgen. "Let me put it another way. I can't afford to fail."

All the fight of the last half hour drained out of me as I grudgingly gave in to the point he'd been trying to make since we'd first arrived here. I sighed, louder than the wind whispering through the trees. "I guess you're right. In a way, it's nice to matter."

He reached out, captured a strand of my unsalvageable hair, and twisted it around his finger before tucking it behind my ear.

He tilted my chin up and eyeballed me. "Let me be there for you."

I barely managed a strangled "Okay," before I spun around and almost skipped down the path. No way could I take much more of that serious eye contact stuff without flinging myself at him.

We traveled down the path in silence. The closer I got to Bel's fire, the stronger the pull. My core temperature shot up by a few degrees as I reached the altar and knelt behind it, the flame burning brighter than ever in the pitch of night.

Joss remained silent—smart guy—while I stared at the flame, semi-hypnotized, centering myself after the crazy day.

I don't know how long we sat there for, me contemplative, Joss just there for me.

Without a vision to miraculously guide me, my mind started to drift to what I'd said earlier. I'd meant every word. I craved normal. All my life, I'd never quite gotten there. Sure, loads of kids at school came from single parent families, but I was the only one raised by my Nan.

While the rest of the kids lived in cool homes in the middle of town, I lived in an ancient wooden cottage on the shores of the lake.

While the rest of the kids couldn't wait to escape Wolfebane, I was happy there.

I liked skiing down the local slopes in the winter.

I liked canoeing on the lake with nothing but the latest paranormal book for company.

I liked hiking through the nearby forest, the smell of damp moss and pine strong in my nose.

Maybe I was a freak before the visions started? But ever since they had, my secret wish of normalcy had been replaced by a wish for something else.

A wish to live up to expectations.

Everyone was depending on me: the Sorority, Brigit, Nan, even my mom in some warped way.

Even though I didn't know her, I refused to believe my mom could be with Cadifor by choice. Which meant she was being held against her will. If I could find Arwen, I knew without a doubt I'd find her too.

"Your *mom*?"

Uh-oh. Until now, I'd been very careful to avoid thinking about her around Joss. I didn't want the Sorority knowing all my secrets just then. Now, in the lulling silence, by the warmth of Bel's fire, I'd screwed up, big time.

When I didn't answer, he grabbed my shoulders and turned me to face him. "Your mom is with Cadifor?"

"I've seen her in a few visions." When he continued to stare at me in disbelief, I added, almost defiantly, "He's violent toward her."

Shaking his head, he said, "You should've told us."

"What difference does it make?"

He shot me another furious glare, repeatedly clenching and unclenching his hands, buying time, getting his emotions under control.

"My mom vanished when I was six months old. Now I suddenly see her with some seriously scary dude, who just happens to be the bad guy I'm supposed to defeat." Leaping to my feet, I searched for the right words to make him understand. "It's nice to finally belong somewhere and that's what I feel with the Sorority, but you don't think I see their doubt every time they gawk at me? It's hard enough to prove my worth without saying up front 'Hey guys, sure, I'll bring down the bad guy but by the way, my mom's hanging out with him.' Bet that would've gone over well."

Mutinous, he glared at me like I'd crossed to the dark side too. "It changes everything."

"Like what? I still have to find Arwen before Cadifor does. If my mom's somehow involved, I find her too."

He shook his head, dragged a hand over his face to ease his

somber expression. It didn't work. "Have you seriously thought this through? If she's on his side and it comes to a battle ... " He didn't need to spell it out. Mom could get killed along with the rest of Cadifor's consorts.

"That's not my only concern," Joss said, touching my arm for a moment before thinking better of it and snatching his hand away. "What if it comes to a final showdown and Cadifor uses your mom as leverage against you? Her in exchange for Arwen? What would you do?"

Panic fluttered in my chest, a familiar I'm-in-over-my-head feeling that squeezed my lungs and made it difficult to breathe. Though somehow, not being prepared for an algebra pop quiz didn't have the same grave consequences as choosing between saving my mom or saving the world.

"This isn't going to be easy," he said, his voice gruff.

"You think I don't know that?" I hissed. A twig snapped; we both ducked behind the altar.

"Stay down," he whispered, edging to the right, one arm holding me back protectively.

If I'd inadvertently exposed him to danger because of my foolhardy hope to come here and conjure a vision, I'd never forgive myself.

He released me and I sagged to the ground. Signaling for me to stay down with his hand, he straightened to his full height.

"What are you doing here?"

"We've come to help the girl." A masculine voice drifted down from the tree line, a voice I'd heard before but couldn't place.

"She doesn't need philosophical guidance right now, Dyfan."

The druidh? What was he doing here?

"No, but she can use my help. She needs to know what she's facing."

I knew that second voice: Lia the witch. I couldn't think of her as a medicine woman, not after the hocus pocus stunt she'd pulled with my wrist earlier.

My wrist! I touched the braided bracelet she'd slipped on my wrist that morning. I'd totally forgotten about it in the dramas since. What had she said? It had a protective charm? Tracing it with my fingertip, I wondered if it had something to do with my escaping Cadifor's henchman. Or was I just buying into a bunch of superstitious nonsense, grasping at anything to help me in this crazy quest?

"Surely whatever we see in her future can help?"

Joss glanced down at me with a raised eyebrow and I shrugged. What could a little more magic crap hurt? "Come," he said, sounding more king than warrior, his bossiness beyond sexy as he ordered Dyfan and Lia to join us.

Joss held out his hand and pulled me up, giving mine a squeeze before he released it as the witch and the druidh made their way down the path.

As Dyfan and Lia approached, the fine hairs on my arms stood to attention. There was something seriously spooky about the two of them in the moonlight, one tall and luminous in head-to-toe white while the other carried a medicine bag half-concealed beneath her swirling crimson-lined cloak.

When they reached us, Dyfan held up his hand in greeting first, leaving me no option but to press palms with him. "Stay warm, Holly." I don't know what creeped me out more, his clammy palm or the fanatical gleam in his beady eyes. Lia repeated the greeting and my skin prickled.

Yep, these two were serious weirdos, but apparently they'd come to help. Considering I had to control my abilities pronto, master lessons both here and at school, and find Arwen before Cadifor, maybe I needed all the help I could get.

Joss stayed close, as if he didn't fully trust them either. "What did you have in mind?"

Lia pulled her medicine bag from beneath her cloak and Joss stiffened as if it were a gun. "A simple psychic scrying. For what she faces, it can only help."

I wanted to ask why here, why now, and how the hell did they know we were here? But I was too intrigued as she started pulling paraphernalia out of her bag like a magician would from his hat. And yeah, I can see the irony in that analogy considering she was kind of one anyway.

As if sensing my doubts, Dyfan said, "We ran into Maeve while conferring over Beltane festivities. She mentioned you may need our guidance."

Yeah, but how did Maeve know we'd be here? She'd left with Mack and Oscar, safe in the assumption Joss would teleport me back to C.U.L.T.

Dyfan didn't flinch as I studied him. Maybe I was extra jumpy, not trusting the people who were trying to help. Or maybe I was honing my intuition, which screamed this guy, druidh philosopher or not, was bogus.

"Have you mastered scrying yet?"

I shook my head at the druidh, not wanting to divulge that so far, the only tasks I'd mastered were becoming one with the Triple Flame inadvertently, a semi-grip on the clairsentience, and some consistent teleporting.

"That's why we're here." Lia laid a large bowl on the altar. "Using this psychic scrying bowl now, you can't fail."

Easy for her to say.

"I've used a spell to harness the power of the moon," Lia said. "This bowl has already been rubbed with a mugwort infusion, kept outside all night to absorb the moon's powers, and then wrapped in a black silk cloth and kept in a dark cupboard for a month."

A month? Wow, whatever happened to waving a magic wand and saying a few words? Spells were more complicated in real life than any fiction I'd read. I snuck a quick peek at Joss, to see what he was making of all of this, but his face remained impassive.

"Add the water from this bottle halfway into the bowl, then add a few drops of ink."

I did as she instructed, grateful when my hands didn't shake.

"Good. Now mentally recite an incantation. A wish, a heartfelt desire, something you want to know, then immediately focus on the water. Focus on the image of the moon reflected there, and after a while, you should find the water swirling."

She paused to study me, and once again something otherworldly brushed fingertips along my skin. "You may see images or symbols.

Hopefully, something to help in your quest. Are you ready?"

I nodded, more spooked than I let on. Joss touched the small of my back, letting me know he was there and giving me a much needed confidence boost. I stepped up to the bowl, grateful the small flame burned brightly beneath the altar—a sign Bel was with me—as I quickly sifted through many wishes and concentrated on one.

Show me what I will face in defeating the Lord of Darkness.

I repeated the phrase in my mind over and over like a chant, rhythmic and eerie. When I stopped, I peered into the bowl, seeing nothing in the inky darkness.

I stared. And stared. And stared, my stomach tumbling with nerves, my face flush with embarrassment.

The water shimmered, took shape. I leaned forward, peered harder, seeing the moon's reflection morph into something else entirely.

Something that made me want to scream.

The baby in the crib I'd seen during the divination experiment in Crane's class? The one with the golden eyes?

It had grown.

Into a girl my age.

And she was staring straight at me with hatred in her topaz eyes.

CHAPTER TWENTY

"What did you see?" Dyfan leaned so far forward across the altar he would've fallen on top of me if he moved an extra inch.

"Yes, tell us," Lia said, glancing between the bowl and me, as if she half expected what I'd seen to materialize before us.

So I did what any sane teen would do when faced with an adult inquisition.

I lied.

Crinkling my forehead, I pretended to ponder. "I saw the Arwen symbol carved into a tree. A huge tree. Not sure what type."

"Anything else?" If Lia had rubbed her hands together in anticipation I wouldn't have been surprised, she appeared that eager.

"A bright sun. Super bright. It blinded me to everything else."

Joss stood behind Dyfan and I glimpsed the flicker of a smile on Joss's stoic face. Times like this, it was handy he could read my mind.

"I see." Dyfan stroked his goatee like a history scholar. He was such a poser. "The sun is symbolic, as is Arwen."

Lia wasn't so trusting. She scanned my face, searching for the tiniest tell I was lying. Too bad for her, I'd mastered the poker face from a young age, masking my sadness every year I didn't hear from Mom on my birthday.

After what seemed like an eternity, Lia nodded, apparently satisfied. "That was an admirable first attempt at scrying. Well done, Holly."

"Thanks."

While Lia gathered her paraphernalia together, Dyfan stepped around the altar and laid a hand on my shoulder. It took all my willpower not to shrug it off.

"You are wise to pay attention to the signs." He indicated the temple around us. "What we just did here? Magic can show you the pathway to achieving your ultimate goal."

What a lot of hooey. Sounded like a generic promise from a fortune cookie. Lucky me, my very own Magic 8 Ball.

He removed his hand and I nodded my thanks.

"Stay warm, Holly." Lia pressed her palm to mine, and unfortunately, I had to repeat the goodbye with Dyfan before they left us alone.

Joss waited before the pair reached the top of the temple steps before speaking. "You don't like him."

"He gives me the creeps," I said, rubbing my arms. "I can't

pinpoint why. It's just a feeling."

"Most of the Sorority has the same feeling. The only one who has any time for him is Maeve, and even then I think it's because she's a natural peacekeeper."

"Yeah, I noticed that the first day you took me to his place."

"Smart girl." I basked under Joss's approval. "So what did you really see in the scrying bowl?"

I pinched the bridge of my nose, remembering where I'd first seen those unnerving golden eyes. "I saw a girl about my age, indistinct features, apart from these freaky, angry eyes the color of amber. The hatred … " I shook my head to dismiss the memory of how I'd felt when she glared at me: numb, icy, terrified.

"Do you know her?"

"Nope." There had been something vaguely familiar about her, like she was an old classmate or something, but I couldn't quite recognize her. "Though I have seen her before."

The puzzled frown on Joss's brow deepened. "When?"

"In divination class at school. We did an ashes experiment and scryed with that. I saw a baby in a crib and the baby had those same weirdo eyes."

"That doesn't make any sense."

"Tell me about it," I said, not liking the permanent confusion that tainted everything about this quest. "I asked the scrying bowl to show me what I'd face in defeating Cadifor and that golden eye chick appeared."

A spark lit Joss's eyes. "Maybe he's going to use her to get to you somehow? A new student at C.U.L.T.?"

"Maybe."

If Joss's guess was accurate, I'd spend a lot of time looking over my shoulder at school because Golden Eyes had radiated palpable hatred.

"Anything else?"

I shook my head.

His hand rested on my waist to steady me while the other made a beeline for my forehead. "Time for you to head back."

"Okay."

But it wasn't. I wanted to linger a little longer with him, to explore the connection we shared here in this sacred place. Every feeling I had seemed amplified somehow, like being closer to Bel's flame accentuated what was important in my life.

Right now, I was looking at him.

I saw a mesmerizing mix of need and admiration and awe in Joss, like he couldn't believe someone like me would be interested in someone like him. If he only knew that's how I felt whenever I was around him.

He grinned, and I wanted to slap myself upside the head. Of course he knew. The guy could read my mind. Argh! "Stop smirking and send me back already."

I braced for his touch on my forehead, for the inevitable heat, for the backward propulsion that made my stomach twist. Instead, his fingers drifted down from my forehead before he traced the outline of my mouth with his fingertip.

My lips parted in shock. His touch was feather-light as it skated across my bottom lip and lingered there for a long, exquisite moment.

I held my breath, wondering what he'd do next. I should've known it would be the responsible thing.

"See you next weekend."

Before I could blink, he'd made the Arwen sign on my forehead and I'd catapulted back to C.U.L.T.

This time the churning in my gut had more to do with growing feelings for my warrior than the astral travel journey.

As I left the shed, I realized I'd be scrambling for another alibi. I'd told Raven I'd be spending the night with Nan. With the time difference between Eiros and Wolfebane negligible—how convenient the Innerworld operated on NYC time, being behind its *veil* and all—it meant only two hours had elapsed since I'd teleported there and back, landing me smack bang back at school after dinner on a Saturday night.

The campus was crawling with kids, some heading into town on special leave passes, some kicking back down by the river, some heading for the farthest corner down near the woods to smoke and drink and party. That corner was not far enough from the shed where I now crouched. I eased open the door and took a peek out to ascertain whether the coast was clear. When nearby voices grew distant, I slipped out and made a run for the dorm.

Too easy. I skidded to a stop outside the corridor leading to my room and entered at a more sedate pace, knowing this would be the hardest part. Raven's room was two doors down from mine, and if she happened to see me again … I'd already lied several times tonight. I didn't want to make it a habit.

Coast clear, I headed toward my room, stopping dead when I spotted Quinn. He straightened from where he'd been squatting. Probably sliding something under my door.

My heart gave a strange twang as I realized I'd missed him, missed his normality. Funny how in a short space of time I'd come to see C.U.L.T. as a safe place to hang out when initially I'd preferred to be elsewhere. For now, it was my sanctuary, and Quinn was a huge part of that.

I took a step back. Too late. Quinn glanced up. "What happened? Raven said you were spending the night with your Nan?"

Hating the glib lie, I shrugged. "The nurses had a full house with relatives taking up spare beds, so I came back."

"Right."

He might've believed me if I followed up by breezing past him, opening the door to my room and entering. Instead, I stood there like a doofus, shuffling my feet, absentmindedly patting the bag of crystals in my pocket, and obviously uncomfortable.

"What's up with you? Really?"

"I've just got a lot going on. With Nan, with trying to keep up here, with getting a handle on the visions."

His lips compressed into a thin line and my heart sank. He didn't believe me. "If that's all it is, why do you radiate guilt, like you've got something major going down?"

I wanted to tell him the truth, every sorry bit of it. But I couldn't. This was my responsibility: finding Arwen, saving the world, yada, yada, yada. Besides, I didn't want to taint the friendship we had. While Quinn seemed accepting enough of the magic stuff that went on here, and even craved a little power of his own, I liked that I could be the old me around him. That we could talk about normal stuff and not have every conversation centered on my stupid quest, which would definitely happen if I blabbed. I spent enough hours in the day focused on Arwen and crystals and Cadifor and teleportation and Eiros and mastering tasks.

"I can't talk about this right now," I said, walking straight up to him, in his face, where he'd have to move to avoid a full-frontal body clash.

He stepped back at the last moment, but not before I glimpsed something that blew me away.

A flicker of excitement in his eyes.

Freaking great. As if my life wasn't complicated enough already.

Quinn was a great guy. We had loads in common, being newbies and all, plus he was nice and was currently here in the town I loved, the town I wanted to spend the rest of my life in. All pretty powerful pros, but the major con? Joss, and my conviction that what was developing between us was special, even fated.

I didn't want to jeopardize my friendship with Quinn by rejecting him, but I didn't want to give him the wrong signals, either. Best to pretend like I'd never seen that giveaway gleam and make a run for it.

I quickly opened the door and stepped inside, increasingly

awkward. Usually I wouldn't think twice about inviting him in. Rules here were pretty lax; Brigit treated us like adults and expected us to act like them, including using complete discretion with the boy/girl thing in dorm rooms. But tonight wasn't the night for chatting or debating the next bestselling YA novel or who had the guts to prank Crane at the end of the semester.

Nuh-uh. Tonight I needed to get rid of him ASAP.

I searched for the right words while he slapped his head. "I'm an idiot. All this secretive behavior? Involves another guy, doesn't it?"

At last I could tell a partial truth. "Sort of."

Frowning, he folded his arms. "Who is he?"

"Just a guy I recently met."

"Where?"

Damn, he wouldn't let this go. "Around."

"Is it serious?"

I shrugged, trying to play it cool. If serious was a warrior connected to me by an ancient bond, a warrior who could read my mind, a warrior who I wanted to hold me in a way I'd never imagined before, hell yeah, it was serious. This too, I could answer honestly. "I don't know. There's too much other stuff going on for it to really work."

This cheered him up. "Can't say I'm not disappointed." I managed a tight smile and he took it as a sign of encouragement. "You know I don't have to spell out how much I like you, right?"

"Uh ... right," I said, flattered by his declaration, but spoiling it with a blush that must've made me look like a beet.

"And I'm always here for you."

"Thanks."

"And if it comes down to a fight, I'll take this other guy down."

Picturing Joss and Quinn locked in mortal combat, I struggled to keep the grin off my face. "My hero."

"You better believe it."

When our smiles faded, we moved back to awkward. I hated it; we'd been so comfortable with each other since the first day I'd arrived.

He turned to go, spinning around at the last minute. "Does Raven know?"

"No."

A slow smile eased the tension. "Well, well, well, Goth Girl's not going to like that."

Happy the tension had eased, I laughed. "I'll tell her. Eventually."

Quinn laughed and tapped the side of his nose before walking away, giving a brief wave over his shoulder. As I watched him turn the corner, my lightheartedness evaporated.

I had friends, real friends, for the first time in my life.

And I was deliberately lying to them.

"Okay, people, get out your crystal balls."

A few nervous titters swept the classroom, no one sure whether Crane was serious or making a rare joke, as he strode to the front of the class.

Planting his hands on his desk, he eyeballed us all, a smirk clueing us in.

"For those of you without a sense of humor, that was a joke. What isn't a joke is the art of crystallomancy, another powerful form of divination you all need to learn."

I balked, none too keen on seeing that golden-eyed freak again.

Raven elbowed me, raising an eyebrow. "You okay?"

I nodded, not willing to draw Crane's attention and his wrath yet again. For some reason, he didn't like me. I'd handed in every assignment on time and took copious notes as he droned on, but it wasn't enough. Whenever he saw me in class, his disdain rippled over me like he'd doused me in water.

"If you haven't done your pre-reading, let me bring you up to speed." He carefully slid a large chunk of sparkling purple amethyst from the black bag on his desk. "Crystals have been used since the dark ages to heal and bring balance. They work through resonance and vibration."

He held the crystal up to the light and rotated it, but the only vibration I felt was Raven's suppressed laughter when a dork from the back made a spooky *woo-woo* sound. "For our purpose, crystals can also open the door to other worlds, especially crystals with fault lines and occlusions like this one." He pointed to a large crack running down the center that only served to enhance its beauty.

"Your homework this week will entail each of you meditating with a crystal, losing yourself in it, seeing what arises from your heightened awareness, and jotting those findings in a journal."

After sliding the purple chunk back into the bag, he pulled out several small shiny crystals shaped like wands. "When you meditate, start with red to energize and awaken your senses, then move through the spectrum of colors. And always, *always*, earth your energy again with a black crystal."

Deathly silence filled the classroom. Not one student was game enough to ask what happened if we forgot this last step.

"Now, on to the most important properties of crystals and how they apply to divination." Crane placed the colored crystals on the desk. He slipped his hand into the bag and pulled out two colorless crystals, one flat like a stone, the other so multifaceted it caught the sun streaming through the window and sent shards of light scattering across the walls. Shame Crane was such an uptight jerk. Divination could easily have been my favorite subject.

He held up the stone first. "This is a seer stone, a natural water-polished stone that is cut to reveal an inner world. It's an invaluable aid to scrying as it can show the past, the present, and the future." He weighed it in his palm and rubbed his thumb over the smooth surface. "Some also believe you can program a seer stone to take you back to a specific timeframe to access knowledge from then."

As he said the words, his beady eyes fixed on me. I stiffened, trying to make sense of his words as they jumbled in my head.

Slowly a vague idea formed, coalescing into something so profound it took all my willpower not to leap from my chair and run from the classroom to head to Eiros this very second. What if I could use a seer stone to access information on Arwen's whereabouts? Somehow get information from the time of Bel himself? I couldn't lose.

"Miss Burton, you appear to be interested in this discussion. Maybe you could answer my next question. What's this?"

He held up the multifaceted stone and I gawped. The crystal matched the one from Drake's bag of tricks, the one I'd been using to teleport to Eiros.

"Trans-channeling crystal," Raven whispered, masked by the fakest sneeze I'd ever heard. At the same time, Quinn's hand shot up as he asked, "Excuse me, can you clarify something about the seer stone? You mentioned programming it. How does that happen?" I could've hugged my friends at that moment.

Crane had no option but to answer Quinn's question before returning to his precious faceted crystal, and by that point, the heat was off me. "Miss Burton?"

"A trans-channeling crystal?"

"Correct." His sneer in Raven's direction clued us in that he hadn't bought my friend's distraction technique. "This crystal is a rare formation of three seven-sided facets. It's highly valued, for as its name suggests, it can channel energy or information from higher sources, and then assist in expressing what it has learned."

Tilting it pointy end up, he said, "The added bonus is that this crystal can also be used to send long-distance energy or thought transmissions, can open intuition, and can attract wisdom and communication from higher realms."

"So it's actually a combination of a channeling and transmitter crystal?" a nerd from the front asked and Crane nodded.

"Exactly. Questions?"

I tuned out as other students fired questions at a rapid rate.

Me? I had a lot to think about. If I could master a seer stone, maybe I could go back in time, even as far back as Bel, and gain vital info on finding Arwen. And mastering the trans-channeling crystal for other uses apart from teleportation would allow me to transmit thoughts to Joss and the Sorority long-distance. While I seemed to have a handle on teleporting between worlds, a part of me was terrified that I might not be able to come back. Spending the rest of my life with Joss might not be a bad thing, but leaving behind everything I'd ever known, everything that was dear to me, especially Nan, wasn't negotiable.

Could I do it, find a way to use a seer stone and a trans-channeling crystal? All very nebulous and far-fetched, but considering I'd managed to recognize incoming visions, teleport with a crystal, become one with the Triple Flame and scry, maybe I wasn't half bad at mastering otherworldly stuff.

Crane cleared his throat. "Now, for our practical session today, we're using amethyst wands and seeing their effect on the third eye."

I perked up at the mention of the third eye and inadvertently swiped a hand across my forehead.

"There are many of you here who have an intuitive gift. Precognitive powers, psychic, what have you." Crane held up a tiny mauve crystal the size of my pinkie. "For those of you with the gift, this amethyst wand is a vital adjunct to gaining control over your ability."

Crane held it aloft so we could all see. "The amethyst wand is the perfect tool for opening your third eye—" He pointed to his forehead. "—And stimulating intuitive visions by activating the pineal gland."

He waved it overhead. "Powerful stuff. Other uses include healing a weak aura and providing protection."

Stimulating visions? Protection? I needed one, now.

"That's enough show and tell for one day." He tapped the wand into his opposite palm like a conductor's baton. "Turn to page ninety-nine of your divination text and list other crystals used to balance the third eye. Choose one you'd like to experiment with. Have your partner take notes. Remember, those with precognitive powers, concentrate on mastering the amethyst wand today." He placed the wand on his desk and clapped his hands. "Get to it, people. Once you've chosen your crystal, come see me for a sample."

"This is so lame," Raven muttered, but she flicked to the appropriate page in the textbook as fast as I did.

The list of crystals to stimulate the third eye blew me away: garnet, kunzite, azurite, moldavite, sodalite, lapis lazuli, royal sapphire, atacamite, azeztulite, and the list went on.

"I'm jealous."

I glanced across at Raven. "Of what?"

"Psychic stuff and crystals are way cooler than moving stuff around."

I grinned. "I thought it was lame a second ago?"

She shrugged, sheepish. "Makes me feel better to diss it."

"Hey, at least you can learn to do some of this stuff. I have no chance of learning telekinesis."

"True. Not everyone has the raw talent to move Crane's precious crystal bag out from under his nose."

"Don't you dare. I want to have a go at this wand thing."

"Teacher's pet," she mumbled.

I chuckled, my attention already snagged by a paragraph on amethysts.

Amethysts are a protective stone with a high spiritual vibration, guarding against psychic attack and enhancing higher states of consciousnesses. A powerful stone, amethysts enhance spiritual awareness and, used at a high level, open the door to spiritual and etheric realms.

Amethysts were *so* my stone.

Amethysts open intuition, enhance psychic gifts, are excellent for meditation and scrying, and can stimulate the third eye if placed on it. They can also facilitate out-of-body experiences and bring intuitive visions.

I hadn't been this excited about anything in ages. Had I found the key to unlocking control over my visions and ultimately finding Arwen?

But if amethysts were so powerful, I didn't want to try out the stone in class. What would happen if I spontaneously teleported? Or opened a communication channel to Joss? Or did something equally stupendously freaky?

Raven nudged me. "Everyone's gone up and picked their stone except us, and Crane keeps giving us the evil eye. You go grab your amethyst while I quickly choose something."

"Okay."

I dragged my feet and trudged to the front of the class. Speaking to Crane one-on-one wasn't high on the list of my favorite things in the world at the best of times; compounding my worries about what amethysts could do for me had me silently freaking out.

When I reached the desk, Crane stepped around it, effectively shielding us from the rest of the class. "Are you ready to unlock your potential, Miss Burton?"

"Uh, yeah, sure, but—"

"You're worried about what might happen."

"Uh-huh." Now I was even more suspicious. Why was he acting human?

"Amethysts are powerful for students with a gift like yours. Your fear is understandable." He handed me a small amethyst wand, and I cradled it in my palm, surprised something so small, so insignificant, had the potential to provide answers I so desperately sought. "For today's experiment, make sure you hold this in your hand while you press the amethyst to your forehead." He pressed a small black stone into my other hand. "Black obsidian will ground you and whatever spiritual forces you unleash."

Yikes! I didn't want to unleash anything I couldn't control.

"It's protective. It will repel negativity." He paused, glowering at me. "You may need it."

Now I was seriously spooked. Was Crane generalizing, or did he know more about me than was safe? Before I could question him, he turned back to the class, dismissing me, so I took my amethyst and my obsidian back to my desk, passing Raven on the way as she mouthed, "Kyanite, woo hoo."

All around me, students were in various stages of experimentation, pressing odd-shaped rocks of various colors to their foreheads, eyes closed, talking softly or not at all while their partners scribbled in notebooks.

I wanted to really try it, but had a problem. I didn't want Raven to take notes on anything I said. I was too scared of what I'd blab, so I hurried to my desk, intent on starting the experiment before she got back. I could always feign misunderstanding the instructions when she returned, though my stomach churned at perpetuating yet another deception on my friend.

With every lie I told, with every truth I withheld, my guilt unfurled, spreading through me like a slow-killing poison. Raven and Quinn stood by me, and how was I repaying them? By telling lies that would surely rip our friendship apart once I told them the truth. And that time would come. I had no doubt that at some point in the future my worlds would collide and the resulting fallout would be catastrophic.

I slipped onto my seat, clutched the obsidian tightly in my left fist, took a deep breath, pressed the amethyst to my forehead, and waited.

CHAPTER TWENTY-ONE

I stand in a cave.

Different from the others I've seen.

Larger, darker, older, with a mystical aura I can almost see, a black haze suffocating me like thick smog.

Joss is behind me, Cadifor and my mom facing us.

He wants Arwen. Mom, too. Malice radiates off them, washing over me, making my skin crawl with fear.

I stand my ground.

I don't move a muscle, don't blink, even when the malevolence rolling off my own mom makes me want to fall to my knees and curl into a protective ball.

Celtic symbols cover the walls, pulsing with a strange light that beckons. I put my hand out to touch and ...

A blast of light from a hole in the ceiling illuminates the cave, bathing it in an eerie glow.

We watch, transfixed as the thin stream of light travels to the floor of the
cave, inching toward a stone altar covered in spiral symbols. Symbols I've seen
somewhere before ...

The moment the light hits the stone, an explosion blinds me.

I plunge into terrifying darkness.

I gasped and my eyes opened, the amethyst burning my
forehead. I dropped it onto the desk, blew on my hot fingers, and
poked it away with a trembling hand, terrified that what I'd just
seen would somehow follow me back.

Had I just foreseen my confrontation with Cadifor for Arwen?

If I had, my faint hope that Mom was being held there against
her will? Blown sky high. I clamped my teeth shut to stop them
from chattering. She'd stood next to him, alongside him, craving
Arwen as badly as the monster she'd hooked up with.

I guess I should have been grateful I'd stood up to them. But
what was that explosion of light about? And was I blinded by it?
That freaked me out as much as the rest of it, the fact I could be
left powerless and not be able to see in the presence of those two.
At their mercy ...

I focused on the crystal and struggled to get my breathing under
control. It lay on the desk, an innocuous piece of purple, as benign
as a curled rattlesnake.

A shadow fell over my books and I sucked in a breath, another,
quelling the waves of nausea that were making me feel lightheaded.

"Well, Miss Burton? Anything to report?"

Some seriously freaky stuff, not that I'd tell Crane. When I'd
taken enough breaths to ensure my voice wouldn't wobble, I said,

"Honestly? I'm not sure if it was part vision, part revelation, or part nonsense."

He folded his arms and didn't budge. "Perhaps if you care to share, I can shed some light on it."

Here I went again with the lying thing, but I had to. No way was I about to tell him I'd just had a frightening glimpse into the future, *my* future. "There was a faceless figure, on the school grounds I think, down by the river. Evil. A guy with an accomplice. They were building some weird altar with the rocks." I shuddered. "They scared me."

Crane's stare could've cut glass it was that sharp, but I widened my eyes and gnawed on my bottom lip, doing my best impression of a nervous kid who didn't have a clue what she was dabbling in.

"Hey, Mr. Crane, is it true kyanite doesn't hold negativity, so it never requires cleaning?"

Crane swung toward Raven, and I silently mouthed "thanks" at my friend for saving my butt yet again in his class.

Another kid claimed his attention after Raven so I was in the clear. Until Raven imitated Crane's death glare.

"Why didn't you wait for me?"

Just when I'd gotten my queasy stomach under control, it rolled again, this time with the increasing guilt of lying to my friend. "Sorry, thought we had to just do it and write notes later."

Her eyes narrowed, shrewd and unforgiving. "What's going on with you?"

Uh-oh, she'd echoed Quinn's words from the other night. Could I use the pseudo-boyfriend excuse to put her off too?

Hating myself more by the minute, I said, "I've got a lot going on. Nan, mastering stuff here."

"Nothing else?"

As much as I wanted to trust her with the truth, I couldn't. The evil in that vision lingered, infusing me with the certainty that whatever I'd face would be bad, really bad. Bad enough that Joss would be there. No way I needed to worry about the other friends I cared about too.

Realizing I was still clutching the obsidian so tight it hurt, I unfurled my fingers and laid it on the desk next to the amethyst wand. "Like what?"

"Oh, I don't know ... " She trailed off, her smile patronizingly sweet. "Something along the lines of Quinn knowing a big fat secret I don't?"

"He told you?"

Her expression changed from curious to indignant in a second. "So that dork *does* know something? I knew it!" Glancing over her shoulder to make sure Crane had moved a good distance away, she muttered, "He's been acting superior and condescending all week. I knew something was up but I was only fishing just now." She paused and picked at a hangnail. "I had no idea you'd share something with him and not me."

I felt lousier by the minute, especially after she'd saved me twice in class. "It's no big deal. He was giving me a hard time, so I told him about this guy I kind of like."

"You have a *boyfriend?*"

She made it sound like the possibility of that ranked right up there with my mastering telekinesis, pyrokinesis, and pyschometry all in one day.

"Nothing that serious. It's just a crush."

"Someone *here?*"

Her hand waved toward the rest of the class and I shook my head. "No, someone I met around."

Someone who made my heart beat faster just by looking at me, who made me want to curl up in his arms and stay there, who made me want to go the whole way when I hadn't even had a first kiss. Someone who infuriated me one second with his stubborn nobility, then made me melt the next with his deep voice, someone who gave me goosebumps with a simple touch, someone who made me feel so good about myself when I was with him I felt invincible.

God, I missed him.

"Ooh ... I get it. He's some guy at the hospital, that's why you've been spending all that extra time with your Nan."

I hated lying, I really, really did, but corroborating her assumption would get them both off my back and explain my continual vanishing act. Playing coy, I shrugged. "Maybe."

"Sneaky. I like it."

Crane glared at us from across the classroom and we stopped the chatter.

Fine by me. Whatever the amethyst had revealed to me, it was significant.

Now I just had to figure out how to use the knowledge.

After Raven's two saves in class, Crane's dislike for me increased. He'd save the hardest questions for me, he'd call me up to demonstrate labs, and he continually glared at me like he expected me to teleport on the spot.

It unnerved me. Like I wasn't nervous enough with everything going on. And it didn't help that Raven came up with nefarious ideas to get back at him in class.

"It's time we pranked Crane."

Quinn and I stopped scribbling notes. It wasn't the first time Raven had suggested this, but it was the first time I was willing to listen after the way Crane had patronized me for my lack of knowledge in front of the entire class ten minutes earlier.

Quinn shook his head. "A few weeks before end of term? You're nuts."

When Quinn resumed studying, Raven reached over and slammed his textbook shut. "The guy's a superior jerk. He needs a shakeup." She jerked a thumb in my direction. "Look how he treats Holly."

"Hey, keep me out of this." I held up my hands.

Raven promptly high-fived them. "Great, you're in."

I laughed and Quinn joined in. "You're insane, but you're right. He's got it in for Holly and needs to be taught a lesson. What did you have in mind?"

Raven grabbed a pen, pulled a notepad in front of her, and

started writing. "Something totally inspired, of course."

"Of course," Quinn said, rolling his eyes. "As long as this ingenious plan doesn't get us caught and consequently expelled."

Raven's derisive snort spoke volumes. "I was the prank queen at my last high school. Never caught."

"Impressive."

When Quinn tried to sneak a peek at her writing, she flipped the notebook shut. "Nuh-uh, no peeking. We brainstorm first and then I'll set out logistics."

"Okay maestro, what's the plan?"

As we huddled and Raven outlined the basics, asking for our input occasionally, I couldn't help but admire the cleverness of it.

"We all clear?"

Quinn and I nodded, our matching grins making her chuckle.

"You guys are naturals," she said, opening the notebook and swinging it around so we could see. "Here, check it out. Any potential problems leap out at you?"

I quickly scanned her list, amazed at her brilliance. "Looks good."

"Quinn?"

"A-okay."

Raven rubbed her hands together. "Then we're in business. Let's get to it."

While their excitement was infectious, I'd never played a prank on anybody in my life. Blending into the background and being a model student didn't exactly endear me to the pranksters at Wolfebane High. In fact, I was probably the last person they'd tell for fear I'd tattle. Yeah, I was that much of a goody-goody. So while being part of this had me excited, I couldn't help but shake the feeling I'd be lousy at it.

"What if I let the team down?" I blurted, absentmindedly doodling sunbursts surrounded by spirals on my notebook.

"You won't." Raven refuted my concern by pointing at her book. "We have a foolproof plan. What can possibly go wrong?"

Famous last words.

Our plan was simple.

Crane had clued us in to tomorrow's lesson. Candles. Not particularly exciting on their own, but if used correctly a great aid to focus and increasing energy in spells and divination.

Thanks to Raven's extensive research, we were aware of what each color represented for the candles, what they could enhance, and what they could do. Throw in Ms. Morris performing a Wiccan ritual in front of the class with the aid of Crane's candles, and we had the perfect stage for a little hocus pocus of our own.

Quinn would ask questions to distract Crane—nothing out of the ordinary there. I would volunteer to participate in the experiment. And Raven would perform a little of her telekinetic magic, swapping candles at the last second and seeing how Crane—who we all thought had a secret crush on Ms. Morris— reacted when the spell using white, silver, and violet candles for enhanced psychic work became a spell using green, pink, and red candles for love, romance and lust.

It worked like a charm—no pun intended—the candles switching flawlessly as both teachers had their eyes closed, chanting some weird rhyme.

We expected Crane to moon over Ms. Morris in front of the whole class and make a general ass of himself—more than usual, that is, while she belittled him. What we didn't expect was Ms. Morris being affected too and both of them indulging in a serious makeout session in front of the whole class.

The result? Brigit being drawn to the classroom by our raucous hoots, catcalls, whistles, and foot stomping, barging in like a stormtrooper and demanding the culprits behind the prank.

We'd relied on safety in numbers to save our butts. What we hadn't counted on was two of the other telekinetic students being ill with food poisoning, leaving Raven and one other dork who sat in the front row under Crane's nose and practically drooled over every assignment as the obvious masterminds.

And considering Quinn and I were Raven's buddies ... well, we all received an interrogation of monumental proportions.

None of us talked. Brigit had no proof. So we walked free.

Crane knew. We could see it in the way he glared at us with barely disguised venom once the spell had been reversed and he'd come storming into Brigit's office.

But I stood by my friends, feeling like I truly, finally belonged.

CHAPTER TWENTY-TWO

Crane treated us like lepers in class, but he couldn't fault my work. I studied my ass off all week, blitzing every assignment and discovering a wealth of information in the process.

Amethysts were good, but a chevron amethyst, a beautiful deep mauve, was best for third eye stimulation, enhancing intuitive vision and out-of-body journeys. They could powerfully focus energy and repel negativity, as well as cleanse auras. And the biggie? They helped the user find positive answers to any problem.

I could use that right about now.

The other vital snippet of information I'd gleaned from my all-night reading sessions was that the shape of a crystal determined its powers. The one that snagged my attention was the gateway—or aperture—shape, a cup-shaped depression within a crystal large enough to hold liquid. Gazing into the liquid center provided a gateway to other worlds and enabled the user to travel through past, present, and future.

After Beltane, with Joss's help, I'd use them all and get the answers I so desperately craved. So I had to play all nice and sucky with Crane, asking pointed questions about chevron amethysts and seer stones and trans-channeling crystals. Crane hated my guts, but he had to answer my questions, and surprisingly, he didn't freak out when I asked if I could obtain three crystals, one an aperture amethyst, to practice.

In addition to busting my ass in divination, I also spent some serious time in the evenings training my third eye. Guided meditations, visualization techniques, you name it, I tried it. I didn't spontaneously create any enlightening visions, but I developed a feel for journeying with my mind. It was like an out-of-body experience, a weird, light, floaty feeling that made everything around me sharper, clearer, and faded once I opened my eyes and found myself sitting on the floor in the middle of my dorm room.

It felt good to be doing something proactive, something that took me closer to gaining control when I traveled to Eiros.

When Dyfan had originally recited the tasks I'd have to master, they seemed impossible. But since I'd managed a decent scrying with Lia, had become one with the Arwen Triple Flame (however inadvertently), could teleport with the aid of a crystal and the sun, and was another step closer to gaining control over my visions, I was hopeful that maybe I could succeed on this ludicrous mission after all.

If I hadn't been studying so hard, the days would've dragged toward Sunday. Of course, Beltane wasn't the only reason I wanted to return.

I missed Joss. Big time.

It wasn't just that he was so hot—I mean, he *was*, but I missed the reassurance he gave me just by being there. I felt truly safe with him, something I valued more and more the closer I got to discovering Arwen. Besides, it sucked not being able to confide in my friends, and he was the only other person I truly trusted; I was desperate to tell him what had been going on. He got me, really *got* me, and that kind of trust was what I really needed right now.

I was getting closer. I'd mulled my first amethyst-induced vision at length and knew that confronting Cadifor and my mom in that cave would be our final battle over Arwen.

Call it intuition, call it whatever you liked, I knew. Which made telling Joss and the Sorority about it all the more important.

So there I sat, Saturday night, alone in my room, cradling the trans-channeling crystal in my palm, desperate to see if I could communicate with Joss, yet terrified I might screw up and fry my brain.

I took a deep breath, rolled my shoulders, and stretched my neck like a boxer about to enter the ring. Holding up the crystal to the light, I rotated it slowly. How could something so small, so insignificant, hold so much power?

I lay on my bed, closed my eyes, and started meditating. Nothing too heavy, just a general relaxation technique, a simple visualization that had me chatting to Joss as if he were right beside me, making small talk, asking questions about school, that sort of thing.

I could see it so clearly in my mind. It had to work. Taking a slow, deep breath, I pressed the crystal to my forehead.

Hey, you out there. Warrior Boy. I've got news. Big news. It can't wait.

Silence. A long, deafening, disappointing silence. I pressed the crystal so hard into my forehead I'd probably walk around with a weird indentation for a week.

So much for our bond. I need you. Now.

Where are you and why are you yelling?

I almost fainted at his response, his voice so clear in my head it was like he was sitting on the bed. A tempting thought ... I resisted the urge to peek and make sure he wasn't actually there.

I thought I told you to stay away from Eiros 'til Beltane? His tone held so much disapproval I could imagine his matching glower. *Tell me where you are right this minute. I need to be there, damn it!*

Chill. I'm at school.

What?

I still couldn't quite believe this had worked. *I'm using a trans-channeling crystal.*

Your powers aren't that advanced yet.

Wrong again, Warrior Boy. Oops, hadn't meant for that to transfer across our neurons.

Warrior Boy?

I chuckled. *Term of endearment.*

Like Dream Boy?

A million miles away, I blushed. *Isn't this cool? We can talk anytime we like.*

Yeah, cool. The edge to his voice was unmistakable.

What's up?

I'd rather you were here.

My heart did a weird little jive and I almost dropped the crystal.

He clarified. *So we could talk strategies.*

Riiiight, strategies …

He cleared his throat. *Had any visions?*

Not a spontaneous vision, but I used an amethyst wand in divination class and I think I know where Arwen might be.

Where?

In an underground cave, where the sun comes through a small hole in the roof and moves along the floor to an altar covered in spiral symbols. Sound like the Cave of the Sun you described to me?

He paused. *We thought it could be the place, but it seems too obvious.*

There's something else.

He waited and I suppressed a shudder at the memory of Cadifor and my mom, their maliciousness in the vision hanging over me like a malignant cloud.

You and I were there. Cadifor and my mom too. I had to tell him the rest. *It felt like a final confrontation. There was an explosion. I could smell …*

What?

I shivered. *Death.*

We didn't speak after that, gathering our thoughts. When he

finally spoke, it didn't reassure me. *If we're to succeed, you may have to initiate this confrontation.*

And how do I do that? Find another crystal that lets me chat to bad dudes and say, "Hey, buttface, you down there, let's meet."

This isn't going to be easy, Holly.

Don't you think I know that? Why was it I ended up losing it with the only person I truly trusted every time this subject came up?

Here are the facts. Winter solstice is December twenty-second, when we celebrate the birth of the Unconquered Sun, a huge festival on a par with Beltane. It's the day the sun enters the Cave of the Sun in the Eiros stone complex.

December? But that's eight months away.

I think the confrontation will be sooner.

Oh, fabulous.

Summer solstice is June twenty-second, the festival of fire. That's our day, because during winter solstice the sun hits the altar first, then travels toward the cave's entrance. You described the opposite, so it has to be summer solstice.

Less than two months? While I wanted to find Arwen, find my mom and get this whole thing over with, confronting Cadifor so soon was seriously scary.

Why so soon?

Because things are escalating here.

What things?

Bad things.

I could imagine. I didn't want to know what Cadifor was capable of, not when I had to confront him to end this thing. *We need to be prepared. I'll confer with the Sorority and we'll lay out the plan after Beltane tomorrow.*

Okay.

But it wasn't, none of this was. Fear clawed at my insides, dying to escape in a screeching scream.

It's okay to be scared.

Freaking great. Even at a distance he could do the mind-reading thing.

Petrified, actually.

Fear is good. Fear keeps you alert and focused. His voice lowered to a whisper, a soothing caress for my frayed nerves. *Fear is what will keep you alive.*

My hand trembled and the crystal slipped. Quickly realigning it, I pulled myself together. Joss was right. Fear was normal, and if it kept me one step ahead of Cadifor, bring it on.

Holly? You're doing brilliantly.

Glad one of us thought so.

Let's concentrate on celebrating Beltane tomorrow and we'll talk afterward, okay?

Yeah, sure.

See you in the morning.

'Night. I removed the crystal quickly, like ripping off a Band-Aid. Less painful that way. The crystal pulsed with a pale golden glow in my hand.

I should have been glad. The trans-channeling had worked and I hadn't given myself brain damage in the process.

But I couldn't forget what Joss had said.

Summer solstice, the festival of fire.

As long as Cadifor was the one burning in the eternal flames of hell and not me.

CHAPTER TWENTY-THREE

Nothing could've prepared me for Beltane.

Not reading all the texts in the library at school, not a half-hour crash course from the Sorority, not all the vivid descriptions Joss had bombarded me with for the ten minutes we strolled toward the Temple of Grian in the soft darkness, awaiting the first streaks of dawn.

I mean, I'd heard about the ritual itself: always at sunrise so the candles lit from Bel's fire are properly illuminated before dawn breaks, people wearing white robes made from cambric—a fine white linen—and crowns of their tree sign, bringing offerings of fresh produce to place at the altar.

The reality of my first glimpse of the temple, filled to capacity with what seemed like a million flickering candles casting a warm glow over the towering stones surrounding it in a protective circle, blew me away.

I stopped and sought Joss's hand in the dark, overcome with a puzzling combination of emotions: awe, excitement, and fear.

He squeezed my hand. "Ready?"

I'd never believed in prayer, but impressed by the reverence of the situation, I closed my eyes and sent a silent plea to Bel. *Please help me.*

I had no idea if he was listening or my subconscious just needed a sign and produced one, but comforting warmth started at my head and seeped downward, spreading through my body like sinking into a bubble bath.

Opening my eyes, I nodded. "Let's do it."

Joss released my hand and we made our way down the spiral path single file to where Mack, Oscar, and Maeve already waited.

The faint tweeting of awakening birds mingled with the fading chirps of crickets. No one in the crowd spoke. When we reached the altar and took our place alongside the others, I could've sworn I heard a collective sigh of relief.

I hadn't realized how badly my knees had been shaking until I stood still, the rustling of my robe no longer a dead giveaway. Sensing my nerves, the Sorority huddled closer, the five of us forming a strong bond around Bel's fire.

On cue, Mack raised his right hand in the Eiros greeting. "Stay warm, my friends. We come together today on this first day of May to celebrate our founding father, Belenus, the Sun God."

I half expected muted cheers, but no one uttered a sound.

"Today is a celebration of light, a pledge to our constant goal: to return to the peaceful existence of the golden age when Bel was among us."

Peace sounded good to me. Wish the dark lord had taken a page out of Bel's book.

"In a moment we will extinguish our flames as one. Following a minute's contemplation, we invite each one of you to come and relight your candle from Bel's fire."

This time the crowd rustled, shifted. The murmurs were quickly quashed when Mack picked up his candle, imprinted with an elaborate gold sunburst, and held it up to the heavens.

The expectant hush roused goosebumps on my arms. I clenched my candle so tight I left a thumbprint. The first strains of a harp so ethereal, so poignant, added to the surrealism, and my throat clogged. A soft pan flute joined in with a haunting melody that evoked images of rolling green meadows and swaying sunflowers and perfect summer days. Freshness and growth and light filled me with joy and uplifted my soul to a place I wanted to be: happy, carefree, and loved.

The final note resonated, hung in the emotion-charged air, and finally faded. We extinguished our candles as one.

The immediate darkness should've been frightening, but the peace from the evocative song lingered, binding us, lending Bel's followers strength.

This is what we needed to defeat Cadifor. Unity. Trust. Safety in numbers.

In the minute's silence, my eyes adjusted to the darkness in time to see the first fingers of dawn flexing across the horizon.

The beat of a drum, low and rhythmic, slowly built to a crescendo and signaled the end of our silence. Mack, the direct descendant of Bel, lit his candle from Bel's fire, a lone flame in a sea of darkness. He held it aloft, the wan light casting shadows across his proud face.

"Bel, father of light, behold our promise to you."

The Sorority relit candles as one, our efforts perfectly synchronized. This time, when I held my candle up I didn't shake.

We stepped back, allowing the crowd to make their way toward the altar single file. No one spoke, but I could see the smiles, the occasional flash of white teeth in the dimness. Standing alongside the Sorority, feeling like I was one of them, made me wish I could do this forever.

I might have found friends in Quinn and Raven, but the Sorority was my destiny.

Corny? Maybe, but after the last person had lit their candle and headed back to their groves so the celebration could commence, I knew that what was about to happen would cement my place in Eiros history.

"You ready, Holly?"

I nodded at Mack, a tingle of excitement at my pending initiation running through me.

"Step forward."

Laying our candles on the altar, we stepped forward as one, joining hands.

Mack tilted his head back toward the heavens. "Bel, your ancient wisdom tells us the elements represent energy around us. Earth, from the north; the trees and plants we honor in your name, symbolize stability, security. Air; blowing on the hilltops surrounding us, carries your inspiration from the east. Water; in the lakes to the west, cleanses, enhancing our healing and psychic abilities."

Mack, who held Oscar and Maeve's hands, brought our hands up to rest on the altar, forming a protective circle around the candles.

"And most importantly fire, bringing energy, power, and passion to all that we do."

He bowed his head and we copied him.

"On this day of Beltane, your sacred celebration, we invoke these elements to welcome a true member of the Sorority."

He paused, raised his head, and looked at me. "Holly Burton, descendant of Bel, welcome to the Sorority of the Sun."

For the first time since I'd been here, the constant grayness was erased as dawn broke in a blaze of gold, crimson, and mauve, bathing everything in a new light and filling me with belief.

This was right.

This was meant to be.

Joss and Maeve released my hands and I stepped forward, knelt on one knee, and pressed my forehead against the altar in honor of my new status.

That's when all Hell broke loose.

CHAPTER TWENTY-FOUR

A high-pitched wailing filled the air, piercing and horrific, leaving my eardrums on the verge of exploding. I clapped my hands over my ears, but that did nothing to dim the ghastly shrieking. I whipped around, trying to see where it was coming from and whether this appalling noise was a prelude to one of Cadifor's tricks.

Maeve screamed. Mack paled. I became the middle of Oscar and Joss's human sandwich as they wedged me between them. The gruesome screeching shot bolts of terror through me and I recoiled, petrified.

"Don't look," Joss hissed, trying to protect me from seeing whatever was making that god-awful noise. The fear in his voice clued me in to the fact that this thing was more horrendous than anything I could possibly imagine.

Oscar glared at Joss in disbelief. "Are you crazy? She invoked the banshee, she has to get rid of it."

"What the hell's a banshee?" I said, remembering in a frightening flash I had to face and banish one.

A *thing* materialized less than five feet in front of me, hovering in the air like one of those lame ghosts in the haunted house at Wolfebane's annual fair. But this was no fake fiend. No, this banshee was the real deal, from the top of its streaming flame hair to the bottom of its ragged gray robes. Bloodred eyes glowed in gaping holes. Its mouth was a wide black canyon emitting the ear-piercing wail, and its deathly pallor was highlighted by nondescript tattered robes hanging from its lifeless body. And then I realized something that had to be a trick, an illusion.

The banshee looked like my mom.

I was transfixed, desperate to look away but horribly drawn to its ugliness. Shudders racked my body, rolling over me in sickening waves. I clutched at Joss to stop from crumbling to the ground.

"You need to do this," he said, his calmness belied by the anguish darkening his eyes to midnight.

"Tell me how to get rid of it!" While my ears bled, the banshee kept coming, closing the distance between us. The closer it drifted, the harder I shook, pain shredding my insides like I'd swallowed a pack of razors. "Freaking tell me or I swear—"

"You need to find the answer within."

I swayed, increasingly dizzy and faint, as Joss held me upright.

"Ground yourself. Concentrate. Think."

Ground yourself.

In an instant I knew. But where was I supposed to find a black obsidian now? Unless I could manufacture obsidian in the next thirty seconds, our eardrums would burst.

I focused on Bel's fire and wished like I'd never wished before. All of those wasted wishes for the tooth fairy to leave dollars rather than cents, for Santa to bring books rather than more scarves, for the Easter Bunny to hide chocolate and not hideous carob, I'd take them back in a heartbeat if this one wish could come true.

Bel, help me, tell me what to do.

As the flame flickered, it cast a shadow on the ground, over a flat, dark rock. ...

"That's it!" Startling Joss, I dropped to my knees, snatched up the rock, and examined it closely. It didn't resemble the obsidian I'd used back at school, but it would have to do.

I had to try it, had to try something. Clutching the stone in my left hand, I faced the banshee, trying not to flinch as those crimson eyes staring straight at me glowed with malevolence.

Invoking the grounding spell, I pressed a fingertip to my forehead while aiming the rock at the ground, effectively closing my third eye while visualizing the banshee trapped underground, surrounded by darkness, as far from the light as possible.

The harder I concentrated, the more the agony eased. The banshee faded, her stumps-for-hands reaching toward me, clutching at air, her wail increasing in pitch and volume until we fell to our knees. Though I wanted to look away, I couldn't, mesmerized by those gleaming red eyes, my forehead and palm holding the rock pulsing with heat. When I thought I couldn't bear the shrieks any longer, the banshee vanished.

"Holly, you okay?"

Joss helped me to my feet, the sudden silence a welcome relief from the wailing, but strangely eerie.

"Yeah, fine," I said, though my voice shook.

Mack touched my arm, his expression dazed. "How did you—"

"She's a fully fledged member of the Sorority now, that's how," Maeve said, hugging me tight.

"Yeah, if ever we had doubts before, guess you put those to rest. That's another task mastered." Oscar nodded, pensive, sizing me up. "What did you do?"

How did I explain something I didn't fully understand? "I grounded myself with black obsidian, then visualized the banshee back underground."

Mack and Maeve beamed like proud parents while Oscar frowned. "You've practiced with black obsidian before?"

"A little." Tired of his condescension, especially after I'd done so well, I squared my shoulders. "I used a trans-channeling crystal for the first time last night too."

"You used a trans-channeling crystal?" Oscar's sneer made me bristle. "No way. You're new to this. You can't be that powerful."

"She is." Joss's clipped tone didn't invite further argument. Mack and Maeve studied me with renewed interest.

"Is anyone going to tell me what that thing was, apart from one of the lesser creatures of the Underworld I had to face and banish?"

I didn't imagine the long pause before Joss nodded.

"Banshees are female spirits who are usually attached to a specific family." Joss paused and glanced at Mack, whose grave expression gave me the creeps.

"Come on, guys, I need to know what I just faced off in case it comes back."

Joss entwined his fingers with mine in such a way the others couldn't see, his simple touch giving me instant comfort.

"Okay." Mack nodded. "You saw the red eyes?"

Hell yeah, I'd seen them. I thought back to meeting Drake on the first day at C.U.L.T. what seemed like an eternity ago, and how the flicker of crimson in his creepy eyes had spooked me. The banshee made Drake look like an innocent kid.

"Uh-huh."

"That's from weeping."

"So she's a big crybaby. I can deal with that."

Nobody laughed, not even a ghost of a smile, and Joss squeezed my hand, his grave expression sending a shiver of foreboding through me despite the reassuring grip.

"A banshee voices her anguish when a death is imminent."

Terror choked me as I deciphered what he'd just said. "You mean—"

"When a member of that family is near death."

Mack, Maeve, and Oscar couldn't meet my eye; only Joss could, as brave, stoic, and supportive as ever. But for a split second, I saw the fear lurking behind his beautiful blues. Somehow that one glimpse of my warrior's vulnerability scared me more than the rest put together.

"So someone in my family is going to die?"

The last word dripped off my tongue like acid. Maeve sucked in her bottom lip and bit down on it.

"It's just part of an old legend," Joss said, his lack of conviction emphasized by the others' silence. He slid an arm around my waist and held on tight while my shaking eased.

Joss was wrong.

That banshee meant business.

I didn't believe in coincidences, didn't believe in random acts. Of all the lesser Underworld creatures I had to face, this banshee had appeared at this point in time for a reason.

As a warning.

To scare the crap out of me.

It had worked. No matter how much Joss tried to placate me, one word echoed through my head.

Death.

My first thought was Nan, wasting away in that hospital bed, non-responsive, a shadow of the woman I knew and loved. Losing her would gut me. I didn't want it to be Nan.

What if it wasn't?

Did the banshee transforming into an image of Mom mean *she* would die? While I didn't feel the same ripping loss at the thought, I didn't want her to die. Not at the hands of Cadifor, and certainly not before I'd gotten my answers. Did that make me heartless? Maybe, but I wasn't the one who ran out on my daughter when she was a baby.

The last option was too creepy to contemplate.

As I raised my stricken gaze to Joss, the possibility too hideous to acknowledge, I saw the same thought lurking in the shadows of his expressive eyes.

What if the person in the Burton family about to die was me?

CHAPTER TWENTY-FIVE

As I accepted my second pewter tankard of mulled apple cider and raised it in a group cheer, I glanced around at the glowing faces, the genuinely happy smiles, the revelers dancing to lively jigs. I'd never been to a celebration like it. Huge banquet tables were covered in fruits and vegetables; flower garlands were strung up between the trees. Musicians strolled through the crowd, and children squealed in delight as they bobbed for apples. Everyone was smiling, chatting, laughing, and dancing.

As hard as I tried to join in and enjoy my first Beltane, I couldn't shake the residual bleakness from the banshee and what she represented.

"Guess who?"

I didn't need to guess. The moment Joss came up behind me, I felt his body warmth. The urge to turn and bury my face in his chest was overwhelming.

"RPatz?"

I swung around in time to see him try a mock frown. "Who?"

"Everyone in the entire universe knows who RPatz is. Robert Pattinson? Edward? *Twilight* movies? Hello?"

The corners of his mouth kicked up. "You know all that vampire stuff is nonsense, right? Underworld creatures, including the undead, aren't heroic or vegetarian." My urge to tease faded at the mention of the undead, and he winced. "Sorry. I'm sure the banshee's still fresh in your mind."

I nodded. "Don't get me wrong, I'm stoked I sent the screamer packing, but that whole death in the family prophecy? A real dampener."

"It's a legend, and many legends are hearsay."

"Arwen's a legend, but you guys seem to take that one pretty seriously."

For once, Joss didn't have an instant comeback.

"And speaking of sending the banshee away, what's Oscar's problem? Even when I get stuff right, nothing seems to please him."

An expression I couldn't decipher flitted across Joss's face, part guilt, part regret, before he rubbed a hand over it and pinned me with a speculative stare. "You really want to know?"

"Know what?"

He sighed and propped himself against a tree trunk, arms

folded, casual and sexy at the same time. "Oscar wanted to protect you."

"Protect me how?"

"By being your warrior."

Confused, I rubbed my forearms to ease the foreboding slinking under my skin. "But you're my warrior. If we're bound, how can he muscle in on your turf?"

Darkness clouded his eyes as that prickle increased tenfold. "Challenges occur within warrior circles. Oscar challenged me for the honor of protecting the Scion. I won."

Joss wasn't telling me everything. I could see it in his clenched jaw, his rigid shoulders, his nervous fingers absentmindedly shredding bark off the tree.

Before I could question him further, he captured my hand. "Let's get out of here."

As a distraction technique, it worked. Having my hand encased within his—strong, warm, solid—I didn't need to be asked twice.

Holding hands, we eased through the crowd, strolling towards the ash grove furthest away. We didn't speak as we picked our way through the grove, watching our step, but it wasn't an uncomfortable silence. Plenty of time for questions later. For now, I was enjoying the stolen pleasure of having him hold my hand.

When the trees grew so thick we couldn't go farther, he stopped and placed both his hands on my waist. "You were brooding back there rather than enjoying yourself."

Not wanting to bring up Oscar again and shatter the mood, I let the conversation flow his way for now. "I was having a good time."

He raised an eyebrow and I shrugged. "Mostly."

"Forget the banshee. There are countless druid legends that never come true."

Don't think about how the banshee looked like Mom … don't think about it …

His hands gripped me tighter, digging into my hips. "The banshee looked like your mom?"

Oops, too late.

"Yeah."

He frowned. "Is that what has you so spooked?"

"That and the fact I have to face off with Cadifor next month, find Arwen before then, and maybe face the death of someone I care about."

Maybe even me.

It came out a mental whimper, a fleeting thought he couldn't possibly have picked up on.

His hands slid all the way around my waist, pulling me almost flush against him. "Don't even think it."

Think? Who could possibly think when pressed against his hard body with my hands resting helplessly against his chest, itching to slide up and pull his head down toward me?

Momentary insanity was my only plea for thinking like that; of course he'd know what a pathetic pining loser I was and release me like he had the last time we'd gotten this close. It didn't happen, and when I finally had the guts to glance up, the hunger in his eyes had my lips parting in a surprised O.

This time, there was no prolonged moment of exquisite

torturous anticipation, no time for second-guessing. This time, we went for broke.

Our lips met in a burst of pure, unadulterated heat. An explosion of longing and of soul-deep need burst over me. I wondered how I could've denied myself this incredible feeling for so long. Were all kisses like this? Or was I just so naïve, so new at this, it felt like the greatest thing in the world?

As the kiss deepened, I couldn't breathe, my mouth consumed by his, my nose pressed against his cheek, but I didn't care. I didn't care about anything but how warm and firm his lips were, how his tongue touching mine set fire to the pit of my stomach, how my skin tingled where it pressed against his chest.

I had no idea how long we kissed for, our mouths fused despite the small shifts in posture, the slight angling of our heads for better positioning. There was no embarrassing clash of teeth or noses as I'd envisioned my first kiss to have, only the sublime pleasure turning my bones to mush as I sagged against him.

A glorious eternity later we eased back, our lips lingering, reluctant to part.

"Wow," I murmured, savoring the moment, my forehead resting on his.

When he didn't answer, my heart sank. Our exquisite moment was over, and it was time for the "this can never happen again" speech I just knew he had rehearsed for moments like this. I could tell by his expression I wasn't far off the mark, so I scrabbled for something to say, something to preempt the inevitable brushoff.

"Been a big day. We got carried away; no big deal, right?" I braced myself for the worst.

When he finally spoke, he said the last thing I expected to hear.

"That was freaking unbelievable."

No, what was unbelievable was the stunned incredulity making his eyes so wide I could've drowned in those endless blue pools.

Blah, where was I getting this corny crap? One kiss and I'd turned into a ... a ... cheerleader!

I used to hate hearing their drivel, fawning over boys, rehashing in great detail every single kiss, makeout session, and beyond. I'd always wanted to block my ears and shout "la la la." Now that I knew the euphoria, I wanted to shout out to the world myself.

Hey, listen up, I kissed the hottest guy on the planet ... and he liked it!

As the silence stretched awkwardly, I blurted the first thing that came into my head. "Let me guess, you enjoyed it, but we can't kiss again because there's a rule against warriors fraternizing with their charges and—"

"There's no rule," he said, dragging a hand through his hair, leaving it sexily mussed. I only just caught his muttered, "Maybe there should be."

Unable to get a read on him, I tried a joke. "Why? Because I'm too much of a distraction?"

"That too," he said, his expression surprisingly grim.

"Apparently the warrior geis is more than protective."

This time he shuffled his feet, appearing embarrassed. "Warriors often bind for life with the chosen one they protect."

"You mean?" I waved a hand between us. "We're *soulmates?*"

Soulmates was too heavy, too romantic. I'd settle for girlfriend/boyfriend, considering I'd never had a relationship before.

"No."

"Either we are or we aren't." I injected false pep into my voice to hide that he was confusing the hell out of me.

"We can't be."

He spoke so softly I thought I'd misheard, and my heart felt like it plummeted all the way to my shoes.

He stared at my lips and I swear it was like he'd reached out and touched them. "It's not you, it's me—"

"You're giving me some lame line? What the—"

"Because we're not really bonded!" His eyes blazed with a fierceness that snatched my breath away. I took a step back, stumbled into the nearest tree.

"What's going on, Joss?"

I half expected him to clam up or give me the brushoff, but the moment he raised his stricken eyes to mine, I knew the truth would be far worse than any lie he could've told me.

"We're not bonded because I'm not your warrior." Pinching the bridge of his nose, he spat out, "I got the job by default."

I sank onto a log, my knees shaky as I waited for him to continue.

"Olwydd, your destined warrior, used to train with me. There was an accident … " He started pacing, as if trying to outrun his demons. "Nothing serious, a flesh wound by my sword, but Olly disappeared after that and people blamed me."

Stunned by his admission, I watched him pick up the pace, scuffing through debris littering the forest floor.

"Not being a warrior by birth is bad enough without the constant cloud of another warrior's 'disappearance under mysterious circumstances' hanging over my head. So I volunteered to protect you, fought Oscar for the honor, to prove I'm blameless in Olly's disappearance. But ... "

He stopped and pinned me with a glare that begged for forgiveness I wasn't ready to give. "People have suggested I got rid of Olly to claim the prestigious job of protecting the Scion. But that's not why I did it. You have to believe me."

I clenched my hands into fists and shoved them into my pockets to stop from thumping him. He'd lied to me. About everything. The one guy who I'd trusted with my life since I'd started on this whole crazy quest turned out to be a phony. Crap. Was any of this real?

"You were right about me earning my stripes. After my previous 'misdemeanor' with Olly, I basically got this assignment because they think I'm guaranteed to fail and they can get rid of the troublemaker forever. But they're wrong." He waved a hand between the two of us. "You and me? We're going to kick serious ass. Initially, I resented you, or resented this assignment, because I had to do a great job or else. But then I met you ... "

"And what? You fell for my many charms?" Seething, I leaped to my feet. "Cut the crap, Joss. I'm nothing more than a means to an end. You do a good job protecting me, you get to stick around

269

in your precious Eiros. So don't make this any worse by implying you actually care about me."

"I do—"

"Bull!" I wanted to hit him, to jab at him, to make him hurt half as much as he'd hurt me with his lies. "Let me guess, that kiss was a distraction technique, right? Because I was getting too close to the truth asking questions about Oscar and why you challenged him to protect me?"

"That kiss was real," he said, his shoulders slumped. "It shouldn't have happened, but it was real." Some of the fight drained out of me as I belatedly realized some good had come out of this disaster. I now knew the truth, and nothing would stop me from finding Arwen, defeating Cadifor, and getting the hell out of Eiros permanently. I planted my hands on my hips. "Tell me this. Are you properly equipped to protect me?"

He staggered as if I'd hit him. "My skills as a warrior are not in question. I'll do whatever it takes to ensure your safety. You have my word."

Like that means much.

He chose that moment to read my mind and he straightened to his full height, his posture proud. "I mean it, Holly. Whatever it takes."

He brushed a fingertip down my cheek, making me want to cry.

I wouldn't give him the satisfaction.

Turning away, I marched back towards the Beltane festivities, blinking back tears of betrayal.

While the Sorority had played down the banshee incident for my benefit, it had rattled them enough to call an emergency strategy meeting.

The Beltane festivities had barely wound down in the early afternoon and I was a mess, high from my first kiss, yet seething at Joss for the rest. I wasn't in the mood for a how-do-we-defeat-Cadifor chat.

I knew a sure way to get this with over quickly. Have a vision. Since I couldn't control when they popped up yet, I'd do the next best thing. Manufacture one with a crystal.

"You sure you're up for this?"

I nodded at Mack, appreciating his concern. "It worked at school. Shouldn't be a problem here."

Maeve slipped an arm around my waist, squeezed. "You're so brave."

"Or stupid," I quipped, earning a wry smile from Oscar.

Joss didn't say a word. Disapproval radiated from him like a bad aura.

I clutched the chevron amethyst in my fist, eased into a chair in Uriel's living room, closed my eyes, and tried to relax.

I focused on my breathing, keeping it deep and steady, visualizing white light and space—the opposite of that dark, dingy cave Cadifor dwelled in. I pressed the amethyst to my forehead, focused on the heat, the energy.

I startled when I was instantly sucked into the darkness.

Cadifor leans over a scrying bowl, filled to the brim with a thick, viscous crimson liquid. My attacker and my mom flank him.

"The blood does not lie. She is the one."

He turns to my attacker. "Keenan. Give me her hair."

Keenan slides a clump of my hair from a black silk bag and hands it over. Cadifor lays the strands in the liquid, where they float like gossamer gold. "Ah yes, there is no doubt. This Holly is the one."

Mom stiffens, her pale face stark against her black robes.

Cadifor turns to her.

"What is it, my Elphame?"

"Nothing."

Cadifor's hand whips out from his draping sleeve so fast she flinches. He grabs a fistful of hair and forces her head back.

"Do. Not. Lie. To. Me."

Mom blinks.

She forces a smile, but the terror in her lying eyes is there all the same.

"Of course not, my lord. I'm merely surprised by your increasing strength. Your scrying skills get more powerful with every passing day."

Ego appeased, he releases her.

"Pity I can't say the same about your honesty."

This time, his attack is more silent, more lethal than before.

He grabs her around the waist, hoists her up onto the altar, forcing her head toward the scrying bowl until her nose almost touches the blood-infused liquid.

She doesn't cry out, but her fingers clutch the hard, unforgiving stone so hard her knuckles stand out, stark and white against the darkness.

"When I showed you the photo of the girl, you professed ignorance."

His frigid voice would've frozen Lake Wolfe twice over.

Shoving her head closer, he yells so loud he could give a banshee baseball team a run for their money.

"Behold."

He shoves her head closer to the liquid until her nose skims the surface and she clamps her lips shut, struggling to turn her head away.

"Now tell me you don't know this girl."

Despite her knuckles so prominent the bone almost split through skin, Mom didn't flinch, didn't hesitate.

"I didn't recognize her. It has been sixteen years—"

"Liar!" he roars, shaking her so hard her teeth rattle. "A mother would know her own daughter."

Mom's ragged breathing, harsh and unnatural, is the only sound to pierce the eerie silence.

"I swear to you, my lord, I didn't recognize her. She was a baby, six months old, I can't remember."

While her voice is steady, Keenan's horrified expression in the background implies this won't end well.

He shuffles his feet, darting furtive glances at the exits, ready to flee the wrath of a monster.

Though Cadifor's face is hidden, the malice radiating off him sends a shudder through Mom and Keenan.

His fingers convulse on the back of Mom's head.

"You will pay for this."

Cadifor plunges Mom's face into the blood and turns to Keenan, who takes a step back.

"Find the girl."

His evil chuckles make Keenan step back again.

"Get Arwen."

Mom starts flailing, her arms scrabbling at nothing, her legs jerking off the floor.

Cadifor laughs louder.

"Then kill her."

I came to with a gasp, a silent scream ripping my throat.

CHAPTER TWENTY-SIX

"I need to find Arwen. Now!"

I leaped from my chair and started pacing.

Mack held up his hands. "Calm down and we'll—"

"No. I will not calm down!" I jabbed a finger in his direction. Maeve and Oscar stared at me in open-mouthed shock. "I need to get to that cave and grab Arwen and confront this evil psycho before—"

Joss shot me a warning glare and I bit back the rest of what I was about to say.

Before it's too late for my mom.

"Before?" Mack prompted.

"Before I go freaking nuts."

I slumped back into the chair, defeated. This was my battle, mine alone. Even when Joss placed a comforting hand on my shoulder it didn't help. I wanted to shrug it off, to tell him where he could stick his false protectiveness, but I was too shaken by my vision for bravado.

I didn't love my mom—far from it. In fact, I hated her deep down inside for abandoning me. But I didn't want her to die. Not like that. And not before I asked her why.

Why did you leave me?

Why have you stayed away?

And the biggie, *Why the hell are you with a monster like him?*

"He knows who I am. He thinks I have Arwen. He wants it. And he wants me dead."

"We won't let that happen." Mack, as cool and unflappable as ever, sat at the table and beckoned us. "No point barging into a confrontation with Cadifor unprepared. Let's sit, strategize."

I respected him for not giving me the brushoff, for not placating me with some lousy meaningless words, but all the planning in the world wouldn't save Mom if I was too late.

The stupid thing was, I had no idea if Cadifor was trying to teach her a lesson or if he did that kind of thing to her all the time. I'd already seen him shove her, and seen his henchman drag her into the cave by her hair. Maybe they played these twisted games all the time for kicks? My stomach rolled at the thought. I needed answers, and Mom was the only one who could provide them. I needed her alive.

As the others assembled at the table, I clutched Joss's arm to hold him back. "He knows who I am and he's killing Mom right now because of it. We have to do something."

Joss motioned at the others. "Stop and think. If he has discovered the link between the two of you, there's no chance he'll kill her. He needs her alive more than ever, to draw you in. So relax, and we'll find her and Arwen, I promise."

Okay, what he said made sense. I dragged in a deep breath, trying to regain control. Being emotionally invested in this search was a bad idea. What Joss said about Cadifor using Mom to get to me could only end badly, but for now, I had to believe him. Despite the fact he'd lied about why he was my warrior and not the chosen Olly, I believed him. I had to. I couldn't do this alone, and in some small way, I guess I was grateful he'd finally told me the truth.

He didn't have to. He could've kept lying to me until the end, making it so much harder if I'd fallen deeper. And I had fallen, no doubt. To forgive him this quickly, I cared, a lot. But that didn't mean I had to forget, and having my trust shattered in the guy I liked was a wake-up call I needed.

"You'll never be alone in this," Joss said. "Ever."

He chose the most inopportune moments to read my mind, and I wanted to yell at him to back off. Until I saw his genuine concern, and my resentment eased. For now, I needed him and if I didn't let go of my anger entirely, it could affect my thinking and jeopardize my chances of getting out of this thing alive.

Nodding, I mouthed "thanks" and headed to the table to plot Cadifor's downfall.

I hoped it wouldn't be mine too.

When I arrived back at school a few hours later, my head spinning with plans and my stomach churning with worry, I ran into the last person I wanted to.

"Hey Holly, how's your Nan?"

I skidded to a stop as Quinn stepped out of the girls' dorm. Of course he'd be visiting Raven on a Sunday evening. We often did that, chilling out, listening to music, going over our schedule for the week. Usually I was back much earlier from Eiros, but tonight my timing sucked.

"The same." I crossed my fingers behind my back, hating the little white lies.

"Too bad."

"I'm really tired. I'll catch you tomorrow."

If I'd been thinking straight, I wouldn't have made the mistake of trying to slide past him in my desperation to escape his interrogation. Giving Quinn the brushoff only piqued his curiosity.

As I stepped around him, he grabbed my arm, too fast for me to shrug off. "What's going on with you?"

"Haven't you given me the third degree before? It's getting tiresome."

His bewilderment soon gave way to anger at my joking response. "I get that you like this other guy, but you're seriously starting to freak me out. You don't eat with us any more, you hole up in your room, or you're at the hospital all the time to see him."

"That's not true—"

"Bull." Shaking his head, he released my arm so quickly I stumbled. "This guy isn't good for you." His glacial tone chilled me.

"This is none of your business—"

"Like hell it's none of my business!" He grabbed hold of both my arms. I'd made a monumental error in continually lying to him; easygoing Quinn had vanished.

As if I hadn't had enough drama for one day. Fighting off a banshee, getting sworn into the Sorority, having my first kiss, seeing my mom being murdered by a monster, and now this.

"We're friends, damn it, and friends care about each other. What I see when I look at you now … " He shook his head.

He didn't deserve the way I'd hurt him, not after the way he'd stood by me from the very beginning. But as much as I would have liked to soothe his ego and tell him the truth, I couldn't do it. Mom's life, maybe all our lives, depended on it.

"You're into some guy who's turning you into a stress-head and you expect me just to stand back and let it happen?"

"You have to trust me—"

"So you said before, but sorry, not buying it this time. Trust is earned. Trust is respected between friends. You don't trust me, so why should I trust you?"

Fair point.

I had to give him some snippet of the truth before I lost him for good. The last few weeks, Quinn and Raven had become the BFFs I'd never had. Being cooped up here until graduation, whenever that was, with my friends not talking to me would be unbearable. Who would've thought a loner could become dependent?

"You can't tell anyone about this."

Lips still compressed in a mutinous line, he nodded. "Promise."

"I've developed another ability. My—" I stumbled, almost saying *boyfriend* and wishing it were true. "My friend's gang is expert in this sort of thing, and that's why I'm hanging around them."

"If they're helping you, why are you so strung out?"

Crap, it was harder coming up with half-truths than full-blown lies.

"Because this ability is … volatile." I fumbled for the right words, hoping my bumbling would convince him I was telling the truth. "Guess I'm strung out because I'm coming to terms with the unpredictability."

Totally true. I had no idea if the Sorority's grand plan would work, whether I'd find Arwen and save Mom or this entire situation would blow up in my face.

For someone who liked everything orderly, this lack of control was driving me nuts.

Then there were the added complications of having a huge crush on my warrior, who had shattered my trust in him, a principal possibly involved in nefarious plots and as anxious as I was to find Arwen, and two best friends I couldn't afford to piss off without losing them.

Unpredictable? My life was a freaking mess.

He scanned my face for the tiniest giveaway I was lying. "Why the secrecy?"

Because people were depending on me.

Because the *world* was depending on me.

And because I cared too much for the guy staring at me with mistrust to put him in danger.

All very noble reasons, but deep down I knew I couldn't completely trust Quinn either. Brigit was his aunt, and until I discovered if Maisey had told the truth about who opened the rift, I couldn't trust Quinn with the complete truth. Which sucked big time, losing faith in my warrior and doubting my best friend in the same day.

"It's complicated."

He snorted. "Everything about this place is complicated." Anger darkened his eyes to moss green. "You know what really pisses me off? That I'm not in on it. You and Raven have your abilities, and I'm boringly normal."

I opened my mouth to respond, but he held up his hand. "And I know there are a bunch of other normal kids here, dabbling in the dark side, but they don't have to sit back and watch a friend get in over her head and know there's not a damn thing they can do to help."

Okay, this situation was getting worse by the minute. I wanted to confide in him so badly, wanted to have someone truly on my side, but I didn't know where this would all end, not when the threat of death hung over me like a constant shroud.

"I can't help if I don't know the full story," he said, reaching out to touch my arm before his hand fell uselessly to his side. "And I want to help, any way I can."

I shook my head, glanced away. "You can't."

"Because you won't let me!"

Frustrated, he thumped the wall with his fist and I immediately reached out to him. "Don't. I'm not worth it."

Horror warred with realization: I'd just blurted my innermost fear out loud.

I didn't feel worthy of this, any of it. Having special abilities that set me apart from everyone, being the only descendant of Bel who could save the world, having an affinity with a hot warrior who liked me back, and having two new friends, one of whom would do anything for me, apparently. How could I be worthy of any of that?

I'd been totally unremarkable my entire life: the model student, the model granddaughter. Quiet, studious, queen of the nerds. Yet here was another amazing guy staring at me with genuine caring and I couldn't handle it. It just didn't seem real. Stuff like this didn't happen to me.

He captured my chin, leaving me no option but to meet his eyes. I forced my feet to stay rooted to the spot. I couldn't speak past the lump in my throat.

The tiny gold flecks in his eyes glowed amid a sea of green. "You really have no idea, do you? You are so worth it." His gaze dropped to my lips and my heart stopped.

A tingle of expectation rippled along my skin. I didn't move as

Quinn continued staring at my lips. His head tilted slightly to one side, and I held my breath, my skittering pulse as out of control as the rest of my life. How was it that I hadn't been kissed my entire teenage life, and now faced the prospect of two in one day?

"Holly?"

"Hmm?"

He stepped forward, so close our bodies almost touched. I could feel warmth radiating off him, could smell coffee and mint and freshly cut grass. He must've been lying outside having a latte while I'd been seeing my mom being tortured by a monster. "I'll always be here for you, whatever happens."

As his head descended, I had a split second to avoid the kiss.

Hating that I'd landed in this predicament, I turned my head a fraction.

"You have real feelings for this guy."

I nodded and bit my lip to stop from blurting platitudes, eventually settling for, "I care about you too—"

"Just not like that." He dragged a hand through his spiky hair, his laugh hollow. "Yeah, I get it."

"So we're cool?"

He stuffed his hands in his pockets, like he didn't want to risk reaching for me. "Hot, more like it."

I blinked several times and shook my head. I wasn't interested in adding another guy to my complicated life. Especially when the guy already complicating it wasn't who I thought he was. Joss had lied to me, and that had tainted my trust in him, but I couldn't ignore what had come before: I'd fallen for him, and no matter how much I'd like to punch him for deceiving me, I needed him to get through this.

"Quinn, I can't—"

"Forgotten."

I didn't buy his fake smile. I could see the lingering hurt in eyes.

"Thanks."

"For?"

"Being a great friend. For understanding. For being here for me."

I wanted to fling myself into his arms, to hug him, really hug him, a full-on genuine bear hug to convey half of what I was feeling. But I didn't. I just stood there, shuffling my weight from one foot to the other, awkward and embarrassed and way out of my depth.

With a solemn nod, he turned and walked away.

I wanted to reach out to him, to say something to make it all better. But what could I say to make this any easier?

Blinking back tears, I fumbled with the lock on my door, half-fell into my room, and flung myself on the bed. I was overwhelmed by the day's events, and fatigue seeped through my body like a sleeping pill.

Nan, lying in her hospital bed, pale and lifeless.

Two people lean over her.

Keenan, evil contorting his twisted features as he fiddles with the tubes keeping her alive.

A second figure, smaller and slighter, a girl, steps around the bed to stand beside him, places a hand on his arm, stopping him.

The girl raises her head, the teenager's creepy golden eyes glowing like a tiger's as she screams "Nooooooo ... "

I sat bolt upright, unsure whether I'd yelled "no" or if that was only part of my vision. After a quick knock, my door flung open and Brigit rushed into the room, panicked. Guess I had my answer.

"What happened? I heard you from the end of the corridor."

"Vision," I spat out, grabbing a bottled water from my mini-cooler and downing it to ease the dryness in my throat.

"Arwen's whereabouts?"

At that moment, with Brigit looming over me, expression hopeful and not in the least concerned for what I went through with each vision or what had just made me scream, I hated her. Ever since I'd walked through her wacky stone arches and been revealed as *the one,* she'd treated me like some giant science experiment. Sure, she'd been solicitous and helpful, but only because it suited her.

"My Nan, actually." I stood and snatched my messenger bag off the chair. "I have to go see her."

"Now?"

She glanced at her watch and frowned. "It's eight on a Sunday night. They won't—"

"I'm going." I didn't add "And you can't stop me." She saw it in the stubborn jut of my chin, my shoulders squared for battle.

"Whatever your mission and talents, Holly, I'm still your principal." Her unsaid warning lingered between us. *And I can make you do anything I want.*

I knew I'd have to give her something for her to let me go. Besides, every moment I wasted here could prove fatal for Nan. "Someone's a threat to Nan, I saw it in the vision. I have to go to her before … "

It's too late.

I couldn't say the words, let alone think them.

"What did you see?"

"We haven't got time for this! Let's go."

Brigit frowned, her glower not nearly enough to intimidate me when all I could think about was getting to Nan. "Holly, I'm well aware teens don't like hearing this, but I've been around a lot longer than you, and one thing I've learned is to not rush headlong into situations that are potentially dangerous."

Chief Crazy thought I'd be leading her into danger. *Welcome to my life, lady.* "Who's rushing? By the time we get there those two could've killed her!"

Concern deepened the crease in her brow. "Who's with her?"

"Some guy fiddling with her tubes, and a girl." Not just some guy. Keenan. Cadifor's right-hand torture instrument. But Brigit didn't need to know that. She'd only want to ask me more questions, and right now I was out of time.

Frantic, I focused on the door. I'd have to bolt past her if she messed around any longer.

She laid a calming hand on my shoulder. "You know your visions are precognitive. They'll happen some time in the future, and very rarely occur in real time."

I hated her smooth, well-modulated tone, hated her

condescension, hated the fact she was probably right.

"Very rarely?" I shook my head and jammed my hands in the pockets of my hoodie to prevent myself from grabbing her and dragging her out the door to her beat-up VW. "I'm not willing to take that risk, so can we please go?"

Some of my desperation, or maybe my uncharacteristic show of manners, must've gotten through to her, because she finally yanked open the door.

"Come on, I'll drive you."

Being holed up in the principal's car as we hurtled down the quiet Wolfebane streets wasn't my idea of fun, but if it saved time I'd put up with it, even tolerate her none-too-subtle probing.

"Your initiation went well today?"

"Uh-huh."

"You enjoyed the Beltane festivities?

"Hmm."

Her eyebrows rose at my monosyllabic answers. "Any progress with finding Arwen?"

Ah ... the real reason behind her mercy dash. She didn't give a damn about me or Nan. Brigit didn't care what happened to me as long as she got her hands on Arwen, and that pissed me off.

I hated being used.

"Holly, I asked you a question."

"Sorry, drifted off for a moment." My snarky tone gave fair indication I wasn't sorry in the least.

"Well? Are you any closer to finding it since the last time we talked?"

When was that? Like, yesterday?

Biting back my real response about where she could stick her questions, I injected enough sweetness in my voice to keep her off my back. "The Sorority and I have a plan."

"You do?"

She was so excited she almost swerved off the road.

"All the signs point to Arwen being revealed during summer solstice." I didn't tell her where. Let the old bat stew.

"That soon? Wonderful." She yanked the steering wheel so hard the car almost slammed into the curb in front of the hospital. I could've sworn her eyes glittered with maniacal fervor as she turned toward me. "Do you want me to come in with you?"

Hell no.

Shaking my head, I said, "Thanks for the lift, but I'd rather be on my own."

"But if there's danger—"

"I won't be alone. The place is packed with doctors and nurses. I'll yell for help."

"As long as you're sure—"

"I'm sure. Thanks." I didn't give her time to respond, leaping from the car like I had a dozen Cadifors on my tail.

Escaping my obsessive principal was the least of my worries as I sprinted toward the front doors, skidding to a stop when an old guy pushing eighty hobbled out, dragging an oxygen tank with one hand and holding a cigarette in the other. I eased past him before bolting up the front steps and through the main entrance.

The place was deserted, the deathly silence immediately raising my spooky antennae. Where was everyone? As I crept down the corridor, I snuck glances into patients' rooms, relieved when I saw TVs flickering and rheumy eyes glaring at me for intruding.

Okay, maybe that vision had me on edge for nothing.

But when I rounded the last corner, the empty nurses station outside Nan's room had me worried. Night shifts were quiet, but the times I'd visited late the nurses were usually clustered around their workstation, chatting about the hottest American Idol contestant or the newest McDreamy doc on their roster.

Holding my breath, I inched toward Nan's room, pushed open the door, and exhaled with a loud whoosh.

Nothing had changed.

Nan's machines still beeped and whirred, all wires and tubes intact.

I entered, headed for the bed, and laid my hand on her chest, relieved at its gentle rise and fall. I touched her cheek with my fingertips, its coolness underlined by residual warmth.

I sank onto the chair next to her bed, clutched her hand, and cried.

It had been building all day and my overwrought emotions finally released in this quiet room while holding the hand of the one woman I'd trusted all these years.

What the hell was I doing, going after my mom and trying to save her? She didn't deserve it. She didn't deserve the time of day.

At that moment, ice trickled through my veins. I held onto

Nan's hand tight, scared by the prospect of having two visions less than twenty minutes apart.

"Nan, I love you," I murmured a second before my eyes slammed shut and I was catapulted into another frightening glimpse of my future.

CHAPTER TWENTY-SEVEN

In the darkness of a cave, Cadifor snaps his fingers and Keenan steps forward.

"The old woman is still alive?"

"As you wished, my lord."

Cadifor nods. "Good. We may have use for her yet."

He flips a photo between his fingers over and over.

"It will be good for the girl to know the power we hold over her loved ones, how we maintain her grandmother's coma so easily."

"Is there anything else, my lord?"

"Yes. My Elphame is displaying worrying behavior. Watch her."

Cadifor withdraws a long, curved bronze blade from within the folds of his robe.

"She has one last chance. If she shows any suspicious behavior, bring her to me."

"She has been loyal—"

"You dare question me?"

Cadifor spins so fast his robes rustle and blow a pile of brittle dead leaves off the altar. They flutter to the ground, falling like teardrops.

Keenan flinches but doesn't step back. "No, my lord, but Rhiannon, your Elphame, has proven her faith in you many times—"

"Except with the girl," Cadifor hisses, his fingers convulsing around the knife hilt. "I can't afford dissension, especially among those closest to me."

Keenan nods, his wary gaze riveted to the knife as Cadifor rolls it in the palm of his hand before flipping it and catching it smoothly.

"I kill traitors in a heartbeat."

He plunges the blade into a pomegranate lying on the altar. Repeatedly. The skin splits, its lush ripeness spilling onto the altar.

As he continues stabbing in frenzy, it splatters the walls with crimson, the same rich garnet of blood.

I opened my eyes to see Nan's pale, lined face. She was in a coma, caught up in all this Arwen crap, because of me.

A wave of nausea rolled over me as I bent to kiss the hand I clutched, whispering, "I'm sorry, Nan. So, so sorry."

I glanced down, horrified to see the crescent-shaped indents my nails had made in her fragile skin where I must've gripped onto her during the vision, and I quickly released her hand, smoothing the skin as if I could magically erase the marks. I loved Nan's hands, the raised veins on the back of them, the short-clipped nails, the skin always smelling of the rose hand cream she used religiously.

I'd held her hand my first day of preschool, the first day of grade school, the first time I'd ridden a pony. How many meals had these hands prepared? How many of my ponytails braided? How many of her horrid bright scarves knitted?

I adored Nan, and to think that monster was somehow responsible for this …

I leaped to my feet and headed for the door, not wasting a second. I needed a foolproof plan. One that would assure I'd find Arwen, defeat Cadifor, and save my Nan and my mom.

Only one place I could do this. Eiros held the answers I needed.

I'd played nice until now, being the good little Sorority student, absorbing everything they'd taught me, doing everything they'd said.

Now it was their turn to listen.

Cadifor was close to losing it. I could see it in every vision; the escalating violence, his tenuous hold on control, his increasing doubts about my mom.

He wanted Arwen; he wanted me.

Well, maybe it was time to give the monster what he wanted.

On *my* terms.

I stopped at the door and turned to blow a kiss at Nan.

"Hang in there, Nan. I'm heading back to Eiros to put a stop to this. Once and for all."

The Sorority didn't like my plan, didn't like me calling the shots. But I left them no option. They did it my way or I walked. Not that I would, not with Nan and Mom's lives hanging in the balance, but the Sorority didn't know that, and what the Sorority didn't know wouldn't hurt them.

With their hands tied, they'd asked for some thinking time and I'd obliged, leaving the meeting convinced that by the next day, I'd have answers one way or the other.

Not that I had a death wish, but I couldn't let another day go by with Nan lying in that hospital bed, not if I could do something about it.

Cadifor wanted Arwen, so I'd bargain him for it. I'd meet him in the Cave of the Sun at summer solstice. He would know the significance of the day, would assume he'd finally gain Arwen and have his revenge on Bel and the rest of Eiros.

After I issued the challenge, he'd send his consort to meet me. I couldn't risk venturing into the underground complex twisting beneath us like a labyrinth, but I could meet him at the main cave's entrance. No way would Cadifor pass up a possible opportunity to discover more about Arwen's whereabouts. Once I fed his consort the story about the Cave of the Sun and summer solstice, I'd buy time for Nan, and hopefully for Mom too.

"Don't wander too far."

I saluted Joss. "Yes, sir."

I'd wanted to rattle his impervious air since I'd returned, the first time since The Kiss. He'd been all business, cool and unflappable, annoyingly professional. While I needed him to protect me, I wanted him to acknowledge there was something more between us, that even though he'd kept the truth from me, I was willing to put my faith in him till the end.

"I'll be back in five minutes."

"No worries."

As he strode through the ash grove and disappeared from sight I sank onto a nearby log and propped my chin on my hands. I could sit and watch that particular view all day. A funny, fuzzy feeling spread in my chest and I absentmindedly rubbed it, wondering if all first loves felt like this, vague and exciting and scary all at the same time.

I heard rustling and turned to see Uriel. "You're a good match." She sat next to me. "I'm glad you're in my son's life, Holly."

I mumbled a noncommittal response, reluctant to discuss my major crush with his mom.

"You know this isn't just about his father?"

"His father?"

Confusion creased her brow. "He said he'd told you the truth."

"Obviously not all of it," I said, twisting the string on my hoodie until I cut off circulation in my fingertip. Better the discomfort there than the awful ache spreading through my chest because Joss had more secrets.

She frowned, staring at me before patting my hand. "He'll hate me telling you this, but I believe you need to know." Uriel picked up a nearby stick and drew a vertical line with three horizontal lines across it in the dirt. "The ogham sign Ur; its tree name is heather." She drew a circle around it, then slashed a line through it, obliterating it, which was kind of scary. "Heather was Joss's biological mother. She insisted her son be a warrior, and Sean, his father, acquiesced to her wishes. Though not a warrior by birth, there are ways for men to become warriors. Facing profound evil is one of them."

Unease trickled down my spine.

"When Heather died, Sean became obsessed with keeping his promise to her. He believed for Joss to one day be a great warrior, he had to set an example." Uriel swallowed, her throat convulsing. "Joss was still a child, seven years old, when he entered the underground labyrinth ... "

Dread blossomed into full-blown dismay. "Cadifor?"

Uriel nodded. "Joss vowed to avenge his father's death. It drove him to be the best warrior, and then there was the incident with Olly."

"Yeah, he told me about that."

Uriel toyed with the cross embroidered on her blouse. "I love Joss as if he were my own son. Sadly, bad luck seems to follow him." She squeezed my hand. "Until now."

Uh-oh. If Uriel thought I was a good luck charm, she was sorely mistaken. If Joss attracted bad luck, what I attracted would be the equivalent of breaking a hundred mirrors, walking under a thousand ladders, and treading on a million black cats.

"Did you know Joss fought to protect you?"

I nodded, not trusting myself to speak, not when the reality of this situation had gone from bad to worse. The warrior who professed to be there for me until the bitter end was in fact using me to get to Cadifor for his personal agenda. Nice. The truth lodged in my throat, a lump of bitterness I couldn't budge no matter how much I swallowed.

"No one can explain it, but despite not being your true warrior bound by geis, the two of you *are* bound." She ticked off points on her fingers. "Joss knew you were coming. His pyrokinesis works on you. He can read your mind. Only a true warrior bound to his charge could do this."

Okay, so his mom made a pretty convincing argument. But that didn't change the fact he wanted revenge on Cadifor and was using me to get it.

"He's determined to prove himself worthy of you."

"Worthy?"

"Deep down, Joss is insecure. He fears he cannot live up to being the protector of the Scion."

I was seriously starting to hate the *Scion* label. As if it wasn't bad enough laying the expectations of the world on my shoulders, it now made my warrior insecure too?

"I guess we all have our fears." Mine included a fear of failing everyone: my Nan, my friends, the Sorority, even my mom. Oh, and the world. Not that I wanted to belittle Joss's fear, but right now I didn't want to acknowledge any vulnerability he might have. I wanted to stay mad at him so I could rant when he came back.

"I'm sorry Joss didn't tell you the entire truth, but he wouldn't want to burden you with his past when you have enough to deal with in the present."

Sounded like another convenient excuse to lie. "I'm glad you told me."

And I was. Now I knew exactly what I was dealing with: one seriously messed up warrior with an agenda and a mysterious past rivaling the bad guys'.

Uriel touched my cheek in an affectionate gesture I would've found condescending coming from anyone else. There was something so sincere about her, so gentle, that she reminded me of Nan. My heart lurched at the thought. "I may not have any supernatural powers but I know you're a sweet, selfless girl. A fitting soulmate for my son."

I opened my mouth to answer and shut it again, not sure how to respond. What do you say when the mom of the guy you like—who also happens to be the guy you'd like to throttle—gives you the all clear?

"Thanks" seemed lacking, so I settled for a mumbled, "okay," and silently cringed at my inadequacy. How come I was such a smartass with trolls like Maisey, yet couldn't string two coherent words together for a cool lady like Uriel?

Smiling, she patted my arm and stood, glancing into the distance. "He'll be returning soon, so I must go." She hesitated. "If you're wondering why I told you all this, it's so you understand what motivates him, and to have patience."

Placing her hand on my head, she spoke so softly I barely caught the words.

"You will be together. It's destiny."

After Uriel left, I picked up the stick she'd dropped and started practicing ogham in the dirt.

One vertical line and one horizontal for Beithe, the letter *B*, birch. Added another horizontal line for Luis, *L*, the rowan tree. Another line for Fern, *F*, the alder. Another line, Sail, *S*, for willow.

I'd learned ogham by rote, its symbols, letters, trees and meanings. While I still struggled with a lot of it, I found the symmetry between the symbols and trees intriguing.

Before I knew it, I'd drawn the symbols for holly and ash within a heart. Grimacing at my corniness, I quickly scrubbed it out as a shadow fell over me, and I blushed, hoping Joss hadn't seen it.

"I was just doodling—"

A hand clamped over my mouth, squashing my lips against my teeth so hard I tasted blood. "Come with me now if you want to see your mother alive."

Terrified, I frantically scanned the grove for signs of Joss as my assailant dragged me upward, ignoring my wriggling and squirming.

"I won't hurt you. Unless you make me." As I contemplated kicking him in the shins, he growled, "Listen. Cadifor is on the verge of killing your mother. Only you can save her."

The fight immediately drained out of me and I sagged like a limp doll.

"I'm going to remove my hand from your mouth so we can talk. If you scream, your mother dies."

I nodded and he eased his hand off my mouth. I immediately swung to face him, gasping in horror at those familiar twisted features. The man who'd come after me that day at Joss's cottage, who'd yanked out half my hair, was the man standing before me.

"Keenan." His odd little formal bow conflicted with the violence emanating from him in petrifying waves. "Come, we need to talk."

With one last desperate glance over my shoulder for Joss, I followed Keenan into the forest, the towering trees soon swallowing us.

We hadn't walked far when he held up his hand. "This is far enough."

I gulped.

"I'm not here to harm you," he said.

"Unlike before, when you almost scalped me?"

He frowned. "It was necessary; I followed orders. Now I come as an old friend of your mother's." My disbelief elicited a slight quirk of his upper lip in what passed for a smile. "Cadifor is using her to get to you. If she doesn't comply, he's going to harm her."

I swallowed past the lump of fear lodged in my throat. "What can I do?" It was easier to play along with him for now, hear what he had to say, and plan how the hell I was going to give him the slip.

"Give up your quest."

"Just like that?" I scoffed, increasingly doubtful Keenan had come here on anything other than another lapdog excursion for Cadifor. His master said jump, sit, roll over, and Keenan performed on cue.

Though—he hadn't harmed me, which blew that theory. If Cadifor had sent him to come after me again, I doubted we'd be standing here talking. I'd probably already be in a body bag.

"It's the only thing that can save your mother." He paused, his beady eyes glittering with malice. "And you want that, don't you?"

"You don't know what I want," I said, looking away.

"Don't waste my time."

He stepped closer and I suppressed a spasm of dread. Standing this close to him was like standing next to an open freezer. My first instinct was to scramble backwards. My second, to run. But I stood my ground and eyeballed him, clamping my jaw to stop my teeth chattering and giving away the waves of terror racking my body.

I couldn't concentrate thanks to his unnerving proximity, but I had to think. This didn't make sense. Cadifor wanted Arwen, and according to legend, I was the one who had to find it. If I called off the quest, wouldn't we all lose?

I folded my arms and glared. "This is crazy. I need to find Arwen."

"Cadifor believes he's close to securing Arwen. If you interfere ... " He shrugged. "He will have no reason to keep your mother alive."

I gulped and jammed my hands under my armpits to stop them from shaking. "You're bluffing."

Malevolence radiated off him. "Am I?"

I wanted to tell him to stick his advice, to crawl back into the dark, dreary hole he'd come from and stay there with the rest of the underground slugs. But all I could muster was a glare. I hated his smugness, hated the fact he'd hurt me once, hated the power he wielded that could hurt me all over again in an instant.

"Are you willing to take the risk? You have a chance to save your mother, to see her for the first time, to ask all those questions burning you up inside."

"How did you—"

His harsh laugh sounded like staccato gunfire. "A girl discovers her mother abandons her as a baby. You must have a thousand questions."

Screw you hovered on my lips, but I wouldn't give him the satisfaction.

I hated every inch of his gloating face: the pockmarked cheeks, the thin lips, the cold eyes, the scar running from his right temple to his chin.

This was the man who had terrorized me.

This man was part of Cadifor's band of merry monsters.

Why the hell should I trust him?

But he was right. I couldn't take the risk of defying him and losing the chance to confront Mom.

"What do you want me to do?"

Before he could respond, something crashed through the undergrowth like a hundred stampeding elephants. I whipped my head around in time to see Joss burst into the small clearing, leap over two logs without breaking stride, and crash into me, sending us both flying.

My hard landing wasn't half as bad as it could've been, considering I landed on top of him. Keenan had already vanished.

"Not a bad cushion," I said, patting his chest as I sat up.

"You're making jokes at a time like this?"

"Adrenalin," I muttered.

He helped me up. "Do you know who that was?"

"Keenan. He introduced himself. Who knew monsters had manners?"

Joss stared at me, stunned, as I peered into the gloom. Part of me was thrilled at his timely arrival, part of me was annoyed I'd lost my chance at hearing the rest of what Keenan had to say.

"What are you doing?"

"Checking to see if he's still around."

"Are you crazy? You sound like you want him to be."

"We were ... talking."

He swore, loudly. "Keenan has killed many people on Cadifor's behalf and here you are, having a leisurely early morning chat?" He grabbed my upper arms, shook me. "What were you thinking? Why didn't you scream? Call for help? Do something?"

Bringing my forearms up, I broke his hold. "Because my mom would be dead if I did that."

"And you *believed* him?" He stalked away before swinging back to face me. "As Cadifor's lackey, it's his job to lie, cheat, manipulate. He'll say anything, do anything, to serve his master. What did he want?"

Feeling more than a little foolish, I murmured, "To give up my quest in exchange for my mom."

Joss shook his head, his pity annoying me more than his high-handedness. "Come on, Holly, you're smarter than this. For all you know, your mom and Cadifor are awaiting Keenan's return right now, laughing at how gullible you are."

"But I saw him threaten her, physically manhandle her—"

"Visions are just that, a vision of the future. Doesn't necessarily mean they're always true. We have the power to change the future."

"Then what's the point of any of this ... " I turned away and swiped a hand across my eyes to stem the angry tears welling there.

"Hey, it'll be okay."

I stiffened when he slid one arm around my waist and the other across my upper chest, holding me close, leaving me no option but to lean back against him. I wanted to struggle, to turn around and thump him for not telling me everything, to release the frustration that nothing I believed in was ever real.

I closed my eyes, sighing when he lowered his head and snuggled into the crook of my neck, willing half his strength to seep into me. I had no idea how long we stood like this, our bodies pressed intimately together, the heat slowly building, words unnecessary.

I turned my head slightly to the right and our eyes locked for a long, loaded moment before the hunger consumed us and we were kissing, hot, open-mouthed kisses that eradicated everything that had come before.

Our hands were everywhere, eager, exploring, tugging at clothes, desperate to touch bare skin. I gasped when his fingers delved between my T-shirt and the top of my jeans, skimming the skin there, trailing up my back, lingering at my bra strap.

When he stopped I pressed against him, showering kisses along his jaw, tasting the salty tang of his skin, eager to lick but not that brazen. In that instant of hesitation he pulled away, holding me at arm's length, his eyes dark as midnight, beautiful yet haunted.

I held up a finger to his lips. "Don't say it."

He didn't say a word, and I traced his lips with my fingertip, a slow, leisurely exploration of the fullness, the softness, the dips in the corners.

It was torture, for both of us. I could see it in his wild-eyed expression, his barely-restrained need struggling to burst forth.

He did what I expected. He stepped back.

That was my moment to tear into him about his hidden agenda, about how I felt betrayed yet again by his withholding the truth.

Instead, all I could think about was how much I wanted this, wanted him. Crazy? Irrational? Absolutely, but nothing about my life made sense anymore; might as well let my hormones throw me into further turmoil.

Ignoring the expected rejection digging sharpened claws into my heart, I cocked my head to one side. "I know we're not *officially* bonded, but it's pretty obvious there's something between us. Maybe we should explore it further?"

"No."

If he'd shouted or yelled or ranted I might've thought we had a chance, but that one, soft, flat refusal scared me more than anything.

"We can't keep ignoring—"

"We can and we will."

I took a step forward; he took a step back in a bizarre avoidance dance.

"Come on, Joss, it won't affect the quest—"

"You're kidding me. Want to know where I was when Keenan grabbed you? Doing something special. For you!"

I took back what I'd thought a moment ago. I preferred words quietly spoken over yelled.

He pulled a necklace out of his pocket. He dangled it on the end of his finger, the silver links impossibly delicate against his strong hands. A white oval crystal hung off the chain and caught the light as he thrust it towards me.

"I was getting this for you. Because I see what this quest is doing to you. Because I want you to have something solid, something tangible, to remind you of how great you're doing. Because I wanted to apologize for keeping the truth from you, for deceiving you into thinking I'm your chosen warrior. Because I still haven't told you the whole truth—"

"I know about your dad."

He swore. "Mom?"

"Yeah, she kinda let it slip. Thought I already knew."

"And you still like me?"

"I'm working on it," I deadpanned. What I felt for my warrior went way beyond "like."

"This is crazy. You should be ripping into me for lying to you. You should be pushing me away."

He was really yelling now, and a flock of nearby birds took flight. "Want to know the real reason I was getting this for you? Because I think you're incredible and I want you to be mine!"

I was beside him in an instant, wrapping my arms around his

waist, burying my face in his chest.

He took a deep breath, and another, and I waited. After a few moments, he slid his arms around my waist and held me tight.

"There's too much at stake for us to complicate things ... " He smoothed my hair and I almost purred. "Wanting you is a distraction I can't afford. It's a miracle Keenan only wanted to talk today. He usually maims first, asks questions later. And I won't put you through that."

Heartsore, I pulled back and glanced up at him.

"You mean too much to me." He cupped my cheek and brushed his thumb along the tear tracks.

"Yeah, I mean, so much you use me to get to Cadifor to avenge your dad's death, and you fake being my bonded warrior for the same reason."

"Holly, don't—"

"Don't what? Speak the truth?"

He winced. "That may've been my motivation at the start, but then I met you ... "

"And you were belligerent and abrupt and standoffish."

A spark lit his eyes. "Didn't you ever have some dorky kid in first grade throw erasers at you or tie your pigtails to the chair?" He tugged my ponytail for emphasis. "Guys are dumb. When we like a girl, really like her, we're horrible."

"You must really like me a lot, considering how distant you've been."

He smiled and I sucked in several breaths to ease the tightness in my chest. "You're a smart girl. I think you've already figured it out." His smile faded all too quickly. "But it doesn't change the fact we can't—"

"Save the excuses, Warrior Boy. I'm going to play things your way for now. But after this quest is over, watch out." Before he could react, I pressed my lips to his in a quick snatched kiss. "Now put this on me as a constant reminder I'm yours, whether you want to admit it or not."

With a shake of his head, he took the necklace from me, closed the clasp around my neck, and stood back. "Beautiful."

I fingered the pendant. "What type of crystal is it?"

"I wasn't talking about the crystal."

Rolling my eyes, I jabbed a finger at his chest. "You can't do that. Can't shout 'hands off,' then say stuff like that, okay?"

"Okay."

From the devilish glint in his eyes, I knew I wasn't the only one making the rules.

"What is it?"

"Snow quartz."

"Meaning?"

I held my breath, wondering if he'd say a deep, abiding love that never died. Yeah, right. His eyes crinkled at the corners as I mentally slapped my head for thinking something he could easily read.

"Snow quartz indicates profound change is coming. It supports you while learning lessons and helps during times of overwhelming responsibility."

"It's perfect." I smoothed the flat stone between my thumb and fingers. "Thanks."

"You're welcome."

He turned away, embarrassed by my gratitude. I snagged his arm. "Joss?"

"Yeah?"

I expected him to shrug me off, but he didn't. I stepped closer, so close I could see indigo flecks in his eyes, could hear his slightly ragged breathing. My grip on his arm eased and my fingers glided over the soft skin, the light smattering of hair tickling my fingertips as my hand slid downward.

He had a chance to pull away, but he didn't; his eyes locked on mine as my hand slid into his, coming home.

I pressed my palm to his, mine so much smaller and insignificant, his callused, the ridges and bumps testament to his devotion to things that mattered to him.

My fingers intertwined with his, a perfect fit. As I glanced down at our hands, I sighed with the rightness of all this.

When he tried to pull away I wouldn't let him, holding on tighter and he shook his head in resignation. "What were you going to say?"

I mustered my bravest smile. "Our time will come."

CHAPTER TWENTY-EIGHT

The Sorority agreed with my plan. With amendments.

I was forbidden to venture anywhere near the underground labyrinth, entrance or not. When they explained the number of people who'd disappeared without a trace—and were probably dead or part of Cadifor's consorts—I agreed with them.

Oscar went in my place. It was mean of me, but I was relieved it wasn't Joss or Mack or Maeve, the three members of the Sorority I was closest to. He met with Keenan, gave him the message, and waited around for a response. It came in less than ten minutes: Cadifor agreed to our terms.

Leave Nan alone.

Meet me in the Cave of the Sun on June twenty-second.

I wished I could've bargained for my mom's safety too, but that would have meant revealing my precognitive ability and my little tête-à-tête with Keenan, so I didn't go there. For now, securing Nan's safety had to be enough. I'd deal with the rest later.

I spent the weeks leading up to summer solstice studying, reading every book on Arwen the library had, and trying to get a feeling for what this mystery icon actually was. Legends guessed—sword, amulet, gold statue, ring—but the fact remained that nobody knew.

Guess I would soon find out.

My weekends at Eiros continued to be enlightening as I threw myself into all things druid, while my weeks at C.U.L.T. focused on lengthy practical sessions to master my abilities as Brigit grew increasingly agitated.

At least the Sorority was clear in their motivations: they wanted Arwen to defeat Cadifor and keep the Innerworld safe. Brigit had professed the same goal—keep the world safe from darkness—but her almost maniacal focus on securing the icon had me seriously doubting her motivations.

I hadn't run into Maisey again; shame, when I wanted to question her further. And when I'd rocked up to her dorm room, some scrawled tacked-on sign announced she was doing some study off campus. My hackles had risen. What if Brigit had done something to Maisey the same way she'd reportedly experimented with Drake? Or had Maisey simply gone off campus to shack up with her biker boyfriend for a while?

Without Maisey to fill my head with conspiracy theories, I analyzed Brigit's obsessive behavior logically. She was America's leading parapsychologist. Wouldn't it be the coup of a lifetime to have access to something like this? To prove biokinesis existed?

I'd done a heap of reading, including the science journals lining her office, and nowhere was there conclusive proof that biokinetics worked. Altering human DNA? Rearranging and controlling genes inside the body? Immortality? Nada. If Brigit could prove it existed, she wouldn't only be famous in this country, she'd be renowned worldwide.

Not that Brigit's motives mattered. As long as I let the Sorority and Brigit think I was the model pupil, an obedient lackey doing their bidding, I could work on my own plans.

As I picked up my trans-channeling crystal to chat with Joss, a brief knock sounded at the door before Quinn and Raven bustled into my room.

"Hey, did you hear RPatz and his latest are on the rocks? We're in with a chance."

I laughed at Raven's optimism, but Quinn, intuitive as ever, knew something was up. "Damn, I was supposed to pick up half a leftover red velvet cake from the dining hall."

Clever ploy. Quinn knew how much Raven loved red velvet cake.

"And you wait 'til now to tell me?" She glared at him. "Back in a sec."

She was out the door in a flurry of black silk before we could blink. Quinn didn't hesitate, crossing the room to sit on the floor next to me. "What's up?"

I wanted to tell him about tomorrow: my fears, my hopes, my insane sense of impending doom. Instead, I mumbled, "Nothing."

"I tried a psychometric analysis in magic-woo-woo class today and I'm not half bad at it, if I do say so myself. So spill before I practice on you."

I glared and he laughed.

"Come on, Holly, I know it's something big. You've been buried in the books for the last few weeks, and on the weekends you're with your Nan. Supposedly."

He wouldn't let up, so I held up my hands in surrender. "Okay, fine. Remember that group I mentioned?"

"Yeah."

He'd lost the teasing sparkle the moment I brought up the Sorority, and I knew why. He was thinking of Joss.

"Something big is going down tomorrow and I'm worried."

He frowned. "Dangerous?"

"Uh-huh."

"Then I'm coming."

His instant protectiveness, his willingness to help, warmed me. But I'd have a hard enough time knowing the guy I loved would be standing beside me when I faced Cadifor, let alone my best friend too. "You can't."

Uh-oh, wrong choice of words. He rarely backed down from a challenge.

"You're in danger. Of course I'm damn well coming!"

Jeez, how would I get myself out of this one? The only thing that would explain why he couldn't come was the truth, but …

"There's nothing you can say that's going to stop me." He folded his arms, his mutinous glare almost funny if I'd been in the mood for laughing.

"Actually, there is something—"

"Nope, nothing. Don't waste your breath. I'm coming."

I would have to tell him. I didn't want to—it would change our friendship forever. But I'd jeopardized our friendship enough. I took a deep breath, and blurted, "When I said you can't, I meant it literally."

Confusion clouded his eyes. "Huh?"

"This group I'm a part of? They're based in Eiros. The Innerworld. Kind of like a parallel existence behind a veil over New York City. I—I—teleport there."

Silence. Long, drawn-out, uncomfortable silence as my best friend stared at me like I'd lost my mind.

"Long story. When the sun or intense heat hits my forehead, I teleport to this place linked to a sun god." His frown deepened and I rushed on. "Apparently I'm a descendant of this sun god, the only one who can find an icon a bad guy wants. So that's what I'm doing tomorrow. Facing off with this guy. In Eiros."

Quinn leaped to his feet and took four steps toward the door before swinging back to glare at me. "You could've just blown me off."

"It's true—"

"Save it!"

Raised voices I could cope with, but the disbelieving glare he shot me, like I'd betrayed him, cut deep. I pushed up off the floor, wanting to … what? Calm him? Hug him? Convey the relief I'd finally told him the truth and bone-deep sadness he didn't believe me?

"It's the truth—"

"The truth is I care about you. The truth is I value our friendship. The truth is you must think I'm an idiot to spin me a story like that just so I don't get to meet your boyfriend and his crazy friends."

His face flushed an angry red. I wanted to shake him, to make him believe me. But if the truth hadn't convinced him, what would? I swallowed my disappointment and tried one last time. "I value our friendship too. It's why I told you the truth."

"Your version of the truth sucks. Screw that."

He stormed out the door and misery wormed its way into my heart.

I didn't sleep all night.

My overactive imagination envisaged how the confrontation with Cadifor would go down, what I would do if Arwen didn't miraculously appear when the sun hit the stone altar covered in spiral symbols I'd seen in my vision. Joss had a backup plan to get me out of there pronto if Arwen didn't materialize, but I knew better.

If I couldn't produce Arwen, I'd die.

The Sorority didn't believe that. When we'd gone through every possible scenario, they thought Cadifor would spare me because I was his main chance at finding Arwen fast. But Joss was wary. Something about this meeting felt off. Like I was walking into a trap.

I closed my eyes, and saw an image of Nan lying helpless in the hospital, closely followed by Mom's face dunked in a bowl of blood emulsion.

I had to do this.

I clutched the trans-channeling crystal in my hand and pressed it to my forehead. Last check-in with Joss before I teleported in an hour. Unnecessary, I thought, but he'd insisted, wanting to ensure everything was in place before I arrived.

Hey, Warrior Boy. This is Scion Chick checking in from the control tower before coming in for a smooth landing shortly.

I smiled at his laughter.

All in readiness. You'll be here in an hour?

Yeah. Meet you at the cave entrance?

Fine.

Our mental conversation came to an abrupt halt. I hated the stilted nature of our chats these days. We used to spar in the midst of all the chaos.

Any more visions?

No.

You've mastered all the tasks. You're ready for this.

'Course I am.

I hesitated, wanting to ensure Joss was clear on who'd be doing the confronting in that cave.

You know this meeting is between me and the monster, right? I know you want to avenge your dad, but I just need you to be there for me.

There was a long pause.

I'm going to be with you every step of the way.

I know.

What we didn't know was how powerful Cadifor really was, or how far he'd go to get his hands on Arwen.

I know I've been a jerk these last few weeks, but it's for our own good. Focusing on what we need to do, you know?

While I didn't agree with his tactics, now wasn't the time to lay a guilt trip on him. *We're focused. We're ready. Let's do it.*

See you soon. And Holly?

Hmm?

I'll always be there for you.

As I eased the crystal from my forehead, I now had another clear motivation to stay alive.

Joss. Soulmates. Entwined destinies.

Keenan met us at the cave entrance, his mouth twisting into an evil grimace that passed for a smile.

"Welcome. You're expected." He held up a lantern, illuminating a narrow, dark passageway. "Follow me."

Fear jagged through me, raw, potent, and I dragged in deep

breaths, trying not to hyperventilate.

Joss touched my arm. "You don't have to do this."

Grateful for his presence, I shook my arms out and squared my shoulders.

"I do."

I hesitated for a second, thinking how great it would be to turn around and walk away from all of this. Back to a time before visions and teleporting and Arwen.

"We can wait—"

"We're out of options." Not a convincing declaration, considering hysteria edged my voice. "I can do this," I muttered.

Keenan swung back to face us, held the lantern high. "Is there a problem?"

"No problem," I said to Keenan, grateful my voice had steadied. No point tipping off the enemy I was scared witless.

"We must hurry. The sun will be in place shortly."

And point the way to Arwen, supposedly. The Sorority, Brigit, and I had been over this a thousand times, had scoured books, the legends, even picked Dyfan's brain. We thought we had all the answers. But how could we, when no one had ever seen Cadifor, let alone knew what he was capable of?

Keenan stopped, held up his hand. "Wait here."

"Don't—" *Leave us in the dark*, I wanted to say, but he'd already vanished, taking the lantern with him. My terror flared, burning bright, threatening to consume me.

"I'm right here." Joss stepped up behind me, so close I could feel him pressing against my back, solid, reassuring, a comfort as always.

"What's he up to?" I whispered, edging closer to Joss as I heard a faint scraping up ahead.

"Trying to intimidate us," he growled, resting both hands on my shoulders as footsteps came towards us in the dark. "Don't let him see your fear. It'll only feed his power trip."

Easy for you to say.

He squeezed my shoulders in response and eased away as Keenan rounded a corner, the lantern illuminating his hateful face. "Cadifor is ready for you."

How nice, the monster is receiving now.

The route we took to the Cave of the Sun was circuitous and winding. Cadifor was taking no chances; he wouldn't want a Sorority army storming down here if things went wrong. The closer we got to the end of the corridor the lighter it became. As we rounded a corner, the passageway widened, the ceiling considerably higher. My eyes slowly adjusted as we stopped on the threshold of a large chamber.

"This is where I leave you." A hint of annoyance flashed across Keenan's face. "Cadifor does not allow anyone to enter the Cave of the Sun without permission."

Uh-oh. What about Mom? I'd seen her there alongside him in my vision. She needed to be there.

Joss touched me lightly in the small of my back. "You expect us to believe the dark lord will be alone?"

Keenan shrugged. "It's not my place to question. I follow orders."

Not buying his dumb act for a second, Joss said, "Let me guess. Your orders are to block the exit just in case we make a run for it."

Straightening to his full height, Keenan glowered. "I don't answer to you." He pointed to a narrow stone archway at the opposite wall of the chamber. "Through that door is another chamber, larger than this one. The Cave of the Sun leads directly off it."

"Is my mom in there?"

"I don't know." Something flickered in Keenan's eyes. A hint of sadness? Of guilt? Who knew, maybe the bad guy had a conscience and there was something humanitarian in his approaching me in the glade.

When he moved to pass me, I stepped in front of him. "Has he harmed her?"

He glanced away. "She's alive."

I clenched my fists, ready to pound something. Joss held me back and I let Keenan go.

"You'll get nothing more out of him, he's a lackey."

"He sidestepped my question." My voice shook. "Must be bad."

Joss cupped my chin. "She's alive. Cadifor will make sure of it."

Only so he can get to me.

Dropping his hand, he glanced over my shoulder. "You know he'll try to use her to manipulate you?"

I nodded.

"You have to stay strong, whatever happens."

All perfectly logical and doable in the light of day, but down here in the cold, dank dimness, my steely backbone had turned to rubber.

But I'd come this far. I had to do this. Now.

"Come on, we're wasting time."

He grinned at my sudden bravado. "That's my girl."

I had to lighten the mood, do anything to detract from the fact my knees had started knocking together. "I could be, if you weren't so damn stubborn."

His thumb brushed my cheek for an all-too-brief moment. "We'll debate it later. For now, we have a job to do." He assumed his usual position, on my right and slightly behind, ready to protect me.

We stepped into the chamber. It was empty, eerily so. We crossed it quickly. Our footsteps were muffled by the dirt floor. If our approach couldn't be heard, that didn't bode well for whatever nasties that might creep up on us.

I paused at the arched doorway. Though Joss stood close, the chill of the stones seeped into me, strumming my spine with frosty fingers. I couldn't see beyond the archway, but the miasma of evil permeating the air raised the fine hairs on my arms.

"Ready?" Joss's steady tone didn't betray an ounce of fear. I admired him for that. With his solid heat at my back, I could do this.

I nodded. "Let's do it."

Willing my legs to stop quaking, I peered into the inky darkness.

One step.

Two.

With my third step, I entered the Cave of the Sun.

And screamed.

CHAPTER TWENTY-NINE

Blood covered the walls.

I stopped dead, gawking at the spirals, triquetras, and triskelions etched in vivid crimson.

"He's trying to psych you out," Joss murmured in my ear.

It's working. I balled my hands into fists to stop from grabbing Joss and making a run for it while we still could.

"Welcome, Holly Burton. So nice of you to finally join me."

I flinched despite my best efforts to appear calm. I hated that voice, that flat, cold monotone, so much scarier live than in my visions. It ripped through my fake bravado and tied my insides in painful knots. Fear churned like scalding acid in the pit of my stomach.

No way would I give *him* the satisfaction of seeing how much he terrified me.

Determined not to show my fear, I took a step forward. I couldn't even see him. "Where's my mom?"

Cadifor's glacial chuckle draped over me like a frigid cloak, intensely suffocating. "Impatience in one so young. Not a good trait to possess if hoping for a long life."

Joss stiffened at my back, his implied threat obvious.

"Let's cut the chitchat. You have something I want, I have something you want. So I repeat, where's my mom?"

"Your mother is awaiting our presence in the next chamber. I will call her in shortly. But first, step forward toward the altar."

I took a step forward and Cadifor bellowed, "Alone!"

Joss stiffened, but didn't budge.

It's okay. We need to do as he says. It's the only way we'll have a chance of getting out of here alive.

Joss traced the word NO on my back.

He won't try anything until I have Arwen, and that won't happen until the sun hits the altar. It'll take a few minutes. Play along.

Joss didn't like it.

"Now!"

We both jumped at Cadifor's shout.

I took the next few steps without Joss. He listened, his presence a comfort despite the increasing distance between us.

"I've waited a long time for this moment, Holly Burton."

It really pissed me off how Cadifor kept saying my surname, but what was I going to do, complain?

"I hear you've been down here a long time."

Oops. Maybe not the smartest move to antagonize the monster.

Joss snickered softly.

I couldn't see Cadifor beyond a robed shadow several very welcome feet away, so when he moved into the light I braced myself.

"As a descendant of the infidel that put me here, you'd know exactly how long I've been incarcerated."

Another step toward me.

"Robbed of my powers."

Another step closer.

"Forced to exist here rather than rule the Inner and Outer worlds as I should."

This time, he didn't yell. He didn't have to. He punctuated every precise word with venom.

I still couldn't see his face beneath the hood and that unnerved me as much as his restrained rage.

"So tell me, descendant of Belenus, how long is too long to wait for justice?"

A loaded question. "You're immortal. Time means nothing."

"Does it now?" He swung away from me, his cloak bellowing out behind him like an oil slick. "If time means nothing, tell me this. Have you spent the last sixteen years wondering where your precious mother was? What she was doing? Who she was doing it with?"

My stomach churned at his taunts, but I couldn't let him see how his poison stung.

He swung around so fast I took a step back. "Take your sixteen years, multiply that by a hundred thousand, and you'll have some idea of the torture I've endured being cooped up here."

"I'm not doing a thing until I see Mom."

"Very well." He inclined his head. "Enter, my Elphame. We have guests."

I'd mentally prepared for this moment for weeks. Years, in fact, counting all those secret wishes I'd harbored that one day I'd get a chance to see Mom again.

Now that the moment was here, I felt empty and drained and unprepared.

My mom stepped into the Cave of the Sun. She looked exactly the same as the photo I had by my bed at the cottage: long auburn hair flowing past her shoulders, blue eyes so dark they bordered on navy, flawless cream complexion. The visions hadn't done her justice. She'd appeared vague, fuzzy, washed out. In reality she was still stunning. And still the woman who'd run out on me and stood by this monster for sixteen years.

"Holly … "

I didn't know her voice. How could I, when she'd abandoned her baby? But somewhere, deep down on an instinctual level, I wanted to hear her talk. I wanted to hear her apologize and say all the comforting words of affection I should've heard all those years.

Cadifor turned to me. "As you can see, Holly Burton, your mother is perfectly well. Now for your end of the bargain."

I couldn't take my eyes off her. Despite Cadifor's reassurance she was well, I didn't buy it. Why was she propped in the doorway like a mannequin? Why was she so pale?

"You said the whole process would take several minutes." I

pointed upward. "And the sun isn't even overhead yet to pierce the hole in the roof. Let me talk to her."

I expected him to refuse, so he surprised me when he said, "As you wish." Turning to Mom, he said, "Rhiannon, my *Elphame*, come greet your long lost daughter properly."

As Mom stepped into the cave, I gasped.

The bastard had lied. She looked like she'd gone ten rounds with a prizefighter and lost. Livid bruises ringed her neck and arms. Finger marks traced from her collarbones to her ears, thumbprints near her carotid arteries. Deep purple edged in blues and golds, like kaleidoscopic proof of his cruelty. Despite my intense dislike for her, I instantly wanted to go to her.

Questions reeled in my head, but only one tumbled from my lips.

"Why?"

Mom didn't respond, her unwavering stare beseeching. For what? Forgiveness? Understanding?

Cadifor's chuckle pierced the silence like a chisel scraping on metal. "Go on, Rhiannon, tell her why you chose to abandon her. Why you took the other one."

The other one ...

She took the wrong one....

I dragged my gaze from Mom to Cadifor, chills racking my body, making me sway. "What did you just say?"

I couldn't see his face, but I could imagine a predatory grin, pure evil.

"It's not my place to tell you about your twin sister, Holly.

That's your dear mother's job."

Twin? *Sister?* No freaking way!

"Mom?"

Blood pounded in my ears, not loud enough. I wanted it to drown out my thoughts, my horrific, catastrophic thoughts, all of them centered around one horrible truth.

I had a sister, a twin, and Mom had taken *her* and left me behind.

Acid bubbled up in my throat. I clutched my stomach and moaned, a low, gut-wrenching groan of pain, of suffering. Joss was beside me in an instant.

"Get back!" Cadifor thundered. Joss didn't listen, sliding his arms around me and pulling me backwards.

"Get back or she dies!" Cadifor pointed at Mom, and in that instant I didn't care. I wanted her to suffer, just like she'd made me suffer all those years, which was nothing compared to what I'd suffered these last few minutes, learning I'd been dumped in favor of a sister I never knew I had.

"Go ahead," Joss said, inching me back towards the exit.

The rest happened in a blur.

Joss's arms were around me one second and gone the next. He crumpled to the floor. Keenan towered over him, holding a club and smacking it against his other palm.

The guy I loved lay on the ground, motionless. I froze, desperate to scream but unable to squeeze air through my closed-off throat.

I can't lose him, not now....

Keenan grabbed my arm and I struck out, swinging and kicking and writhing. It did nothing. Keenan dragged me toward the altar as the sun trickled through the roof aperture.

Cadifor laughed, an eerie humorless sound that chilled my blood.

Mom crossed to stand by Cadifor's side, so close they were touching.

I wanted to be brave, to face the monsters head on, but one glance at Joss lying stationary on the ground had me clutching the altar for support.

All eyes were on me as the sliver of sunlight started inching along the floor, creeping closer ...

None of us saw another person in the archway.

None of us saw her enter the cave.

None of us registered she was close until she uttered one word.

"Mom?"

CHAPTER THIRTY

"Shona, leave us!" Mom swung toward the girl in the doorway, fear twisting her face. Ironic, the first sentence I ever heard my mom utter was directed to my sister, not me. She cared about the girl. A hell of a lot more than she'd ever cared about me.

The girl frowned, a tiny crease that lowered one eyebrow and tilted the other. I sagged, my knees turning to mush, as the truth slammed into me like a wrecking ball.

Those visions ... two cribs, one empty ... the girl with the topaz eyes, trying to protect Nan from Keenan, hating me ...

Pieces of the puzzle slid into place, realigning to paint a picture I couldn't comprehend. My gaze swung from Mom to the girl in the doorway.

The girl, Shona, stared straight at me.

With luminous golden eyes.

Shock peppered my body like shrapnel from a bomb blast as I struggled to come to terms with the truth, and stupidly, I picked up on an insignificant thing: the sunburst medallion she'd been wearing in my vision had vanished.

"I'll explain later, honey. Just let me take care of things here." Mom smiled at Shona and the stab of betrayal sliced deep. Honey. Mom called her *honey*.

She'd abandoned me, chosen to take my sister over me, and now she stood there having a nice little chat with her precious *Shona* right in front of me, like I didn't exist. The rage I'd bottled for years erupted like a silent volcano.

I clenched and unclenched my hands, flushed and shaking, wanting to kill someone.

Shona glared at me. "Who's she?"

Nobody spoke, not even Cadifor, the bearer of glad tidings.

"Shona, sweetheart—"

I snapped. Seething, I launched myself at Mom, yelling obscenities, desperate to vent every ounce of pent-up bitterness that had been building for years.

"No! Get back to the altar!" Cadifor roared, roughly pushing Mom aside, making her stumble and fall.

I laughed, a loud, hysterical cackle I couldn't control as she crumpled in a heap, exactly where I wanted her.

I didn't feel pity. I felt nothing but rage, a frenzied storm of jealousy fuelling my temper and urging me to kick her while she was down.

She'd *left* me.

She'd chosen one child over another.

What kind of a maternal monster did that?

Guess I had my answer right there. She *was* a monster. Little wonder she kept the company she did.

Shona and Keenan rushed to Mom's side and I sniggered at their misplaced devotion.

Mom clutched my sister's hand for support, while I went face to face with a monster.

Cadifor's face remained hidden. He didn't speak, his silence unnerving me as much as his proximity. His fetid breath washed over me from his faceless cowl. I clenched the snow quartz around my neck, wishing I could miraculously conjure an army to stand alongside me.

But I didn't get an army. I got one better: the reedy voice of a lone warrior.

Use the stone.

Joss was okay. Relief shimmered through me—but then I realized he hadn't uttered the words. They'd come from somewhere deep in my head, like a seed of knowledge bursting and sprouting and growing.

Cadifor lunged for me.

I scrabbled backwards, clutching the snow quartz.

The stone. Of course!

"Go. Run away. Escape back to your false safety." His eerie monotone washed over me like sleet. "Do you think the real Queen of Elphame will allow you to rest?"

His harsh cackle raked nails of dread down my spine. "Beware, if she gets her hands on Arwen she'll create her own race of immortals, banish the Trio, and rule all worlds forever."

I had no idea who this crazy queen of death was and I wasn't planning on sticking around to find out. I grasped the pendant between my thumb and forefinger and pressed it to my forehead, summoning the heat of Bel that flowed through my veins. An instant flash of light slashed the gloom, a radiant sunburst like someone had scooped out the entire roof and let the sun in.

"Don't let Elphame gain control ... " Cadifor whispered, diving for the tunnel from where he'd come.

Blinded, I squinted in Mom's direction and saw a frozen tableau: Mom, Keenan, and Shona like one big happy family, all staring at me like I'd lost my mind.

Though she didn't deserve one second of my time, I knew I'd kick myself for the rest of my life if I didn't take this chance. "Mom, you've got one shot at making this right. Come with me."

Shona stumbled and grabbed at Mom to steady her. "What's she talking about?"

"I'll tell you later, honey."

Still with the barf-worthy sentiments. *Sweetheart. Honey.* I wanted to puke.

Mom didn't say anything to me. She merely shook her head, turned away, and followed Cadifor, taking the last sliver of my faith in the bonds of family with her.

Shona glared at me, her hatred staggeringly intense.

In that moment Keenan lunged at me. I fell, scrabbling backward on my hands and feet.

I connected with something solid—Joss—and Keenan flung himself at me. To protect myself from the incoming assault I rolled onto my side, into the fetal position, and found myself inches away from Joss, our faces almost touching.

Joss's expressive blue eyes sparked with approval, long enough for me to know I was doing the right thing. I closed my own as I held the snow quartz to my forehead, tilting my head so the sunlight I'd created could stream down upon us.

And let the comforting heat come.

CHAPTER THIRTY-ONE

When I opened my eyes, Quinn and Raven towered over me.

I squeezed my eyes shut, willing my rolling stomach to subside.

I had a sister I never knew existed who hated my guts. And a mom who hated me just as much. What else could explain what she'd done all those years ago? And why she'd done it again, choosing to stay with the devil and her other daughter dearest over me?

I could hear Raven whispering to Quinn. It struck me that my friends must've followed me to the shed. My eyes eased open. Raven waved her hand in front of my face. "Anyone home?"

I swatted her hand away. "I'm fine. But I need you to give me a moment while I do something."

"Something other than lose consciousness for the last two

hours?" Quinn's sarcasm was welcome. At least he was talking to me again.

I held up my hand. "Give me five minutes and I'll explain everything."

Raven shrugged. "Fine. You've kept your friends in the dark this long, what's another few minutes?"

Quinn merely snorted.

Patting down my pockets, I found the trans-channeling crystal and yanked it free. "I'm going to be out of it again for a little while but I'll be back soon. Promise."

I didn't wait for their response, desperate to talk to Joss and see if he'd survived. I'd used my powers to escape because he'd made me promise to do so if I faced a life-or-death confrontation. I couldn't believe I'd left him there, injured, battling Keenan. I couldn't lose him, not now. I needed him more than ever.

Pressing the crystal to my forehead, I closed my eyes, focused.

Joss? You okay?

My blood ran cold at the silence.

Hey, Warrior Boy. Stop taking the heroic act to extremes and check in.

Nothing. Not a whisper of a smartass retort.

Joss, please. Speak to me. Tell me you're okay. I've got to annoy you about that soulmate thing, remember? And I still have to kick your ass for lying to me about everything. And I still don't trust you like me for any other reason than you're using me to get to Cadifor so you can kill him yourself. But I'm pathetic and you're the first guy I've really been into and that kiss ... you were great and I really, really want to do it again soon. I don't know what to do. I mean, I know what I want to do with you, but that scares me too, you know?

I've never done it before. And I want you to be my first. So answer me, dammit, before I teleport back there right this very instant and kill you myself.

My voice cracked, tears stinging my eyes, and then I heard a faint gasp.

Joss?

I heard a drawn out wheeze, the pained sound of someone dragging in air.

You're alive!

Another long, agonizing indrawn breath, a hiss out. *'Course I'm alive. Someone's gotta have your back.*

Have me back, you mean?

He grunted and I smiled, beyond relieved. *How did you get out of there?*

Whipped Keenan's ass good.

And Cadifor?

Didn't reappear. He couldn't, with that sunlight trick you pulled.

I hesitated, the hurt too raw for me to even speak their names.

I didn't see your mom or Shona either. They fled along with him.

Disgust churned in my stomach. Mom had chosen Shona over me. What sort of a mother did that?

Holly, I got the truth out of Keenan before he lost consciousness.

The truth?

About your mom and Shona.

I didn't want to hear platitudes. I didn't want to hear excuses. What I wanted to hear was this was all some bizarre dream and I'd wake up back at Nan's cottage with her baking banana bread while I re-read *The Hunger Games* for the umpteenth time.

Maybe hearing the truth would calm me. Anything was better than this edgy, spiky feeling I was about to explode. *Tell me.*

Because your mom's a direct descendant of Bel, any female child of hers would be watched closely by Cadifor. When she had twins, he knew one of you could be the chosen one, so he ordered Keenan to kidnap your mom and the Scion.

I hated that word, Scion. *Go on.*

When Keenan came for your mother, he made her choose which child to take.

"*She took the wrong one.*" Nan's words made perfect sense now. No wonder she was shocked into a stroke when I told her about the visions. She'd raised me the last sixteen years believing I was the normal one, only to discover my mom had botched big time.

Apparently, Shona had those weird golden eyes and exhibited advancements beyond her age, even at six months, so your mom thought she was the one.

Well, well, well, the joke's on her. My bitterness didn't help ease the rage seething just beneath the surface. I'd managed to put a lid on it during that confrontation, but only because I'd had no choice. If Cadifor hadn't lunged at me, I would've taken another shot at Mom. And that round, she wouldn't have gotten up off the canvas. I would've given TKO a whole new meaning.

So why did Cadifor keep her and Mom alive all these years? If he knew where I was, why not come and snatch me?

Because he didn't know Shona wasn't the one 'til you came along. She could've exhibited abilities any second, but then you showed up in Eiros. Cadifor got curious with the rumors flying around about the newest Sorority member, and then your mom recognized you in a photo and he knew.

Good old Mom, landing me in the crap again. *He had Shona, so why keep Mom around?*

Joss's lengthy pause indicated I wouldn't like the answer.

He calls her his Elphame. The original Queen of Elphame ruled the Otherworld. She presided over death and destruction. You know Cadifor's buddies, Mider and Nemain, are part of the Dark Trio? Elphame was Mider's consort. She felt like the slighted, inferior female to the powerful trio, so she was intent on ruling on her own. Rumor has it Elphame has reincarnated yet again, and taken on a human body to continue her quest for domination of the worlds.

This echoed what the monster had told me before he'd vanished, something about me returning to false safety, and in that instant I wondered if this reincarnated queen was someone I knew. But for now, I needed to hear it spelled out why Cadifor kept Mom around to completely eradicate any lingering sympathy I might have had for her being kidnapped.

So why does he call her Elphame when she clearly isn't?

Because she stood by him, he considers her his queen. Initially a captive, she has roamed the labyrinth freely for many years.

And Shona?

Keenan wouldn't elaborate. I got the impression he has a soft spot for your mother and has tried to protect her when things got rough with Cadifor.

How touching. I wanted to puke. My mom, with a bad case of Stockholm syndrome, falls for a monster like Cadifor?

What was she thinking?

As for my sister, I had no idea what her story was, but surely she'd want to escape that hellhole? I couldn't begin to comprehend what it would've been like for her, being raised by two monsters, trapped underground. It was like something out of *America's Most Wanted*, one of those horrific, heart-wrenching stories involving kids being locked up and abused for years.

My sister had been like those victims.

And that's when I started to feel sorry for her.

No one deserved that kind of treatment, and while I'd disliked her on sight due to the simple fact Mom didn't, that wasn't Shona's fault. She simply hadn't known any better. While I couldn't understand her hatred for me, and had no intention of trying to figure it out, I could excuse it. I was free. She was still cooped up with those lunatics.

Then another annoying twinge of remorse niggled at me. While Wolfebane High had sucked most days, at least I'd had the opportunity to attend school. Was she educated? Did she have hobbies? Was she aware another world existed above ground?

Throwing a pity party for the *unchosen one* was getting me nowhere, so I refocused.

So my mom's shacked up with a monster and has a not-so-secret admirer. Anything else?

You were amazing. Joss's voice, barely above a whisper, filtered through my mind, warming me despite our distance apart.

I almost lost it at the end there.

But you came through.

Without Arwen, though.

Doesn't matter. We don't have it, but neither does Cadifor. Time to reevaluate, plan a new strategy.

The thought of going through it all again turned my stomach, because essentially nothing had changed.

I was still the Scion.

I still had to find Arwen before Cadifor did.

As for the answers I'd so desperately craved from my mom, guess I had the big one answered when she ignored my invitation to escape and walked away from me.

First she chose Shona over me; now she'd chosen Cadifor over me.

Thanks, Mom, got the message loud and clear. You don't give a rat's ass about me. You never did.

Have you ever thought your mom's doing what she can to survive and to keep Shona safe?

You're not supposed to read my mind from a distance.

Lucky guess. It probably killed her to leave you behind, but what if she had no option? Keenan would've threatened her somehow, maybe even threatened to kill you, the one she left behind, perhaps your Nan too, if she didn't go with him. What choice would she have?

She could've fought back, she could've fought for *me*, I wanted to scream at him. But I knew that wasn't true. I'd stood against the monsters now, knew what they were capable of. No way could Mom have fought Keenan, not when she had two babies to protect.

Joss might have been right, but it didn't change what had happened less than thirty minutes earlier.

I'd given Mom a choice.

Me or the monster.

And she'd walked away from me a second time without a backward glance.

Holly, you okay?

Yeah, just thinking about happy families.

And how through all of this, the Sorority, Quinn, and Raven had stood by me. They'd been more of a family to me than my mom ever had. At least at C.U.L.T. and at Eiros I'd gained the acceptance I'd craved for so long.

Mack, Maeve, and Oscar are here. They say hi and thanks for everything.

I didn't do anything. Not really.

You did plenty. Lowering his voice, he said, *You're amazing, Holly. I want you to know that.*

Right back at you, Warrior Boy.

He chuckled. *Lie low for a day or two, let us check out the fallout here, then contact me and we'll talk about how soon you can come back, okay?*

Okay.

I didn't want our chat to end yet, not when I had so much to say but no idea how to say it.

Joss, about that soulmate thing—

You weren't the only one who learned a thing or two today. I had this fear I'd fail, that not being a born warrior, I wouldn't be able to protect you when it counted, that maybe my feelings would get in the way, but you know something? No matter how much I stay away from you and treat you like my protégé, I still care.

My heart did a somersault and a goofy grin spread across my face.

In fact, I used my feelings for you to summon strength after Keenan clubbed me, so ultimately this thing between us? It's kinda special.

Cool! I silently cringed. Could I sound any dorkier?

Stay warm, my Holly. Until we meet again.

Soon, I added, easing the crystal from my forehead with regret. *My Holly* echoed through my heart and made me want to go back this very minute.

"About damn time. A girl can't wait around all day, you know."

My eyelids cranked open to find Raven grinning at me, her heavily kohled eyes sparkling with mischief. "Whatever you were just doing, whoever you were talking to? Must've been some chat."

I glanced at a stony-faced Quinn. "Why?"

"Because you had the soppiest smile on your face. And you kept blushing."

I fanned myself. "That's because it's hot in here."

Raven jerked a thumb at the carefully arranged stone roof. "I'm not surprised, with all those rocks. It's spooky and claustrophobic in here."

Quinn darted a knowing glance overhead, obviously connecting the shape of the stones in the roof to the stone archways around the school. "Though something tells me you haven't exactly been conscious when you hang out here."

I raised an eyebrow. "Did you tell her?"

He nodded, his mouth in an obstinate twist, while Raven bounced on her heels.

"Can't understand how that moron didn't believe you could teleport. With the range of abilities in this place you'd think he'd accept whatever you said." She glared at Quinn, poked her tongue out. "Especially from a *friend*."

"It's okay," I said, "I don't blame Quinn for not believing me, considering all I've kept from you."

Raven shrugged. "You must've had your reasons."

My heart twanged for the second time in as many minutes. This was the true meaning of family: acceptance, non-judgment, loyalty, being there through good times and bad.

I'd never shut my friends out again.

"Yeah, there was some heavy stuff going on for a while, and I wished I could tell you, but it wasn't safe."

Understanding lit Quinn's eyes as the familiar quirky smile I'd missed curved his lips. I had my friend back and I could've hugged him. "You were protecting us?"

"Uh-huh."

He took a deep breath and puffed out his chest, stopping just short of beating it, and Raven rolled her eyes. "Those bumps on your chest? Not muscles. They're the start of man-boobs 'cause you acted like such a girl and wouldn't give Holly the benefit of the doubt."

Quinn flipped her the bird. I snorted. If he'd had Drake's talent, Raven would've been ashes. As it was, she blew him a kiss and we started laughing.

I'd needed the tension release, and once I started laughing I couldn't stop. Raven didn't help when she made cupping actions on Quinn's chest and mimed snapping his bra straps, which set us off again.

"You're an idiot," he said, his wide grin telling us he'd enjoyed the joke as much as we did. "But can Holly continue the story?"

Raven poked her tongue at Quinn before focusing on me.

Thankful to be back here, surrounded by my friends, I hugged my knees to my chest. "Cutting a long story short, I'm a descendant of Belenus, the Celtic sun god. Apparently I'm the Scion, the only one who can find Arwen, a biokinetic icon capable of achieving immortality."

Raven's eye lit up. "Just like the philosopher's stone. Wicked!"

I chuckled. "Harry Potter I ain't, because I didn't find it and I didn't defeat my version of Voldemort."

Raven patted me on the arm. "Not to worry. Harry had seven books to do it. You'll get another chance."

Just like that, the magnitude of what I still faced hit me.

I had to find Arwen, defeat Cadifor, and save the world. To do so, I had to continue my studies at Eiros and learn what being a true Sorority member meant—all while mastering my abilities at C.U.L.T. and passing high school.

Not to mention the other questions bugging me: Was there a deeper reason behind my mom's defection to the dark side? What was Shona's story? Who was this mysterious Queen of Elphame? How soon would Cadifor come after me again?

Quinn offered me his hand and I took it, allowing him to pull me to my feet. He didn't release it when we stood almost toe-to-toe.

"I'm sorry for doubting you, for not being there for you when you needed me most."

I squeezed his hand. "You're here now, aren't you?"

"But—"

"Listen up, you two. You're the best friends I've ever had and just knowing you're on my side is enough."

I could've sworn Raven sniffled, which made me tear up. Quinn rolled his eyes. "If you two start blubbering, I'm out of here."

Raven and I smiled through our tears. In that moment, the bond between us and the friendship we shared gave me courage.

I would find Arwen.

I would conquer Cadifor.

Or die trying.

LIFE, A.D.
Life, After. Dez.

MICHELLE E. REED

A Preview from LIFE, A.D. (Life, After. Dez.)

by Michelle E. Reed

Coming from Month9Books in December 2013

CHAPTER ONE

The world around me is fuzzy.

I'm lying on the ground and my face is wet. I blink. Drawing in a shot of frigid air, I shudder at the sensation of a million needles in my throat. Pain sets fire to my leg and shoots up my spine. My left arm is numb, useless. And my right arm is—gone? Mangled?

I don't know.

Don't panic. The fear grows and festers, running through my bloodstream like a virus.

My breath comes in short, desperate gasps. The drumbeat rhythm of my heart pounds against my chest, sending shockwaves to my fingers and toes.

My thoughts reach across five years, coming to rest on my last memory of Aaron. His lifeless body was still and silent, an empty shell of the boy I loved. I'm not ready to be with you. Not yet.

I jerk my head off the ground. A scream escapes my lips as

burning pain engulfs my every molecule. I fight to move. My unresponsive limbs refuse to help me shift position.

I need help.

Panic steals my concentration and threatens to drag me away. Blackness creeps into the edges of my vision, sending my labored breathing into overdrive.

I'm going to die here.

"Somebody, please ... " My voice is unrecognizable, deep and gurgling. I gag on blood and saliva.

Where am I?

I lift my head again in a frantic effort to get my bearings. I'm on the side of the road by a forest. Only the tiniest of buds peek from the trees and shrubs, and after staring at them for a bit, I swear I can see them shiver. I, too, tremble, cold and shaken.

A chickadee sings out its springtime call from a nearby tree, whistling "sweet weather" and waiting for a reply. A crunch of snow from the nearby forest signals a passing animal.

Frost is still rooted in the ground, and the sky refuses to allow sunshine through the thick layer of haze. There is a freshness to the air. That must be what people mean when they say it smells like spring.

The deserted stretch of highway offers little hope; the animals and forest are the only witnesses as life slips from my grasp.

No one is coming.

The blackness advances. I'm getting colder, the numbness spreading down my body from my arms.

The sound of my ringtone snaps me back to reality. Where's my

phone? My teeth clench in agony. I manage to turn my head.

How did I get here?

The phone is well out of reach—ten feet or so away, ringing despite being trapped under the crumpled remains of the overturned car. My shoulder spasms, and what's left of my mangled right arm flops into view. My mind resists the image: twisted, bloodied flesh ripped from the visible bones of my forearm.

My outstretched fingers refuse to budge, even to escape the slow-moving pool of red creeping toward them.

My ragged breathing accelerates, my heart races, and I do something I've never done before: I pray.

Stay calm.

Survive.

The sound of a distant whistle breaks through my raspy, disjointed plea for mercy, for life.

***

My breath fogs up the window as I stare into the dark night from my seat. The landscape is a stark and eerie blur whipping past with unimaginable speed.

"A train?" A strange echo distorts my voice. Terror threatens to roll over me like a tidal wave.

How did I get here?

There was a crash. A car accident. It was early morning.

Why is it dark out?

I cover my face with my hands, and it hits me: my arms work again. I stretch out my hands and wiggle my fingers. Both of my arms are unharmed. Pristine.

What's happening to me?

The vast expanse of nothingness outside the window provides no clues—no hint of place, time, or destination. The only certainty is my need to get home.

A pale hand comes to rest on my shoulder. An older man in an immaculate suit and overcoat braces against me for support as he sits down. "Sorry about that, sweetheart." His voice is distant, hollow.

I close my eyes. The scream of crumpling metal rings in my ears.

I smell gasoline. Burned rubber. The engine hisses as fluids trickle through the overturned car to the pavement.

There's the rumble of an approaching diesel engine. The gravel pops as the vehicle comes to a stop. A door opens and shuts.

"Aw, shit," a man says. His footfalls are quick as he approaches. His phone beeps three times. "I need an ambulance! I'm on County D, about half a mile north ... "

"Haven't used my legs in a long time," says the man in the suit. He tips his hat as he settles in his seat. "Looks like I need a refresher course." The hollow ring to his voice is gone. He turns his attention to the window and shakes his head, his eyes bright with fascination. "There are more things in heaven and earth, Horatio, than are dreamt of in your philosophy."

A moan seeps from me like a toxic cloud.

He puts a gentle hand on my arm. "Oh, now, everything's going to be fine. You'll see."

"I need to get out of here. My mom must be getting worried by now."

"She'll be okay."

"No, she won't! I wrecked the car. I have to explain. I have to get home."

"I don't think we get to go home—not from this." He gives the car a calm, methodical appraisal and nods.

Why isn't he panicking?

"Don't say that." Grief and terror shake my body as I lean into this stranger's shoulder and allow myself to fall apart.

Time eludes me. For five minutes, or perhaps five hours, I cry ugly, desperate tears.

"Feel better?" he finally asks.

My breakdown has reduced from a crescendo of panic to a quiet sniffle. I nod, catching my breath. "A little." My tears have run dry, but the feeling of dread remains. I try to wipe the mess I've made of his lapel clean with the back of my hand. "Your coat's ruined."

He waves off my concern. "Don't worry about it. They may have sent me in my best suit, but I don't think it will matter where we're going."

Panic grabs me again. "No. God, no. We can't be—"

"Ten minutes ago, I was lying in the hospital bed that's crammed into my living room. Now I'm on a train."

His words are a punch in the gut, driving me to my feet. "I have

5

to find my mom."

Even if it's to say goodbye.

His blue eyes are calm as he looks up from his seat. "Doesn't seem right, you being so young and all." He extends a steady hand to me. "The name's Sam, by the way."

"I'm Dez."

"Nice to meet you, Dez. The train's a bit of a shocker, huh? Did you hear it coming? The distant rumble before it all went ... " He trails off as he searches for the right word. " ... lopsided?"

I collapse back into my seat. "Can we please talk about something else?"

"We sure can."

"This is all so ... " I scan the car, still looking for answers. Gleaming hardwood moldings in a rich, deep red run the length of the car. I run my fingers across the repeating lotus flower pattern. The wood is smooth as glass. Soft light filters down from the octagonal stained-glass fixtures above, leaving multi-hued patterns on the royal purple seats and plush emerald carpet. The colorful lights shift and dance on my arms.

This must be what it's like inside a kaleidoscope.

Sam settles back into his seat. "Have you ever been on a train before?"

"No," I say, but a memory flashes in my mind. "Wait, that's not true. When I was little. My parents took me to Chicago on a train."

"I wonder if this one has an observation car."

"Who cares? I just want to find a way off."

"I don't think you want to go out there, dear girl, all alone, and

no idea where we are. It sounds like a bad idea to me."

"Worse than just sitting here, waiting for god knows what?"

"Let's at least find out if there's an observation car. That way we might be able to get the lay of the land."

"Fine," I concede.

Sam leads the way, and it seems we have the place to ourselves. Following close behind, I catch our reflections in the window and notice I'm wearing my favorite sundress. It's the color of a ripe peach, and I've always loved the way it pops against my dark skin. It gives me an odd feeling of comfort to be joined in this place by something so simple that I love. I pause for a moment to smooth the gauzy fabric against my thighs.

Sam slides open the door to the next car. The two cars are swaying in slightly different rhythms as we speed down the track. I take an unsteady step across the threshold.

As the second door clicks behind me, I'm astonished to find an ancient-looking man falling asleep in his seat. His hat is tipped down over his eyes, and his breathing is slow and heavy. A pale, gaunt woman sits two rows ahead of him. She's murmuring to herself and rocking back and forth in a daze with her arms wrapped around her body. She doesn't seem to notice us as we pass.

We find our way to a car with picture windows running its length on both sides. Sam takes a seat on a vibrant plum-colored couch, and I join him.

He squints as he stares out the window. "Well, I can't see a damn thing."

"Does it matter? I'm not sure I want to see where we're going."

"Pessimism doesn't suit you."

I roll my eyes. "You don't even know me." An idea pops into my head, and I sit up from my slouch. "Then again, maybe you do. Maybe you're some sort of reaper, and you've been following me my whole life." I shake my head. "Problem is, I don't believe in any of that crap."

"I assure you, I am quite real, and not a reaper. Or at least I was real. I'm not so sure what we are right now."

From the next car we hear the muffled voice of an approaching man.

"I'd wager that's the conductor," Sam offers.

The man enters our car, walking through as though on patrol. "Next stop, Atman Station! This is our final destination. Upon arrival, exit on the left side of the train. Please have your ticket out and ready for inspection. You will be given further instructions on the platform. This is the four-thirteen express to Atman Station!" The door shuts with a click as he leaves.

Sam reaches into his coat pocket and pulls out a boarding pass tucked into a ticket sleeve. "Looks like I'm going to track eight, platform R, train ... " He scratches the stubble on his chin as he searches. " ... twenty-six. How about you?"

I make a quick inventory of my surroundings. "I never got a ticket."

Sam smiles. "I'm sure it's just an oversight."

Something's wrong. "I'm going to go check back at our seats. Maybe I left my ticket there." I hurry to the door.

My speed increases as I move through the cars. I'm almost at a run as I rush past the catatonic woman and the sleepy old man.

Back at my seat, I take a frantic, hopeless inventory. On hands and knees, I search the floor and the crevices between the seat cushions.

It's not here.

The door clicks as someone enters the car. I jump to my feet and pivot, nearly crashing headlong into the conductor.

"I—I don't have a ticket."

He frowns. "You'll receive instructions at the station. Now if you don't mind … " He sidesteps in an attempt to get around me.

I grab his arm. "Wait. Maybe I'm not supposed to be here. I could be on the wrong train, or maybe it's just a mistake."

He stares down at my hand.

"If you're here, young lady, it's because you're meant to be."

"But—"

"We don't make mistakes. Now take a seat. We'll be at the station shortly."

I trudge back to the observation car and collapse on the couch next to Sam.

"Didn't find it?" he asks.

"No."

"I'm sure they'll get it straightened out once we get there."

We fall silent, staring out into the vast darkness.

Sam lets out a deep sigh. "That bastard cancer got me. How about you?"

I shake my head, refusing to answer.

Forget everything you know.
Let the fire consume you.

INTO THE FIRE

BOOK 1 IN THE BIRTH OF THE PHOENIX SERIES

KELLY HASHWAY

Nicola Marsh

USA TODAY bestselling author Nicola Marsh writes flirty fiction with flair for adults and riveting, eerie stories for young adults.

Based in Melbourne, she has published 40 books and sold over 4 million copies worldwide. She writes contemporary romances for Harlequin Mills & Boon and Entangled Publishing. Her first indie release, *Crazy Love*, was a 2012 ARRA (Australian Romance Readers Award) finalist. *Banish*, a thriller with Harlequin Teen Australia, was her young adult debut, closely followed by the release of a paranormal YA series starting with *Scion of the Sun* from Month9Books.

She's also a Waldenbooks and BookScan bestseller, a National Readers' Choice Award winner, a multi-finalist for awards including the Romantic Times Reviewers' Choice Award, RBY

ACKNOWLEDGEMENTS

Thanks to the following people who were onboard for this book's publication ride:

Georgia McBride, founder of Month9Books, who fell in love with my story super fast and snapped up the entire series. Great working with you, Georgia.

Hallie Tibbetts, my editor, for her insight and wisdom. (And invaluable assistance in showing me the difference between Aussie-isms and Americanisms!)

My writing buddies Natalie Anderson and Soraya Lane, who are with me every step of the way with every book I write. Your support is invaluable. Thanks from the bottom of my heart.

Jennifer L. Armentrout, who took time out of her busy schedule to read *Scion of the Sun* and provide a fabulous cover quote. Much appreciated.

To all the supremely talented YA authors out there, like Suzanne Collins, Cassandra Clare, Richelle Mead, and many others, who sparked my love for all things YA.

To my supportive readers, who buy my books, whether contemporary romance or spooky YA. You're the best!

To my hubby Martin, keep the laughs coming, babe. You keep me on my toes and young enough to write YA.

To my amazing sons, you're my inspiration for everything I do. I can't wait until you're old enough to read this book! Love you infinity plus infinity. And then some more.

(RWAus Romantic Book of the Year), HOLT Medallion, Booksellers' Best Award, Golden Quill, Laurel Wreath, and More than Magic, and has won several CataRomance Reviewers' Choice Awards.

A physiotherapist for thirteen years, she now adores writing full time, chasing after her two little heroes, barracking loudly for her North Melbourne Kangaroos footy team, and her favorite, curling up with a good book!

She also loves interacting with readers. She blogs at http://nicolamarsh.blogspot.com, Tweets incessantly at http://twitter.com/NicolaMarsh, chatters on Facebook at http://facebook.com/NicolaMarshAuthor, and answers emails at nicola@nicolamarsh.com. Come say hi!

A Preview from INTO THE FIRE

by Kelly Hashway

Coming from Month9Books in February 2014

CHAPTER ONE

Cara

In one month, I'm going to die and be reborn from my own ashes. I'll forget everything and nearly everyone I know. But I can't worry about that right now. Jeremy needs me. And I need him to remember. Remember me.

The smoke wafts up from the basement. This is more than just Jeremy setting his pillow on fire again. It's time. He's going to be reborn. Mom and I rush downstairs to find him standing next to his bed, staring at his arms, already beginning to ripple with the first signs of fire. I'm not sure who's more freaked out right now, Jeremy or me.

"We have to get him to the bathtub before he burns the whole room down with him." Mom's voice is calm, and she's already leading Jeremy to the bathroom. I follow, not having a clue what to do or how to help. He steps into the tub and stares at Mom, looking like a scared toddler.

"Relax, Jeremy. The flames won't harm you. Keep telling yourself that. There's no pain during a rebirth, and your body will know what to do on its own. Don't fight it."

"Remember," he chokes out. The word is followed by a puff of smoke. The only people he'll remember when he's reborn are other Phoenixes like us. Everyone else will be a stranger to him, no matter how close they once were.

"You'll remember us. I promise." Mom reaches for his hand, but flames rise from his fingers and palm. She grabs the shower curtain, yanking it down before it catches fire.

I bite my tongue to hold back my tears as the flames spread up Jeremy's arms and across his chest. They dance and flicker until only his head is visible.

"I'm so proud of you, Jeremy." Mom's eyes fill with tears.

I'm terrified for Jeremy but jealous at the same time. He's my little brother, but in a way, going through the rebirthing process makes him the older one now. I shudder as the flames shoot from where Jeremy's eyes used to be. It's like something straight out of a horror movie. My eyes close, unable to watch anymore. When I force them open again, Jeremy is gone. Nothing but a pile of ashes.

"What's going to happen?" I ask, even though I already know the answer. He'll be reborn. I never stopped to think about the whole rising out of the ashes part. I kind of assumed that was just a metaphorical thing, that the flames would die out and he'd still be standing there, only different somehow. But Jeremy is gone.

Mom squeezes my hand. "It will be okay. Give him time."

My heart hammers with each passing second. Why is this taking so long? I count in my head. Forty-five seconds. Fifty. Fifty-five. The ashes stir and take shape. "Jeremy!" In moments, he's lying in the bathtub in the same pajamas he was wearing when this began. I'm afraid to touch him. Afraid he's not real.

Mom reaches for his hand, but he backs away. A vague recognition flashes on his face, but there's nothing behind it. No feeling. He knows who we are, but it's clear he doesn't remember much else, like the fact that he loves us and we love him. "You did beautifully, honey."

What's so beautiful about watching my fifteen-year-old brother burst into flames, turn to a pile of ashes, and rise up out of them, reborn? I can still smell the smoke. See it in the air. Mom disabled the smoke alarms when we moved in—otherwise, we'd set them off on a regular basis. Jeremy looks around the room, disoriented. Everything is unfamiliar to him. I thought I'd feel better seeing Jeremy is okay, but I don't think he is. Not really.

He grips the tub and finally stands. His eyes go up to the black mark on the ceiling, the only physical sign of his rebirth. The ashes are gone—a part of him again. He shuts his eyes, and I wonder if he's reliving the experience.

"How do you feel?" That's not really what I want to ask, but Mom's giving me the look. The one that says, watch your tongue. Forget that *I'm* freaking out. I have so many questions. What does the fire feel like? Will I be aware of what's happening while I'm being reborn, or is it really like dying and coming back to life? I

3

wish the questions could drown out the sound of my heart breaking.

Jeremy looks at me like he doesn't know me. Like I'm a complete stranger. "I feel fine. A little hot."

"Let's check your temperature to make sure everything is as it should be." Mom grabs the thermometer from the medicine cabinet and presses it to Jeremy's forehead. He pulls away for a second but gives in when Mom smiles at him. How can he not remember us? "Your temperature is one hundred thirty degrees," the mechanical voice says.

"Perfectly normal." Mom puts the thermometer away and motions for Jeremy to step out of the bathtub. He's barely moved since he rose from his ashes. Mom's careful not to touch him, and I can't help wondering why. Is he sensitive to touch because of the fire? Or will he freak out having people he doesn't really know anymore holding his hand?

My palms sweat, and I don't know if it's because the room is still so hot from the fire or if my temperature is rising again. I woke up with a fever yesterday. The first sign of my rebirth. My temperature was one hundred and nine degrees, nothing compared to Jeremy's, but that's how I know I have one month left in this life. First it's the fever, then come the dreams. I'm not looking forward to those. After having a front row seat to Jeremy's rebirth, I'm not sure how I'm going to handle having visions of my own.

Jeremy looks around the room, his face darkening. I reach for him, but he stares at me, expressionless. I swallow the lump in my throat. "Come on. Let's look around your room." Mom said he'd pick up on things pretty quickly, but we're going to have to remind him of what he likes and dislikes, who his friends are, how much he loves us. That last one rips what's left of my heart to shreds. How do you relearn feelings? How do I make him understand that he and I are inseparable? My friends are his friends. We share everything. We're a year apart, but we may as well be twins. We know each other that well. Or at least we did.

He comes with me, but his eyes are jumping from one object to another. Posters of bands litter his walls. His laptop is open but in sleep mode. Dirty clothes are piled in a corner. He runs his hands over everything—books, the basketball on his desk chair, his guitar—testing how each object feels. He walks right by his iPod on his nightstand without even looking at it or the play lists he loves so much.

"Cara." My name on Jeremy's lips is like a knife to the heart. There's no feeling behind it. He's saying it like he's trying to commit it to memory, which means Mom had to *tell him* my name. I was too lost in my own misery to hear her. A tear trickles from my eye, sizzling and turning to smoke before it can fall to the floor. One month. One month, and I'll be like Jeremy. I'll forget everything. The only positive I can cling to is knowing this ache in my chest will go away because I won't remember this feeling.

"Mom." My voice shakes. I feel like I'm five again because I just want my mommy.

Jeremy stares at me. "Why are you crying?" His eyes are sympathetic, but the emotion stops there.

"I—" I don't know the words to say what I'm feeling, not that he'll understand anyway. To him, I'm just Cara, his sister. That's all he knows about me.

"Here." Mom hands Jeremy the scrapbook she helped him make. Pictures of our friends with their names written under them litter the pages. His memory book. I have one, too. Mom and I started making it when I was six. "Study the names and faces. The sooner you can remember who your friends are, the sooner you can start being around people again."

Jeremy squints at the faces staring up at him from the page. "This girl …" He points. "She has her arm around me. Is she my girlfriend?"

It's Rachel. Jeremy's crush of the last two years and my best friend. "No, she's a friend."

"She's pretty." That's a good sign. He's still attracted to her. Maybe the pictures will jog other feelings, memories even. Jeremy had hand selected each photo, filling the book with things that meant the most to him. If anything is going to remind him of his old life, it's this.

"Do you know who this is?" I point to Nick, another mutual friend. "He gave you the posters on your walls. Do you remember? He taught you to play the guitar."

Jeremy shakes his head. "I feel like I woke up in someone else's life." He throws the memory book on the bed and walks to the window, looking out. "Will they come back at all? The memories? Or do I have to relearn them and just smile and nod when my *friends* bring them up?" The word "friends" is laced with sarcasm.

I put my hand on his shoulder. "They'll be your friends again.

As soon as you spend time with them, you'll see how well you get along."

"She's right, sweetie." How can Mom sound so calm? Every word I say is shaky and uneven. "You'll understand why you became friends with them in your first life, and you'll fit in with them again."

He looks down at my hand, and I pull it away. He doesn't want me touching him. "If I can't even remember my own family, how will I remember people who couldn't have meant nearly as much to me?"

I swallow hard. Hearing him say he doesn't remember me is like having my insides stomped on. "Do you remember anything about me? What you used to call me?"

He puts his hand to his forehead and shuts his eyes. He's trying to force the memories to come, but they aren't there. He punches the wall, his fist going right through it. I jump. Jeremy's never been violent.

Mom rushes to him. "I can heal this for you."

"No." He stares at his hand, holding it up in front of his face. "*This* I can feel. It's the *only* thing I feel—other than confusion. I don't want the pain to go away."

Mom nods and backs away from him. Even if he broke a few bones, she can heal him later, once he doesn't cringe at our touch anymore.

"Cara-bird," I say. "You used to call me Cara-bird." My God, I'm falling to pieces.

Jeremy looks at me, studies the tears running down my cheeks, and laughs. "Wow, that's a stupid nickname. I really came up with that?"

"It's not stupid. You were six when you started calling me that. You'd just found out we were Phoenixes. Remember? You were upset that we weren't something tougher, like bears. So I called you Jer-bear. You loved it, and you called me Cara-bird."

His laughter fades. "We were close?"

I nod. "Always have been." I bite my lip to keep from losing it. Nothing short of my own rebirth can make me forget what I lost the moment Jeremy turned to ashes. Part of me died with him. I take a deep breath and walk to Jeremy's bed. I pick up his iPod. "Maybe you should listen to some music. It might help jog your memory." I try to place an ear bud in his ear, but he backs away. "Oh God, Jeremy, I'd never hurt you. You have to know that."

"Cara-bird." Hearing him say my nickname makes my insides crumble to pieces because the blank expression on his face means he doesn't remember ever calling me that before.

"I can't." I turn and run up the steps. It's too much. I can't handle watching Jeremy suffer like this, struggle to remember who he is. The memory book, the iPod, the stories—they don't mean anything to him. They're only breaking his heart and mine. "I'm going to the falls," I yell to Mom without looking back.

I need to escape. Need to get away from Jeremy—the brother I lost.